After time at medical college, Martin worked as a labourer, showman, pancake chef, fire technician, and design engineer for London Underground. From years living in South London, his writing explores a world where wealth and poverty exist side by side, and paradise can be a place to stay, a change of identity or a wall of lager cans, and the biggest mistake a person can make is to start believing their own myths.

A PLACE OF SAFETY

MARTIN NATHAN

SALT

CROMER

PUBLISHED BY SALT PUBLISHING 2018

2 4 6 8 10 9 7 5 3 1

Copyright © Martin Nathan 2018

First published in Great Britain in 2018 by
Salt Publishing Ltd
12 Norwich Road, Cromer, Norfolk NR27 0AX United Kingdom

www.saltpublishing.com

Salt Publishing Limited Reg. No. 5293401

A CIP catalogue record for this book is available from the British Library

ISBN 978 1 78463 122 2 (Paperback edition)
ISBN 978 1 78463 123 9 (Electronic edition)

Typeset in Neacademia by Salt Publishing

Printed and bound in Great Britain by Clays Ltd, St Ives plc

. . . their tears issue from the innermost
and farthest places of their hearts,
and the entire world is perplexed . . .
—The Zohar - Book of Radiance

ALICE: THE WORLD IS PERPLEXED

'THE HORROR. THE horror.' That is what Terry, the office junior says, the morning we hear the news. He sees our shocked faces but he says it anyway. It is his catchphrase. He will come in on a Monday morning, eyes still drawn in misery from the weekend's excesses and as he stretches out in his chair, clutching his head and rubbing his brow, he mutters these words. On his return from viewing a house with a difficult client, he will slink off to make a cup of tea and we hear him muttering that inevitable phrase. At lunchtime, as he unpeels his unsavoury construction of cheese, tomato, collapsed meat and foil from its Subway box, you can see him mouthing the shape of the words. So when something really bad happens there is nowhere for him to go. The horror. The horror.

We all look round at each other and we have no words to offer as an alternative.

I am tired. There were dangerous prayers all night at the church behind my flat, with determined fasting, wilderness shouting, fitful rest, punctuated by chanting through darkness into dawn, when dazed children were carried to cars having given in to sleep, and men gripped hands and embraced, before slamming their car doors and gunning the engines, while their wives glided out through the crowd in long purple dresses and aerofoil hats. Fulfilment of wishes, then the final call of mercy. My rest was also fitful last night. I fire a glare in Terry's direction long enough for him to notice.

He moves over to Mr Guralnick's desk to dig out the nameplate, from its burial place under stacks of paper, and creates a little monumental area for it at the front of the desk, with a pencil holder at one end and the phone at the other. Everyone watches in a moment of awed reverence.

The South London Press hangs half-delivered in the letter-box; I pull it through and drop it straight in the bin. One of the things I stopped after taking over the business was having the South London Press in the waiting area. If you're moving into an area, dreaming of creating a home there, you do not want to read about the gruesome crimes in the adjacent roads. But for Mr Guralnick this was an act of dishonesty and he kept putting our office copy out for everyone to read. 'They should know about the area they're moving into,' he would say, as if highlighting the neighbourhood crimes was his civic duty. But even he would have drawn the line at displaying this particular front page. If he had been in a position to.

Outside the office a big black tree creaks in the wind. It died a year ago, the onslaught of attacks from the environment eventually too much for it, but it still stands there, its branches catching whatever debris blows by at the right height. A blue plastic bag rattles and twists in the breeze, sometimes revealing its bloodied interior. This morning it has a new decoration. Someone has thrown clothes up into it overnight and now they hang there, swaying gently, awaiting rescue or a strong wind. There are no messages of love carved below in its trunk, just long gouges in the bark as if a clawed hand has dragged down it, leaving lines that have blackened over the months.

Something remarkable happens and it undermines the sense of order, the rough hierarchy of values that applies: family, friends, colleagues. Suddenly it has their attention and the more they look the more confusing it is. The story changes whichever way you look at it.

I can see myself watching the scene unfolding, the bewildered faces in the office, no-one quite sure what action to take, and then pulling back, that constant ferment on the streets; people on the edge, fizzing, cracking, explosive close-up, when you look into their eyes but from a distance just part of the everyday noise, the rumble of life. Nothing worth reporting.

I go into the kitchen to make some coffee and my hands shake as I sprinkle the granules of instant into the cup. Stretching out my fingers, suddenly I see my mother's hands in place of my own, with week-old nail varnish and a permanent scrubbed pink colour to the skin, as if they have aged in the last few days. Pouring boiled water into a hissing brown froth, I stir it and then throw the murky liquid straight down the sink. I take out the little stainless steel brik, unfold the silver pack with a picture of Cyprus topped by an outsize sailing boat and I mix the powdered coffee, sugar, and the water, spinning it round until I get a sludgy foam and put it on the cooker ring. The spiral of metal turns red, a suddenly active instrument of torture and the hissing and popping of the heat underneath triggers the familiar sad Greek melody playing in my head, jangling repeated notes that always come in a fraction too early: they cannot wait. First you let the coffee rise once, lift it off the heat, let it sink, then you wait for the foam to rise again. The third time it rises, you pour. An essence of sweet bitterness with a deep sediment, topped with a curl of steam.

So he is gone.

Is that all there is to a fire? I hear the notes of a song my father would sing when he'd tired of Greek music and moved on to Peggy Lee.

I'm back in the office, my cup on an outsize saucer, while the staff are crouched over the paper they've retrieved from the bin. I have never seen them gathered like this, showing such intensity and focus. But something remarkable has to have happened to get on the cover of the South London Press.

'What about the house? Is that still there? Will it have to be demolished?' Someone, Yvonne, says the words. Always the estate agent.

Beth shudders, clutching her arms around her. 'I couldn't live in the house, not after that.'

I leave them to it and go back to the kitchen, sipping my coffee and hearing the sweet sad melody as it plays in my head.

I cannot imagine how it happened. Having thrown the paper away, I now itch to read it, to see what they said. I still can't quite believe it. An arson attack. Mr Guralnick had his peculiarities; he could drive me into a rage sometimes, but this? And Esme, his wife. A tragedy. My tragedy.

It begins to unfold in my head: it isn't extraordinary, in fact it was inevitable, once the right sequence of events had been put in place. A shudder runs through my body. I had made it inevitable.

Was it really my fault? Were there signs I should have spotted, that I deliberately overlooked? It is hard to believe it was only four weeks ago that it began. It feels like a different era of my life now.

Times of emotional significance . . . sipping Greek coffee laden with sugar . . . like when Mr Guralnick announced his departure. He had told me and then looked me in the eye, his lip gripped defiantly under his teeth, waiting. Did he think I might beg him not to go? I smiled, shaking his hand vigorously, sealing the deal, 'That's wonderful. You've earned it,' hoping he wouldn't notice my sense of relief as I turned it into a celebration and sent Terry out for a bottle of champagne and cakes. But he was no fool: he knew the truth. He had chosen to go because actually he had no choice. So we ate cakes and drank champagne. And then I made Greek coffee and drank it alone.

I remember Andrew's and Carol's arrival here very clearly. It had been a quiet morning, undisturbed by customers, and I was at first struck by the open physical affection between them. In this area most human interaction consists of confrontation, even between couples: especially between couples, so when I noticed them outside the shop I nodded to Yvonne, who smiled back. She saw it as part of her role to encourage the pairing off of all humanity, regardless of whether the couples were compatible. She had been enlivened by Terry's flirtations with Beth and was mentally plotting the course of their romance. She spent her lunchtimes reading romantic novels, sighing sometimes at a world that was such a disappointment when compared with her fictional domain. But her faith was briefly restored by seeing this couple holding hands; their snatched kisses made her smile, and when Carol gazed at Andrew with her eyes wide in adoration, Yvonne beamed at me.

I have to confess to feeling a twinge of envy as this embodiment of the perfect relationship unfolded before me.

It's bit of a shock now. I used to think my ability to read people was one of my strengths, but in fact I only see the surface. I have no special insight into what goes on inside. We are all trapped in our private isolation. Until there is some action.

Andrew swung the door wide and strode in. He stood in front of the display boards, oblivious to a woman whose view he blocked, as he scanned the properties. Carol followed and stood beside him; she was watching his response to each one. She pointed to one or two, and there was a twitch of irritation on his cheek as he listened to her suggestions.

He was tall, with a rigid upright physicality which made me wonder if he had been in the army, but his arms swung with a careless swagger, suggesting if he had, it must have been a while ago. They were not married; she was touching his arm too much for that and he was at ease with the contact, even though he would move away as soon as something else had grabbed his interest.

I watched them a little longer before approaching them with my usual, 'Is there anything that you'd like to know more about?' He swept a copy of the South London Press from his pocket and opened it flat on the table.

'Can you tell me about the area?' he said. 'What kind of area is it?' His eyes fixed on mine, challenging me to hold his stare.

I was thrown and looked down at the cover of the paper. It featured a story I had read earlier. Someone was killing dogs in the local park, leaving poisoned meat under benches. The animals had suffered a quick but agonising death. 'Dog killer at large'. The poisoner chose only benches with memorial plaques, so the police thought the motive must be revenge and were checking recent incidents involving dog attacks.

My voicebox felt tight, so my reply was strained. 'It's a nice area, quiet but well connected.' That was my stock reply. 'You can be in the centre of town in . . . twenty minutes, but you can almost believe you're living in a village, not in the city at all.'

'Right,' he said. 'Because I noticed the guy with the facial tattoos on the corner of the high street. He seemed pretty angry, the way he was shouting. Is it an angry place?'

His girlfriend's face creased in dismay and she raised an arm behind his back, resting her hand on his shoulder, calming him. I smiled at her as I reassured him. 'It's London. It's a mix. All of London is a mix. It's not an angry place.'

Terry looked up from his desk and added helpfully, 'It's not an angry place. It's just the people that are angry.' He caught my eye and realised I had just become one of them. I would speak to him later.

You catch a glimpse of the core relationship as it's played out in front of all this property; it is the counterpoint to the altar. The altar is the idyll, the heightened dream on the edge of a new life, but buying the house is the reality, the harshness of the possible, and you watch their dreams collapse in front of you when they see what they can afford and their resentment emerges: beneath everything, basic grievances. "Why don't you earn more? Why haven't you saved up? Why have you been wasting your life?" You see the raw conflict suddenly exposed.

I saw Carol gripping his shoulder, stroking his arm as he became calmer.

I saw in Carol things I lacked. I had always been aware of my deficiencies: while my older sisters were getting excited about make-up and dresses and doing each other's hair, I watched them, feeling bored, drawing lines of flowers in the margins of my notebook. I was never a part of all that. Occasionally I would fake the same constructed glamour myself, and they would gather encouragingly, but I never fooled anyone. Carol was different; she had a natural look that she carried with a confidence that I wanted to emulate. I was envious, and seeing her enthusiasm for this dream, I wanted to be a part of it.

She had an optimism, a hopefulness that I envied. She pointed to the details of some awful damp one-bedroom flat above a kebab shop and she smiled and said, 'I'm sure we could do something with it.'

Andrew was grim-faced, hardly able to look at anything.

I drew him aside, gently probing about their budget. He was evasive, as if puzzled by my questions. 'We just need to see the place . . . the right place' was all he said.

'Do you have mortgage approval in place? We have someone who's very good . . . who can advise . . .'

He shook his head. The faintest smile appearing at the corner of his lips. 'I don't need a mortgage.'

It was surprising. He lacked the swagger and the sense of entitlement of those used to wealth.

'Compensation,' was all he said.

'That's nice . . . well not needing compensation, but it's good not to need a mortgage.'

I watched as he moved, looking for the signs of an injury, an artificial leg. But even losing a leg doesn't get you get enough for a house. Maybe some mind-damaging event, some kind of trauma, could result in that much compensation?

He swung round and caught me staring at the back of his legs. 'Sorry,' I said, 'someone left something . . .' I walked over to the desk, grabbing an arbitrary piece of paper. He nodded and grinned.

'Would you like to sit down?' I gestured to the chairs: plastic bucket seats in lime green that someone had convinced me were stylish, but now looked cheap. 'Terry, could you get us some coffee?'

Terry pulled a face and made a resentful gesture behind Andrew's back, but Andrew turned to glare at him, pointing at his eyes. 'I see everything,' he said, narrowing them a little, 'Day or night. In the army they got spooked out because I sleep with my eyes open.'

Terry skulked off to the kitchen.

'He does,' said Carol. 'It is so strange . . . It's like you can see thoughts from another world when you look into them.

'I told them all Jews sleep with their eyes open. We have to. It's the only way we survive.'

Strange . . . That wasn't the word for it. The longer I watched him the more obsessed I became; and he sensed the atmosphere of apprehension and relished it. All that time I never saw him blink.

'I asked about the area because I like to get the mood of a place. I hope it didn't seem . . . too direct.'

'No, of course not. Everyone gets along here. People just get on with their business, however unusual that might be elsewhere.'

He was nodding.

Still Andrew gave nothing away. 'I'll know it when I see it.'

'I really need some idea of budget.'

He frowned disapprovingly at even the most expensive luxury places. 'You see I have it in my head . . . there was one place I saw in the window . . .'

I was about to give up when he pointed to the picture of the Guralnicks' house on my desk. 'What about this one?'

The Guralnicks. I had put the photo up with just the price and 'Three-bedroom house – Details to follow'. The photos I took made it look dark and awful.

'That one? It's only just became available. We don't have the details yet.'

'We could never afford that . . .' Carol said, but as she examined the photograph her face creased into a smile.

'It is much nicer than the photo. That was just taken by me with my phone.'

Andrew appeared to grow in front of my eyes, rising up to his full height. 'The first thing is to get the goal in your head. Then you make things happen . . .'

Normally talk of visions and goals rings alarm bells straight away for me, but his smile encouraged confidence.

I checked the notes and the price Mr Guralnick had scrawled there. It was way too high. 'It could be a starting point . . .' I had said to him. Mr Guralnick had looked genuinely puzzled by the concept of negotiation.

'A starting point for what?'

Many significant moments in my life are accompanied by the cloying sensation of sipping sweet liquids; for example, the previous owner of the business had poured me sherry as he'd introduced me to Mr Guralnick. David. 'Our most senior member of the team. Any problems you encounter, he will be able to help you.'

As he smiled I thought to myself, but what if he is the problem?

My father had been with me as we were marched through a guided tour of the three rooms. I followed behind, fascinated by the owner's brown check suit, with its shiny patches, and observing the way it fell into well-established creases.

When my father left he passed me a slip of paper with a number on it:the maximum amount we would pay. I watched the battle of emotions on the owner's face: joy at the prospect of easy negotiation, sensing that he might be able to sweep a deal through with a bit of charm and bluster, but also concern that any deal with me might still need further parental approval.

The office was a padded cell whose walls were lined with plush green Dralon. I stood in front of the hard leather sofa no-one ever sat on, while he sank into an executive chair the other side of the desk, interleaving his fingers as if about to conduct an interview. 'We have a relaxed atmosphere in this office,' he said, thinking this was what I wanted to hear, before inviting me to sit on a creaking wooden chair.

'Calm. Friendly.' He poured me more sweet sherry, stopping, a protective father turned seducer as he poured an inch more amber fluid. 'It's from Cyprus . . .' he said, tapping the bottle as if that would clinch the deal.

'Tell me about the staff.'

He went through them, one by one, flicking through their CVs and summarizing their skills and expendability in a few short sentences. 'Mr Guralnick is our most reliable and trusted employee,' he said, giving a hint of problems, maybe, but anxious to get rid of the place. I would have to find out for myself. 'Solid and reliable. Trustworthy. One thing you can rely on, David will always tell you the truth, however uncomfortable,' he said, smiling, playing with his pen, anxious. Did he think I would cancel the deal over one man, near retirement, stuck in his ways, too honest for his own good? 'His value may not be obvious at first.'

He leaned back in his chair. 'It's good to have a private office. Very few places have them these days, but if you bring a person here at the right time they know they are being treated with respect. It's old school. Like this business. But it works.'

He was more successful at burying the secrets of his staff than the secrets of his accounting. He pretended it was his traditional time-honoured method as I probed the figures, but I sensed his desperation. I had an advantage: he under-estimated me. He figured if he couldn't fool me, he couldn't fool anyone. I got the business for a good price. I could manage any problems. I could make them go away.

Everyone knew why I was there: they muttered to each other and exchanged anxious glances as we passed. They understood the significance of clinking sherry glasses. I could sense them listening outside, each of them assessing what future that clinking of glasses contained.

We shook on the deal and he led me into the main office to meet the staff.

I took them in, assessing each one in that moment: the cocky sales types, eager and confident; the timid admin woman, her world balanced on a pinnacle, any disturbance likely to lead to collapse; Mr Guralnick, standing upright beside his desk, his nameplate asserting its position in front of a neat pile of paper, not hidden like the others. I could see in that moment his absolute unshakeability . . . whatever happened, he was not going to change.

They were thinking how has this woman, how has this girl got the money to buy a business like this? But for Mr Guralnick the question did not arise. Nothing was happening, as far as he was concerned. The change others perceived was an illusion. The world was exactly as it was yesterday and as it would be tomorrow. It took more than a Greek girl with too much money to change it.

I tried to smile in a friendly manner, but somehow my friendly smile always comes out scary. The owner, who had a short time before been so keen to introduce me, had disappeared to make a start on packing up his office.

I was sure I could turn the business round. I thought the problem was just their old school way of working. But what did I know?

What did I know? It was always falling away, my confidence, every time a decision had to be made, but I had to keep going, even though I was standing on a column of sand and feeling it drop away as the sea rose around me. There was nowhere for me to go if I wanted to step off.

❧

You can spend a lot of time and effort making Greek coffee, just to achieve a brief moment of joy that will disappear in three sips, leaving a mere lingering touch of coffee grit on your lips and tongue. But the reward is in the making as much as the result. The last time I went back to my father's village, the café had taken delivery of a large red Gaggia machine. The owner introduced it to me as if it was a new member of the family, making it perform, the steam shooting out, and he showed me a device for warming the cups as if it was something miraculous. But that was all he used it for. The stainless steel shelf served as a stand for his little Calor gas burner and I heard the busy stirring of a brik as he made coffee the way he always had. He sprayed cream on top and a sprinkle of cinnamon, and presented it to me, the perfect cappuccino.

It was all about the presentation.

I swill the cup out and pour the dregs down the sink, despite the sign I had put up warning people not to put coffee grounds down the drain. This is different, it's powder. I dry the brik and put it away in the cupboard, then I take the nameplate from Mr Guralnick's desk and put it in my drawer. We don't need stupid gestures. They look at me as if I have done something shocking, then carry on working in silence.

I would not say anything bad about Mr Guralnick. I liked him. Yes, he had an annoying straggly beard, bad breath, brown teeth and glasses that made his eyes focus on a different dimension from mine. His suits never quite fitted and his shirt collar was always making a bid for freedom. He was stuck in his ways. Old guard. When I went on viewings with him he would talk endlessly, pointing out defects in the paintwork, patches of damp, lumpy plaster. Prospective buyers would stand back, amazed that he talked without a pause, without any nod towards what they might be interested in. If he had been a surgeon breaking news to a patient of a fatal disease, he would also have told them of the other interesting but non-threatening bodily defects he had discovered during the course of his investigation.

'You're supposed to be selling the property, not putting them off,' I said, and he looked hurt. He drove me mad but I liked him. There was something about his self-assuredness, his unwavering self-belief. He never argued if challenged but would instead fall into a resolute silence.

᳇

Terry comes in clutching a sandwich, chatting with Beth. There is something conspiratorial in the way they talk together and when he sees me he looks away too quickly and rushes over to pick up the ringing phone. Whoever is calling gives up and he mimes bewilderment. Beth giggles and Terry catches my eye, embarrassed.

'So where did you two go just now?'

'I thought I saw one of our exclusive properties in Savile's window . . . I went to check.'

'Right. And you needed Beth to come with you for that?'

Beth is pale and terrified, Terry flushed but defiant. 'Tell me, Terry, where did you really go?'

'I was just showing Beth some of the local streets. Giving her a feel for the area. Just for a few minutes while things are slow.'

I move over to Beth while Terry watches apprehensively. 'Right. So, Beth, did you feel you needed Terry's training tour right now?'

She doesn't speak, keeps looking down, gripping her lip.

'You went to the Guralnicks' house, didn't you? You went to gawp at it, didn't you?'

He looks around, desperate to find an alternative lie. I let the silence hang. Beth looks as if she were going to explode and the tears start to appear.

'I'm ashamed. This is not a scene from one of your horror films to give you cheap thrills. This is real life. He was a valued colleague . . .'

The phone rings again and Terry rushes over to pick it up.

'Miss . . . Alice . . . there's someone enquiring about . . . about the Guralnicks . . .'

I take the phone from him. I hold it, then I slam it down.

'Is the house still on the website?'

Terry and Beth look at each other. Yvonne is about to speak, but thinks better of it, leaving her mouth in a suspended 'O'. The rest of the people in the office suddenly become very busy. I click on the page and there it is.

'So no-one thought to . . . ?'

I look at it. What details. Honed and crafted. Pages of description unfolding. Twists of language. The magic teased out from every fitting, every design feature. The photograph of the all-too-familiar terrace, tweaked to make it into sunny day. In every photo, it's a sunny day. I feel like laughing. The fourteen pages Mr Guralnick produced describing his house!

I clicked the button and it was all gone.

Terry pushes at his jacket, trying to settle the shoulders. He always looks as if he is about to break free of his suit; having squeezed himself in first thing in the morning, he struggles against every seam throughout the day. Then at night he can burst out of it into a tracksuit and be restored to his natural form.

Beth and Terry are still looking at me, not sure if I've finished with them.

'Go away. I don't want to see you for a while.'

Terry looks confused. 'Does that mean . . . ?'

I stride past them, leaving them in a suspended state. Beth trembles and moves away, as if I need clearance of ten feet. Yvonne holds out a piece of paper for me to sign, and watches in dismay as I step into the high street.

I push past the impromptu market that has set up outside the butcher's, with its trays of trotters nestling together like severed baby's arms, the dilute blood gathering beneath them, and pigs' tails wrapped over each other, finally liberated from the body that restrained them, while the stall-holder waves kilo bags of chicken wings at the small but passionate crowd. Next to the butcher's, the vegetable stall, drumsticks and finger aubergines, yard-long beans and mammoth yams and egusi seeds. Beneath the counter are baskets containing mysterious brown shapes, life-forms that have been smoked and desiccated to an ochred shiny curve and with little arms that reach up and hide faces.

A man blocks my exit from the crowd, standing in front of me, chewing a piece of wire, his gums bleeding. His shoes have the fronts cut off so you can see his grimy toes and the yellow horn of nail. 'It's the bleeping . . .' he says to me. 'It drives me crazy.' The windows of his flat above are decorated with placards protesting about the pedestrian crossing: Stop the bleeping. Lambeth Council – Stop the bleeping.

I turn to walk up the hill as he places a pamphlet in my hand. Behind him on the pavement is a semi-circle of pamphlets discarded after a glance, trodden into the mud, but he maintains a sunny smile and his constant refrain, 'I really fucking love Cheesus. I really fucking love him.'

The first time I came across him I thought he was saying

'cheeses' and took his hand-printed sheets, expecting an offering of artisan dairy products rather than his own personal Jesus who blamed women for the world's wrongs: he had cursed them with a monthly cycle to remind them of the damage they did with the constant temptations they offered.

Now he has widened the blame. 'You may think Cheesus is your friend. He's not your friend. You may think he forgives you, but you will feel his wrath before you feel his love . . . Muslims . . . Jews . . . non-believers.' He points his finger at me. 'I am the way, he said. There is no other. They will perish . . . the wrath of God abideth in him. Feel the wrath.'

The Guralnicks' house is in one of those London streets of Victorian terraces which have until recently changed little since the day they were built. A few years ago these were still houses with outside toilets and no central heating whose occupants had been born there, had their families and still lived there now, never feeling the need to rip up the floorboards to replace them with polished white oak. They hadn't changed the kitchen every ten years, going from Shaker to Contemporary and back. They accepted what was there, fixing the odd thing and putting a coat of paint on now and again, but other than that leaving the place be.

Sometimes I feel guilty showing people a house, offering them the promise that whatever it is like now, it will be so much better in the future. It is a dream of possibilities . . . of whatever you want it to be. There is a mix of extremities in this area, a tension from door to door. There's the rawness of the conjunction of the moneyed with those just barely hanging on. You can fool yourself all is tranquil, but it could be on the point of exploding.

A policeman stands outside. What kind of job is that, to

stand guard day after day . . . protecting what? The place is a charred wreck. The windows are void of glass, but still clad with the metal bars. I had told David he ought to take them down if he wanted to sell the house. 'People don't want to see bars when they're viewing a house,' I said, and he looked at me as if I was naïve.

'If I leave them they have the option to keep them or take them down.' So he left them.

Now they protect the emptiness and you can see the black rafters inside where the ceilings have collapsed and the floor boards have burnt away. I think of the Guralnicks trapped inside, fighting to escape, the terror on their faces, unable to climb through those bars. I imagine their desperation as they realised that the bars David put up to keep them safe were what would destroy them.

Glimmers of light come from the gaps in the roof; the burnt timber creaks still, and there is the deep overpowering smell of charred wood, a smell that always bears testimony to misfortune.

'I knew him . . . them,' I say to the policeman, feeling embarrassed, sensing his disgust at my attentions, assuming I'm merely showing ghoulish fascination. He shrugs his lack of interest. 'I just wanted to . . . see.'

Then, with a groan and a crack, a tile smashes through to the floor, raising a cloud of dust among the rubble in the living room. The room where I'd sat and had conversations with the Guralnicks and drunk coffee and heard their plans, even at the time thinking how their lives were embedded in the walls of that house, in its fabric.

'I guess they're going to have to knock it down.'

'I'm not a builder.'

'No, but . . . it looks pretty bad . . . there's not a lot to save.'

He walks over, happy to take advantage of a break in the tedium of his lonely guarding. 'If you're interested, I can pass your details on to the solicitors who are handling it . . .'

'No, I'm not a developer, I'm just . . .'

I don't know what to say. Why was I there? I just wanted to share in the horror. The horror, the horror.

I look through the window into the living room. I can see the horse's head David was carving from that lump of wood we found, lying on its side. Blackened.

A moment was passing in my life: dreams had exploded, people had disappeared. That is what I really could not understand. How it is possible for people to disappear like that?

'So I guess you'll be getting forensic people in. To discover what happened.'

He nods and beckons me closer. He speaks in a hushed voice. 'We are carrying out an investigation. At the moment, though, we're working on the basis that we think there's been a fire.'

A comedy policeman. I go back to the office.

David had helped me a lot in the early days, always accompanied by his patient, amused look, watching every change as if he were witnessing the march of folly, but could only shake his head and observe. I kept the take-over low key. On my first day we had a little party with cake and a bottle of champagne, and I explained how there would be a name-change, a minor rebranding, but apart from that they would notice little difference. As I spoke the sign fitter was up his ladder, replacing the signage above the window. Mr Guralnick shook his head as if his world was collapsing and said one word, quietly epitomising for him the horror of my takeover. 'Purple.'

The sign fitter hacked away some of the branches of the tree outside that had blocked his progress and left the stack of dismembered wood in the street. I brought my car in the next day to take the wood to the dump, but someone had cleared it already, unable to resist free kindling.

Any change I chose to implement would be observed by David with that pained expression . . . the half-cocked eyebrow . . . I started to hate that eyebrow, fantasising about shaving it off or stabbing him in the eye, just to put a stop to that expression. I'm not a violent person, I never actually would do anything like that. I just liked to imagine it.

I set up a sales board and on Friday mornings we gathered to look at the week's sales, the person doing best getting a bottle of wine. The person doing worst had to bake a cake for the next week. It was intended to be a bit of fun, but also to keep the focus on what we were there for.

That first week I supplied the cake from the high street baker's, the woman there persuading me to let them put a picture in the icing. 'Whatever you want,' she kept saying. 'Just send us the picture.' So I sent the team picture taken on the first day, but when I went to fetch the cake I realised that amongst the happy fake smiles, David was gripping his temples, grimacing as though emoting despair for an acting class.

So that first Friday I sliced through his head and hands and closed tragic eyes, hoping no one had noticed them, and I handed him the first slice. Mr Guralnick. David. I called everyone by their first name, but it was always a conscious effort with him.

When I wrote up the week's sales figures I was unpleasantly surprised. 'A couple of things have been slow coming through,' David said. 'It'll be better next week.' But it wasn't. Three weeks running we ate his orange and almond cake and Terry gloated over his bottle of wine.

'Do you mind me saying something?' He didn't pause for an answer. 'We are a partnership, not a mob. People come here because they want something more . . . relaxed. Not pushy. They can get that down the road. But we have always offered . . . something different.'

I don't know why I felt the need to justify it. 'The sales chart is just a bit of fun, to keep up focus and enthusiasm, for the younger ones, especially.' He turned away from his teapot and looked at me as though I had emitted a smell or evoked an unpleasant memory. 'And what,' he said, 'will they do with this enthusiasm?'

He did not say anything more until suddenly he smiled and said, 'You think I am from another age, don't you? An age that you can barely comprehend. But we survived for many years with those values and I can't believe they are completely worthless now.'

I caught sight of his troubled teeth, the long brown cracks in them, the side incisors bending over the middle to protect them from onslaught.

'Sometimes in discussions with clients you can be a little too honest . . .'

'You mean, because I believe in telling the truth?' A little bit of spittle shot out to emphasise the point. We both watched its journey onto my arm.

'I mean when you are selling something you don't have to stress all the things that might be wrong with a place . . .'

'This is the most important purchase of their lives . . .'

'And for everyone that buys there's someone selling . . . the most important sale of their life. We help our client, not the rest of the world. I do really value your help and experience, but we also need to sell.'

The cocked eyebrow of disapproval. I hated that eyebrow. I could imagine what it must have been like to have him as your father . . . that infuriating eyebrow of disapproval.

On the fourth week I set up a rota for cake-making instead of awarding the prize. What surprised me about David was not his performance, but his lack of embarrassment about it.

He still made the cake, but now as part of the rota. It was always the same, but it was a good cake. Orange and almond: a Passover cake. Like one of my mother's Greek cakes when she still baked, before bitterness took over all her cooking and made everything taste sour or burnt.

'You didn't make this, did you? It was your wife. You can't fool me.'

'My wife makes many things, but not cakes.'

It always struck me as a curiously isolating story, the story of Passover, not something to celebrate. Everyone else dies.

When he brought his yeast for Passover to store in the fridge I was puzzled. 'I thought you weren't observant.'

'No,' he said, 'but it's such a little thing.'

He must have sensed that things would come to a head eventually and decided to forestall it. I was in the kitchen one day when he approached me. He was making his tea, using a teapot and strainer as always, pushing those extra droplets through with a spoon as if they were vital. He had his back to me as he swirled the water in the pot. He stopped to speak, clutching the teapot in front of him.

It became clear very quickly to me that I would have to get rid of him. When I looked at the figures, his employment made no sense. He was paid an inflated salary out of sentimentality.

I had built myself up for the inevitable battle.

⚘

The clothes in the tree outside hang from the branches, human fragments, shrivelled, sucked dry. The sun shines on to my desk through the tree and the shadows move with the wind.

Now that he has gone I feel an emptiness. I miss him, but in the way I miss living at home with my family: I remember the good parts without ever wanting to go back, yet never admitting the huge relief of having escaped. It was life at the funfair, always riding someone's turmoil, shrieking from behind someone's door, my mother's face drawn with her personal drama, dragging us into her own Greek tragedy.

But knowing that I will never see him again, the finality of that and the awful way his life ended grips me. I cannot purge the image of that burnt-out house, the three of them trapped there. I hide behind my computer monitor, and sort through the pile of post. Sales literature. A world of so much talking and so little listening: but that's the kind of thing David would say. He is becoming a commentating voice in my head.

'Beth, what is it?' Beth is standing in front of my desk, held-back tears at the point when they will emerge with the slightest encouragement. She had only known him a couple of weeks and she behaves as if it was the major tragedy of her life.

24

'I'm sorry about earlier . . .'

'Yes, well . . .' I remembered how my sisters used tears to get their own way with my father, to wheedle money, lifts, permission to stay out late; how they would make a plan of attack and then blatantly ambush him, eyes moist already in case he tried to refuse them.

Beth's voice quivers. 'If only you hadn't . . . the sale . . . if only you hadn't . . . they'd still be alive.'

She goes back to her desk and sits, watching me occasionally, shaking with sobs. She is on borrowed time. I made a mistake in taking her on; she's a distraction for Terry and she will never have the hard-nosed drive to clinch sales. I won't procrastinate with her the way I did with David.

Sometimes I can almost imagine what it was like being part of David's family, look into the kaleidoscope of their relationships. Things don't emerge from nothing and David could provoke a perplexing rage that you did not know what to do with. So it festered. It built. Then it exploded.

❧

The doorbell jangles and I catch a waft of a terrible, rancid smell. It takes me a moment to register. One of our regular visitors. Peter. He wears a blue suit and from the front he looks relatively smart. You can imagine he is a wealthy trader, successful enough not to have to wear a tie, with his grey hair drawn back tight behind his head, those eyes looking at you intently. A constant stream of words emerges, as if he might be discussing a business deal on a phone clipped to his ear. But as you look you realise there are stains down the front of his suit and when you see him from behind there is a thick matt of grey hair down his back. There are rips in his trousers and the seams of his jacket are split. The backs of his shoes are cut off to expose his blackened heels and he has that familiar smell of street people, a mix of piss, shit, vomit and sweat mellowed by the months and years into something more heady and disturbing.

He came into the shop on that first day, as I was clearing the empties from the celebration party, and the left-over cake was gradually collapsing on my desk. The smell hit me straight away but I had no idea where it was coming from.

I signalled to Terry to close the kitchen door, thinking it might be a problem with the drains. I still thought he might be an important client; he engaged me in a bizarre, breathless conversation about his potential property investments. 'It's all about realisation . . . when you realise your assets . . . the time is right . . . boom . . . the time is wrong . . . bang . . . it's all in flux . . . you can never stop . . . Never get off . . . bang.'

He was a bit too close and I realised I was trapped. I looked for someone to help me, to give me some clue as to what to do as I struggled to breathe, the smell choking me; but everyone had moved away, looking on from afar with embarrassed smiles.

He was becoming increasingly intense, shouting, and his face was getting closer and closer. 'Is it now?' he was saying. 'Is now good?'

'Now is a very good time . . .'

'But are you just saying that? Are you just telling me that?'

Whatever I said got him more agitated. The place had cleared out, the staff had all moved to the kitchen, the toilet, the stationery cupboard.

He was scrutinising our sales board. 'These. Are these

good? These are my investments. You're stealing my money. I own that street and you're selling the houses on it . . .'

He was waving a threatening finger. I could hardly breathe: that grey finger with its alarming yellow horn fingernail was getting close. His eyes were red and staring, both of them directed at points somewhere inside my head.

Then the door opened. It was Mr Guralnick, back from a viewing. He looked across the empty office, taking in the cake debris, and saw me and smiled. He strode over and put a friendly arm around the man's shoulder. 'Come on Peter, I think Alice is busy,' he said. 'Shall we get a coffee?'

He led our visitor through the door. Peter was smiling at him, as if grateful to have been rescued from me, while I stood at the entrance, breathing wonderful fresh air. I was overcome by a surge of gratitude.

David came back and gave me a cup of coffee; although I don't like milky coffee, I gulped it down as we sat together at my desk. 'Thanks. That really helped.'

He nodded. 'We attract a wide variety of customers, maybe a little too wide. Peter has a story. I get a fragment of it each time he comes in. When I have the whole thing, I'll tell it you. But the emerging moral is that self-belief should always be tempered by a degree of scepticism.'

'You're very good with people. You get them to respond to you. You get them to like you.'

He smiled, wary of any attempt to butter him up. 'Maybe not everyone. We all have enemies.'

It didn't strike me as strange at the time, but now it does. Do we all have enemies? How many of us have enemies?

'I was worried that we got off on the wrong foot. I do respect your way of doing things. And I like you.'

He smiled. 'It's fine. You're right. This place needs shaking up a bit. It was drifting like a liner whose captain got off three ports earlier.'

'Have you been painting?' I noticed he had paint on his hands.

'I was touching up my front door.'

'What, last night? That's a bit keen. You're not thinking of selling, are you?'

He shifted awkwardly, 'It was a bit . . . let's say it wasn't something I felt happy to leave.'

As he looked at his watch, the other staff were beginning to emerge from their various hiding places.

'Is everything okay? Do you need some time off?'

'I'm going to take an early lunch, so I can put another coat on the door. It'll only take ten minutes.'

'Is there something you want to tell me?'

His face creased, his lips began to move and form words. I was apprehensive at what I may have unleashed. If he started to talk, how would it end? What details of his life might he reveal? But the words were never uttered; instead he got up and walked out.

⁂

The smell from Peter does not fade and I realise I am still expecting David to appear and sort it out. I stride over. 'Come on Peter,' I say, gripping his arm with two fingers to minimise contact and guide him out into fresh air. It is easy and he smiles at me, as if this is a journey he enjoys. I am about to buy him a coffee when my phone rings, so I give him a pound and rush back inside.

My sister Helena is reminding me about my mother's seventieth birthday. 'You are coming, aren't you?'

'I said I would. I've got it in my diary.'

'You won't cancel? You won't let something crop up at the last minute? It's important to her.'

'Everything's important to her. If I don't call her every other day, it's a betrayal of the family. I'm coming. I'll make a cake.'

'What? You mean you'll buy one?'

'I can bake a cake. In fact, I've made one already.'

I hear her snort down the phone. 'Just come. All right? I'll worry about the food. And one more thing?'

'Yes.'

'Anna's coming to see you. Tomorrow.'

'Can't she tell me that herself?'

'I'm telling you now.'

'What's it about?'

'She'll see you tomorrow. In the shop.'

I put the phone down and begin to think of what excuses I might be able to get away with. I really cannot face hours of my mother bemoaning the tragedy of her life, my sisters competitively boasting about their perfect lives, and the blatant put-downs directed at me, delivered as if by accident.

It is not like Anna to visit me without a reason. She will not be coming to exchange cake recipes.

I do have a cake though, one that I baked with David, wrapped in foil, and bundled in greaseproof paper and string: the sole occupant of my fridge.

Beth was right: I should have seen it coming. There were enough signs. My father told me that events don't come out of nothing; the signs are clearly there but we choose to ignore them. She was annoyingly right, sitting there with her blonde fringe in her eyes and freckles on her nose.

I go into the back office to dig out the accounts. I had intended to knock down its walls, open up the space, but now I am happy to own a quiet space where I can sit and be away from it all. I know what I will find, even without doing precise calculations. David's departure will have helped, but it won't be enough.

Unconsciously I have screwed up balls of paper from my pad and lined them in a row. I flick them off the desk towards the bin, one by one, then pick up the balls that missed the bin and try again.

Once when I was a girl my father sat me on his knee and produced a scrunched-up piece of paper bearing a few words. 'What does it say?' He began to unfold it, bit by bit, and gradually one word appeared and then the next, fragments building until he had smoothed the paper flat on the table.

'It's like a life unfolding, gradually it becomes plain . . . everything is clear, but by then you are old and wrinkled and no good for anything.' I looked at his face, at the wrinkles around his eyes he said he'd got from too much smiling, wondering if he was talking about himself. I read the words from his piece of paper.

"Wherefore all these things are but the names which mortals have given, believing them to be true..." On the reverse side, the same words, more succinctly, in Greek.

'What does it mean?'

'It means you come from a great tradition . . .'

That perplexing epigram made no sense to me then and it doesn't now, despite my heritage. But I kept the ball of paper. I sometimes bring it out from my desk drawer and look at it, as if it might offer help to my failing business. My father's respect for the Ancient Greek philosophers gave him an air of superiority, a belief that he existed on a higher intellectual plane. I had a teacher who said if you can't explain something you don't understand it, but my father believed in innate knowledge: an unconscious understanding.

He held up the ball of paper, hiding it first then revealing it in his palm, a look of amazement on his face. My mother came in and snatched up the piece of paper, flashed her miserable scowl at us, tossed it in the bin. The wisdom was lost, coated in zucchini scrapings and olive oil, when later I fished it out. I don't know how old she would have been then. Early forties, I guess, but she had adopted the role of a miserable old woman early, anticipating her own decline.

Unfolding.

Those days of family life, all the lies; everyone knew what my father was up to, even his customers. We had to skirt around the issue of where he was and cover up for him. We had to endure the knowing looks, the embarrassed silences.

'I'm just telling you, if your mother comes in the shop I am down at the wholesalers. Tell her that because that's where I am. And I will go tomorrow and the day after if necessary. Owning a shop is not just about serving customers. It's about stock, and where does stock come from? Thank you.'

It would not have been so bad if he had not stuck that little piece of mirror on the stock room door and spent five minutes combing his moustache every time he left. 'They're very particular about the way your moustache looks down at that wholesalers, Dad.'

I loved that shop when I was young. It was a piece of Greece brought to this country; the skylight in the back captured the Greek sunshine, a shaft lighting up the shop even when it was grey outside. The smells were so powerful . . . mountain rigani hanging in bunches from hooks all around, twisting bay leaves, and big tubs of brine containing pickled olives, strips of lemon, vegetables whose colour was gradually being leached from them. Mysterious jars of mehlab, mastic, rose-petals. Those rolls, plump soft dough pillows stuffed with cheese and mint, baked to a dark brown shiny dome that exploded in many flavours when you bit into them. He baked them in the oven out in the back and their smell hung in the shop in a permanent haze, transporting you to more exotic places.

'Stand there. Tell me how they are . . .'

I would stand with my eyes closed and he would tear a piece off one of rolls.

'Tell me if they're good enough.'

'Give me some, then. I'm hungry.'

'They're too hot. Just wait a moment.'

If my sisters had been there, they would have put a chilli on my tongue, or something worse. The rolls were always good, a miracle in the form of baked goods.

Every shelf held secrets. The labels of the tins were decorated with paintings of their contents, as if executed by a child with poor brush control, rendering the contents all the more intriguing. Some told stories of far-off places, ships on un-named oceans, depicting fishermen waving to their distant customers, or farmers harvesting corn, their scythes clutched over their shoulders, dangerously close to decapitating themselves. Some jars contained translucent blobs that seemed like tiny preserved embryos. Sometimes I imagined someone had delicately painted little black nails on them to create an illusion of fingers; it was hard to convince myself they were merely vegetables.

Every space in that shop was occupied. You looked up and there would be rows of imported aluminium ladles in all conceivable sizes hanging from bits of string. Griddles and solid rectangular barbecues crafted from galvanised steel were stacked at the back.

The stock began to have a jaded look, dust gathering everywhere, the labels fading in the light. The vegetables became sad and wrinkled: long purple aubergines sagged in the middle; bloated tomatoes seemed on the point of exploding, limp bunches of herbs were black and slimy when you touched them. The smell of the bread faded, to be replaced by the odour of decay. Customers would come in and turn things over hopefully as if the underside might reveal a better prospect, but always it concealed something yet more rotten.

Still he kept the shop open from early morning until way after all his customers had gone home, other than the odd drunkard looking for matches and cigarettes. He liked to keep out of my mother's way; more than that, he could not bear his own lies.

Finally, it all caught up with him. It was on a Boxing Day visit to Hastings. The whole family was traipsing along the seafront. There was a wind whipping foam up from the sea. The jabbering electronic voices of the casino machines tried to lure us inside. 'We're a set of bad crabs – Let's play – crack-the-crab. Ow – oof- urgh- oooh.'

My mother had just found out about one of his affairs; someone had inadvertently let slip some comment and her world had collapsed from its usual misery into one of eternal recrimination. We had all thought she must have known – how could she not have guessed – all those years? The terrible realisation that he had found pleasure beyond her bitter existence was what hurt her. He was marching ahead, grim-faced in the wind, while my sisters crowded around her in a defensive wall of consolation that blocked me out. I wanted to walk alongside him, because for all the lies, and the affectations, the pretence that he was five years younger than he was (as if five years made a difference), at least he was doing something: not just accepting what the world dished up, not just stumbling into oblivion.

'Now you're talking . . . let's have . . . some crazy time.' Those crabs knew how to have fun.

At least, at least. My mother had turned into an angry grass widow so many years before, with little pretence that there was any affection left for him. They didn't split up for years, continuing to live around each other in silent hatred.

For us to acknowledge one of them was to betray the other. My sisters all ignored my father. I was the one who tried to talk to both of them. The other females of the family shunned me. I was the real threat to their family life, because I would tolerate his behaviour.

My mother trapped him in her sullen silence. When I could, I would speak to him, just ask him the odd thing and he would grab my hand as he told me about his days in the shop, mundane stuff, but precious. If anyone witnessed this moment, I would have to join him in his exile for a day or two.

My other time of making contact with him was late in the evenings.

I was often awake late at night, but I shared a room with Anna and would lie in the darkness, rigid, still, desperate not to wake her. Sometimes I would get up to read in the bathroom, sitting in the cold until I was shivering too much, or someone wanted the toilet. I would read horror fiction, usually tales of demonic possession. The image of wild children writhing, abusing parents whose only defence was prayer and a flick of holy water, struck a chord with me.

I would go back to bed and shiver, until I felt warm enough to fall asleep. But sometimes I could hear my father moving and I would get up again, carefully walking with bare feet cold on the floor to avoid waking my sisters. I would wait at the top of the stairs, rehearsing the words in case I needed them. 'I can't sleep. There's too much going on in my head.' I would watch out of the window for a while, at the yellow cast of the street light, figures scurrying past in a world that only contained yellow and black. When I was sure everyone was asleep and I could hear the cycles of gasping that seemed to take over my mother's breathing in slumber, I would creep down the stairs to find my father in the dining room, listening intently to the old tape player, his eyes staring into the clouds of a faraway mountain. He would be standing there with a glass of Metaxa. Not quite daring to dance, he would shift his weight from one leg to the other, swaying, dipping at the knee, twisting his fingers, his eyes closed, not drinking from the glass, just holding it in front of him, the wafts of the spirit enough to stir his memories. His skin was now dry and creased, but his eyes still shone.

I was watching once when he looked up, saw me and smiled, beckoning. I walked towards him, not sure whether he wanted to dance, for us to dance. I had not tried Greek dancing for so long. I felt my hips begin to move. I stepped forward, towards his hand. Suddenly the music became snarled and distorted. That clear jangling melody disappeared into muddy sound, was engulfed in chaos, then became silent. He rushed over to the tape player and pulled out the cassette, its brown entrails spilling in widening tangles. He glared at me. 'Let me . . .' I said, but he pulled the tape and snapped it off angrily, leaving the shreds on the table.

In the morning I picked up the cassette and cleared away the coils of damaged tape. I tried to buy another copy, but it was a Greek Island label. I was offered Greek holiday music instead. I did buy a tape, but not one that he wanted. It sat in the dining room, unplayed, for months, until eventually I threw it away.

That shop, the familiar smells of my youth, the brine of the feta and olives, enough to knock you back if you inhaled too deeply, the cucumbers, cheap misshapen ones coiled over each other in yellowing hugs and ridged ones, short, crisp and bitter green, slightly covered by fronds of dill and huge bunches of coriander, still with their roots clutching soil as if they had just been hauled out of the ground. All was gone. When he sold it, it was not the business he'd built that had made it valuable. It was the property. He could have kept the place empty all those years and built up nothing. He made his money from the dimensions of that space that he had packed with his lies and my mother's bitterness. A space filled with crushed dreams.

Mr Guralnick would never have done that to his wife. All those lies.

When I'd told my father I wanted to start a business and asked him for help, he was amused, and when he agreed to help it was as though he was indulging me. I battled, dreading that he would say yes, and that I would have to do as I said, yet terrified that I would fail. Secretly I thought there must be some quality I lacked to make a success of it, something fundamental that my father couldn't detect.

The thing I lacked was the very thing responsible for the failure of his business.

⁂

I drag myself out of the back office, and when I re-emerge it is clear from the sudden silence that the others have been gossiping. Their mouths are open, suspended mid-chat.

I go to the shop door, flip the latch and turn the sign to 'Closed'. I gather the staff in an arc and they glance nervously at each other.

'Right. While I've got your attention . . . I just wanted to say . . . it's the end of the day and I know it's been difficult. So thank you. And it's a new day tomorrow.'

They relax.

'Just one more thing. At lunchtime I went down to the little patch of grass on the corner of the high street, and there is a lonely old man who sits muttering to himself with just a can of Dread Stripe to see him through each day . . . It's very sad. If I hear one more word of gossip or disrespect, about Mr Guralnick or anyone else in this office, that person will be joining him for company.'

⁂

When I get home the flat is cold. I had left the window open and the building is in shade, so the heat is rapidly sucked out when darkness falls. As I look around the living room, it strikes me how bleak it is. I remember someone told me how dentists have the worst teeth; spending all their days fixing other peoples' teeth they begrudge the time getting their own fixed. Anna once bullied me into a speed dating session. I had three minutes with a dentist and spent the whole time looking at his teeth to see if this was true. His teeth were fine. It was his personality that was the problem.

That principle does apply to my flat, though: I give it little attention. Coming home late in the evenings, I flop down with a takeaway and a glass of wine. I never think about making it look appealing. I pay someone to clean. I never cook. It has barely changed since the day I moved in.

I settle down on the sofa, warm some half-finished Thai noodles from yesterday, and drink the remains of a caustic Bulgarian red bought from the corner shop. 'Very good, very good choice.' The owner had nodded enthusiastically, probably because it had been hanging around for a long time. The dust on that bottle hadn't come from careful ageing in a cellar.

The noodles burn my mouth, hot zones bubble volcanically, but surrounded by a fridge-cold mass. I push the food aside and grab my laptop.

I had not been able to concentrate on the accounts earlier, but I knew my financial problems had not disappeared with David. However I manipulate the figures, I know I am still in trouble.

I shall have to ask my father for help.

⁂

I had spent the best part of the year worrying about how to get rid of Mr Guralnick. I would wake up at night sweating: it was the stuff of nightmares. I mentally rehearsed the speech I would make, practising my intonation, imagining his reaction. Sometimes cold fury. Sometimes collapse, emotional wreckage. Sometimes sheer disbelief, his refusal to accept.

When eventually it happened, he caught me out.

I had spent the morning with a client who, I had finally realised, just wanted to spend time with me; he was never going to buy anything. At the third property we looked at, he began asking about the private schools.

'There's quite a good range of options. For London, anyway. I thought you said you didn't have any children.'

He'd stretched his arms out and yawned. I could see all this was a waste of my time.

'Not at the moment. But who knows what the future will bring?' He cleared his throat and stood in front of me, blocking my path to the door. ' . . . speaking of which . . . do you have dinner plans?'

I nodded. 'Yes, I do, I'm afraid.'

'Not necessarily tonight. Any night, really.'

'Yes, I have plans for those nights too. All of them.'

'Oh. I see. All of them.' He looked down sadly and began to open the door, and as the sunlight lit up the room, it struck him with false hope. 'How about lunch?'

I was tired. I left him in the street and drove back to the office.

I was preparing myself for that moment with Mr Guralnick, fighting my urge to make a diversionary cup of coffee. There was never going to be a good time. I had to face it. It was going to be awful.

As I sat there, Mr Guralnick came over to my desk and stood before me.

'Could I have a private word?' he said.

We went into the back office.

I was still thinking about how I should make the most of this opportunity to broach the subject of his departure when he made a dramatic sweep with his hand. 'I've come to a decision. The time has come . . .'

'What time?'

'For me to leave.' He paused theatrically, to allow for my gasp of horror. 'I am going to go.'

I wanted to go over and hug him. 'Of course, I'll be very sad to see you go . . .' I hoped he didn't hear the relief in my voice.

'You'll get over it . . .' He smiled. He knew the truth.

'I do value your experience. I'm glad you've been here.'

His head rocked a little, as if he was waiting for a punchline, something to undermine the compliment. 'So what are you going to do?'

'No more work. We've got no mortgage. We're moving . . . out to the coast. We'll get something cheaper.'

'Really?'

'You're surprised?'

'You never seemed like the moving-to-the-coast types. Esme with all her visits to art galleries. I just imagined you would stay here forever.'

'The thing is . . . I've been here so . . . sometimes it feels like everything accumulates . . . all the memories. They trap you, but it's a liberation to leave it all behind. And for the first time in our lives, we'll have some money.'

'You'll come back and see us, won't you?'

He shook his head. 'When I'm gone, I'm gone.'

'What, you'll never come back?'

It didn't strike me at that point to wonder what memories

he wanted to leave behind, why after all those years he had nothing to come back for.

'Selling up? We'll do the sale for you, of course.'

He nodded. 'Promise me one thing? Don't let that fool Terry do it just because there's no commission in it for you.'

'I'll handle it myself. In fact, I'll come over this afternoon and prepare the details.'

'This afternoon could be tricky.'

'Are you out with clients? I can get someone to cover it if you are.'

'No, the thing is . . .' He was embarrassed, apologetic. 'I want to prepare the details myself. All these years of selling houses and writing up the blurbs, this time I get to write something I know is true. I know the history of everything in that house, when every fitting was installed, checked, serviced, repaired.'

'Are you sure you want to do it? You could just sit back and relax.'

He bristled. I realised what an ordeal this would be for him. The biggest sale of his life.

When he prepared details, he liked to include everything. The make and capabilities of the central heating controller, the type of pump and its capacity, the thermostat and its resolution for controlling temperature. The number of sockets in each room, how many had switches, the manufacturer. Nothing was excluded from the wad of pages he produced.

He would not gloss over anything negative, either: a crack on a light switch, a trace of damp under the window, chips in the paintwork; all were detailed. And when I removed them it was as if I was committing the ultimate act of bad faith.

'Okay. But if it's fifteen pages long, I'll have to cut it down.'

'You can do what you want. But I'll write it how I like.'

I had thought he would go home then, but he sat at his desk and stared into space for hours. He became a dark presence I had to work with, the author of his own epitaph, finding words inadequate but having nothing else.

The other staff discovered a need to whisper around him, troubled that they might disturb his thoughts. Day after day he sat there, rigid, occasionally letting out a huge heavy sigh, perhaps writing three words, crossing them out and staring aloft again.

Beth and Terry would go into the kitchen area and explode into giggles. Even Yvonne found it difficult.

I took him into the office; I heard Terry begin to mimic the heavy sighing and grunting as we passed the kitchen.

'Are you finding it too difficult? I'm happy to write up the details for you.'

He shook his head.

'David, how does Esme feel about the move?'

He looked at me as if he didn't understand the question.

'She's very keen on the arts and everything. Won't she feel a bit isolated out there?'

He didn't answer.

'Don't you think you'd be better doing this at home?'

He got up with a tragic air, and swung his arm across his brow, like a silent film hero. He went walked the door, step by heavy step.

'I . . . I . . .'

You never know what sadness can create in a person, buried deep inside until some event causes it to rise to the surface. That controlled anger building up pressure within. So many years, and then one day . . . one day.

He did not come into the office again. We moved Beth to his desk the next day, but left the nameplate, just in case he returned.

I knew he would never come back.

⸙

The noodles are cold. The wine is awful. Exposure to air has not helped it.

Beth was right. I set in train a course of events that led to this whole tragedy. If the figures hadn't been so bad, if I had been able to keep David on, he would still be alive. If I had trusted my instinct with Andrew . . . if I hadn't overlooked the strangeness of his behaviour. As my father would have said, all the signs were there. But in the context of everything else...

Three people dead. The police came to the office that afternoon, asking about David, having gained a clue from the singed 'For Sale' sign that lay on its side at the front of the house.

'So, let me get this right . . .' the policeman said for the third time, in a very calm voice. 'He worked for you, and you took this person to buy the house . . . and what exactly was the relationship between him and the client?'

I caught the policeman looking at his partner, a fleeting glance. My speed dating experiences also included three minutes with a policeman. 'When you're questioning someone, how can you tell if they're lying?' I asked him.

'It's easy,' he said. 'Their lips move.'

The policewoman looked back at her notes. 'When did you say you found out about their relationship?'

At one point in my life, I had thought about joining the

43

police. It was probably caused by the frustrations of my secondary school, which existed in a state of perpetual anarchy. I had wanted to take control of it, to make something of it.

I wanted these police to like me as we sat conducting this calm, but carefully recorded, conversation. I could see they were suspicious.

'It's a bit of a long story . . .'

🦋

I tip the noodles in the bin and pour the dregs of the wine down the sink. The taxi standing outside the minicab office is running its engine, the driver revving it up occasionally so that the diesel fumes seep into my bedroom. I push the window tighter shut, but still the fumes penetrate the gap round the sash, and I think of myself drifting away into oblivion, intoxicated by carbon monoxide poisoning. I shout out to the driver, but he is on the phone, lost to the world. Then he drives off and it is quiet. Now there are just the sounds of a distant car alarm, foxes having sex behind the communal bins, the clicking of someone's lighter outside the minicab office. Further along the road, I can hear the constantly simmering battle being waged between drunken customers at the kebab shop.

And in my head? The figures. The figures. The numbers.

🦋

My phone rings as I walk to work. It is Anna. I ignore it. Then it rings again as I arrive in the office. Trembling, I leave the phone on my desk on silent; her name flashes up and I can see

44

the others in the office looking at me, willing me to answer it.

She finally gives up and sends a text. Then another arrives.

'Terry, have you written up those details for that house you viewed yesterday?'

He scowls sullenly. 'Not yet. I'll do them later.'

'I want them done today. Also, I've got three viewings this morning that I want you to cover.'

He nods as I give him the details.

'And, Terry, buy yourself a razor. You've only shaved half your face.'

Beth sniggers, and I realise he is growing a moustache.

'I'm going to be working in the back office. I've got some strategy stuff to work out.'

⸎

I hadn't really known David's wife Esme until the last couple of weeks he worked for me, but I'd seen her occasionally when she popped into the office. She had a self-assuredness that impressed me when she asked me questions, always precise and to the point. Where was David? When would he be back? Occasionally she would have a note prepared for him that she would leave in the centre of his desk. If I tried to talk to her I could see her shift her mindset and make an effort, but her heart was never in small talk. She would engage with me for a few minutes, focusing on a specific topic, talk intently about it and then leave. She was totally unlike my mother, whose raison d'être was to be a victim and to make the most of it. Esme had presence. And she understood philosophy.

A week had passed and there had been no word from David, so I decided to go to his house. We were a bit low on

45

properties, so even though selling it meant no commission for us, I was still keen to put the photo in the window.

Esme opened the door. She scared me a little, with her intelligence. You could feel it: when she spoke it was not just in sentences, it was in whole paragraphs, a part of a whole system of thought. But she didn't talk down to you, unlike the teachers I'd known at school who had used their cleverness to make you feel small and stupid. She spoke to you in a way that made you think the exact same interesting idea had occurred to you, it was just that you hadn't actually said it.

'Alice, nice to see you.'

'I kept meaning to pop in, but you know how it is.'

I followed her into the kitchen. She looked smart, elegant, in her grey suit and stiff white blouse. I admired her for wearing what pleased her best.

'I get stuck here for days on end, marking essays and then I start to disappear into a dark place.' She moved across to the back door and opened it, peering out into the garden. 'Just me and the dunnocks. It's a relief to have someone to help me break out of it.'

She assembled a Moka coffee pot. She pressed the coffee down tight, smiling as I watched her. She put it on the cooker.

'I'll miss this old thing when we move, but I don't think it would survive being dismantled. The gas man would say it should be condemned.' She looked sad, then laughed. 'It's we who should be condemned. Let them move the cooker to a new house instead of us.'

I smiled. It didn't seem like her voice speaking.

Through the kitchen window I could see a little shed that had been painted bright blue. The door was open: it was stacked with a lawnmower, spades, rakes, columns of plant pots.

'I envy you the prospect of a new beginning. Have you been to see any houses yet?'

She fiddled with the gas tap as the flame went out. She lit a match and it popped back to life.

'We went down to the coast the other day . . . but when I started to visit houses . . . there were so many possibilities; a dimension of limitless possibility, and that is very dangerous.'

'It must be exciting . . .'

She looked at me in surprise. 'Oh God, no,' she said. 'I have a horror of the unbounded.'

I wanted to grab her, shake her, stop her slipping into this world that was engulfing her. 'Esme, don't do it if you don't want to. He wouldn't want you to do it just for him. He gets carried away by his enthusiasm.' But I didn't say it: I stayed silent.

As she stacked the cups on the tray, the jacket became creased around her neck. 'I can read anywhere, but I've always been . . . metropolitan. I don't know how I'll survive away from the city, but I do get weary these days . . . you hear about this new art sensation . . . that fantastic discovery . . . and it's always something that was done before, and with more heart, in the sixties, before technology destroyed everything.'

'I don't know anything about art . . .'

'Alice, no-one knows anything about art. That's why they talk so much about it, they need to fill the void. These days I feel relieved when something gets a bad review. I think great, I don't need to bother seeing that . . . They should found a paper that just prints bad reviews, so that you never need to worry about seeing anything.'

The coffee pot began to hiss as the thick syrupy coffee began its journey to its upper chamber. The smell of coffee filled the room, making me a little light-headed.

'I wish I could understand art. I've always felt uneducated when I go to peoples' houses and see the paintings on their walls. I just can't understand what they see in half of that stuff.'

She laughed. 'I often feel the same. Except I don't go to so many houses as you.'

'I went to a house the other day, it belonged to City guy and his wife, lots of money, moving away, going up in the world. Every wall was covered with pictures of the wife naked. Some of them were pencil sketches, some were paintings, and there were oils, crayon, photos. In some of them she looked coy, in some she had her legs splayed wide so you could see all her business. I couldn't look at the woman herself, I really couldn't. I didn't know what to say to him.'

'Alice, you're such a prude. It's your Greek heritage coming through . . .'

'Well there's a time and a place, and for me it's not the hallway and halfway up the stairs.'

She led me through to the living room and crouched down, settling the tray on the table and pouring the coffee. 'I would never have been able to drag David to all those private views if it hadn't been for the prospect of some gratuitous nudity.'

The thought of him walking round art galleries to appreciate the naked form made me uncomfortable. She moved her stack of books away from the arm of her chair.

'You're so lucky. I wish I was clever like you. I'd never have imagined I'd end up an estate agent.'

'If you applied yourself to the subject . . . it's just a discipline like any other.'

'My father was always proud of our Greek heritage in philosophy. He would raise a finger as if teaching a lesson, "One day," he'd say, "one day I'm going to sit down and read this stuff until I understand it all."'

'He could be sitting down for a long time. Don't be envious of me, though: I spend my days marking essays by people who make everything up because they can't be bothered to read the text they're discussing.'

'My father was to blame for my choice of career . . . I used to find his businessman demeanour so impressive . . . using the force of his will to build up a business from nothing.'

Esme was nodding. 'I admire that natural cunning, too . . .'

'I never got on at school, I think it was my accent . . . it was thick in those days and they assumed that I wasn't academic because I didn't speak well; and it turned into a self-fulfilling prophecy. I should study again. You could teach me.'

'What? You want to learn philosophy?'

'It'd be a place to start.'

'I'd start with something useful.' She gave me a little Italian biscuit and poured another trickle of coffee into my cup. The coffee was bitter. I stirred in some sugar, but when I tasted it it still made me wince a little.

'I should do something. I keep thinking . . . here am I, thirty-four, no husband, I'm going to end up alone, childless. I should do something.'

'Believe me, there's worse things . . .'

'Sorry I didn't mean . . .'

She looked surprised. 'Didn't mean what . . . ?'

'I wasn't thinking of you. When I said that.'

Her teeth had been coated brown from the coffee. 'Why would you be? I'm not childless. We had a . . . have a son.'

I was taken aback. 'You have a son? Really? David has never mentioned him.'

She looked sad. 'No, he probably hasn't. He found it all very difficult.'

I was on awkward territory. The picture I had created of them . . . an independent couple, sufficient in themselves . . . evidently wasn't correct at all.

'Of course, he moved away years ago.'

'Do you still see him?'

There came a shouted greeting from David and suddenly he was in the living room. I felt bad, as if we were schoolgirls who'd been caught conspiring in a prank.

'Esme . . . Esme . . . Do you know where the torch is?' There he was, flustered, dark smuts on his forehead and his hair sticking up on end.

'Hello, David. Are you missing us?'

He didn't answer but crouched down to look in a cupboard.

'Why do you need a torch?'

'I was checking the ceiling voids. I saw signs of bark borer beetles a few years ago.'

'You wanted to include those on the details?'

I hadn't noticed until then that Esme often spoke to him in a gently mocking tone.

He met my eyes and gave me the briefest nod.

'I just wondered how you were getting on with those details. There are some people who are looking for a place just like this. I'd really like to be able to put a photo in the window.'

He scowled. Esme reached into a drawer and gave him a

torch. Abruptly, he left the room. 'Sorry, I've just got to do this.'

'Esme, tell me, do you think David really will finish writing up the details?'

Esme shrugged. 'You know what he's like. It could be weeks . . . months. It's the culmination of his whole career, his big chance to get the details perfect . . . a story in every room . . .'

I went over to her and knelt by her chair, dropping my voice. 'Do you think at the heart of it he doesn't want to sell it?'

'He wants to sell. He wants to go.'

'What about you?"

She looked sad. 'I worry that if we lose our connection to the world . . . that everything we had will be broken. We'll drift away; all will be gone.'

What I didn't realise then was that she was actually talking about her son, about cutting off any opportunity he might have had to return. If she and David were no longer at the same address, how could he find them if he wanted to?

'Shall I sort the sales details out? I can knock something together quickly.'

She nodded.

'Esme, I really do have some people who are interested . . .'

She smiled, as if knowing this wasn't true, but happy to pretend.

'And can I ask you a favour? When I bring them to view, can you take David out somewhere? I think he's . . . too close to it.'

She smiled again and I knew she understood.

'Give me a call. I'll sort it out.'

She kicked the pile of papers at her foot as she stood up. 'Believe me, if these students are going to be awarded degrees for writing this nonsense, you have nothing to worry about. When should we start our classes?'

Not for the first time, she scared me with her directness.

As I walked back down the road, I felt disappointed. I had thought of Esme as an ally, someone who had gone through life with no children, and no sense of loss that she had none. I had envisaged her life as a maelstrom of activity, too busy to fit in a child; visits to theatre, art exhibitions, cocktail parties, lectures, philosophical debates, a world distant from the kind of domesticity that had dominated my childhood. My illusion had been snatched away. My discovery that she had a son diminished us both.

⁂

I buy a sandwich and sit in the kitchen to eat it. When I return to the main office I sense I am interrupting something.

Beth comes over to my desk and stands by me. I look up and smile, my best, definitely-not-impatient smile.

'Beth. Can I help?'

'I need to show you something,' she blurts out.

I know they are plotting something and I decide to go along with it. She leads me down the street to a rival agency and we stand looking in at the window as she tries desperately to gabble the excuse she has been rehearsing in her head. The ends of her blonde bob curl towards the corners of her mouth, as if trying to encourage her to smile. 'It's here . . .' She points at the property cards, trying to find the right words.

In front of us a man is chaining his bike to a lamp post. It has a box on the front with a sign on it that says, 'Any needs required? Post details in box.'

'You brought me here to look at a man with a bicycle?'

She looks terrified. 'I thought you might want to see if he could fix those shelves for us.'

I've seen him before. He always wears a brown cloth jacket, like an old-fashioned supervisor's jacket, and cotton gloves with leather patches. After parking his bike, he always hastens away, as if on very important business.

'Got anything today needs doing? Any odd jobs?' He pushes a fist across his brow, wiping away imaginary sweat.

'I put a note in the other day. Last week. We had a blocked sink. You never contacted me. I had to get someone else.'

'Yes. Just put a note in the box.'

'I did. You ignored it.'

He starts fiddling with his bike chain. 'Just a note in the box. That's all. I can't deal with direct requests. I'd get overwhelmed.'

I turn to Beth. 'They told you to get me out of the way for a few minutes, didn't they?'

She nods.

'Do you think we can go back now?'

She nods again.

A gold banner has been strung across the back wall of the shop. There is a bottle of Cava cooling in an ice-bucket. They count down from ten and Terry flips the door sign to 'Closed'. Someone pops the cork. Yvonne thrusts a glass in my hand. 'Celebration Wednesday . . .'

'What are we celebrating?'

'I'm surprised you've forgotten. It's a year since you took over here.'

I force a smile. I hadn't forgotten. I should have laid on something myself, at least bought some better wine than this. I take a sip, willing myself to say a few words, but instead I rush out to the toilet and hide. No one follows me. I listen to their voices; they are getting more raucous by the minute.

I sit in the kitchen, shutting them out, and make myself some coffee. I've run out of Greek coffee, so I stir Co-op filter coffee into the brik, knowing it won't work. As I hear the hiss and pop of the heating pot, I feel the tears rising.

Beth comes in; when she sees my tears, she freezes.

'What is it?'

'Someone's here to see you. She says she's your sister.' Her voice is a nervous whisper.

'Why would she lie about that?'

I am angry. I know Anna has come to check up on me, to make sure I go to my mother's party.

I return to the main office. I am heralded by more popping as they open more sparkling wine. Anna is leaning on a desk, holding out her glass for a refill.

'Anna. Nice you could come and join in the celebration.'

She raises the glass and laughs, then swallows half of its contents. 'Never miss a chance.' I can feel my staff looking back and forth between her and me. She shakes her head and her mass of black curls falls across her face. She pushes them back. 'One year already . . .' she says.

'I'm sure you've got it marked on your calendar.'

She looks puzzled. 'No . . .' Her voice is soft, the words pronounced erratically, indicating to me that she had started on the drinks before she arrived here. She pokes me with a finger. 'At least you've built something with your life.'

She walks over to the property notices, running her fingers across the racks of pictures. 'Look at them all.'

'Do you want to move?'

She sits at my desk. 'It's your party; I'm gate-crashing.' Then, 'Have you got anything to rent?'

Her fingers tremble against the glass, those sculpted nails curling round it as if she's terrified she'll drop it. She knocks back more of the wine, and her eyes close, transported somewhere miraculous by this cheap, metallic fizz. Her shoulders heave and she puts down the glass and pushes out her hand, making a grand operatic gesture.

I take her into the kitchen. 'Why don't you tell me about it?'

⁂

'It's the lies that get me. How can he spend so much time creating lies? How can he live with himself?'

'You'd be amazed the worlds that people create for themselves. They construct the mental spaces they need to inhabit.'

We have been talking for a long time. I want to grab her, shake her, get her to tell me what happened, but I have watched this scene many times before, my sisters embracing the challenge to rise to an emotional trauma and glory in it. It reminds me of a long distant blowy Sunday afternoon when my father took me fishing. We sat sipping coffee from a flask contaminated by the residual odour of mushroom soup, and I stared out over the ripples of the lake, battling with boredom, while he watched the float, which was at that moment the most important thing in his life. When he leapt up after sitting so still, I was taken by that sudden action: drawing, teasing, playing with the invisible fish. I was standing beside him. As he explained to me what it was thinking, half-whispering as he told me how he would outwit the fish, cautious in case it heard his words and so could outsmart him, I imagined myself in that carp's head looking up from the water at the strange scene above.

When we finally held up the twitching brown lump of flesh and its sad eye glared at me, I felt only sadness at our triumph.

My battle with Anna is far briefer. She yields her story with little attempt at a struggle. She presents the evidence: the credit card slips her husband claimed were all part of business entertainment; the phone bill; the secret extra phone; his renewed interest in his appearance. 'He was a slob. He never bought new clothes. Now he spends more than me.'

I don't know what to say, whether I should join in the attack, or whether I am being prompted to try to defend him, tell her she is wrong. When my sisters gathered they were often on the attack, even when the man in question was not suspected of any misdeeds.

'I really need to move out. Now.'

'Are you sure? I thought you were trying to get pregnant.'

She scowls with contempt. 'Not any more. The bastard. I should, though. Just to punish him. But I need somewhere to stay. Can you help me?'

'I'll see what we've got. There's not much at the moment. We don't really do rental. How much can you afford?'

She stares at me and I am not sure if she has heard or if she is absorbed by some mental calculation. She raises her fingers in the air and folds them down one by one.

'The thing is . . . I don't really have any money at the moment. Not until we've got things sorted: arrived at some kind of agreement. And I'm not going begging to that bastard.'

'It's not begging. It's demanding what you're entitled to.'

Her lip quivers and I worry she will explode into tears again. 'Let me stay with you. Just until I can sort something out.'

I recoil. I hate the idea of someone else living in my flat. She reaches forward and grabs my hands. 'It'll be fun. I've decided to move into interior design. You can be my first project.'

My breathing is slow, measured, as I keep it under control. I don't answer. I don't refuse her and in a moment she has wrapped herself around me in a hug of gratitude.

'Tomorrow night, then,' she says as she leaves, and I feel more of a jolt than before. Suddenly this thing that I've tried to resist is happening. There is no escape.

After everyone has gone I clear up the debris.

The cycle of our lives. You put the details up, you take them away. One moment it's there, in all its punchy sentences, drawing you in, promising to fulfil your dreams, then there's just a blank white space.

I look at my calendar, the mesh of appointments filling every day except the blank white space of Sunday. My mother's party. Then I put shading around it and set a succession of alarms. As if I was going to forget it.

The cake. I will make it. I have my back-up cake that I baked with David, but I will bake my own.

I stand at the sink, relieved to be standing there alone, and wash up the glasses.

꧁

I rang the bell, just to make sure that the Guralnicks were out, then let myself in and waited. It was one of those roads on the brink of respectability: you felt that it could go either way: one month there were new buyers sorting out a run-down place, putting in work and money and making it look nice, the next month someone was renting an unloved, rundown house and feeling the need to collect washing machines and broken bicycles in its front garden. But you had to convince people it was an area on the up. It was my job to assist its journey up, rather than get it to the point of arrival.

I went into the living room and waited. There was a wad of paper on the table: Mr Guralnick's carefully-prepared details. Twenty-one pages. Four pages about 'the exquisitely hand-crafted kitchen units'; I knew they would be in a skip the first week after the purchase had been completed.

I went upstairs and entered their bedroom. Spinoza on Esme's bedside table. A crossword on David's side. How was that issue of the side of the bed decided? Does it ever change? With a new partner? If you both were used to the right side and one of you had to give way, what would happen? 'Your mother sleeps on the right side and I sleep on the wrong side.'

The bell rang. I went down to let in the viewers; I could see Carol was excited. She gripped my hand in a kind of failed handshake as I led her into the living room. Andrew was subdued. He held my hand in a handshake that went on too long.

As I turned round, I felt a huge responsibility for their dreams. And as I looked back I thought the house was letting me down. The hallway was dingy, the sole light coming from the glass panel above the front door. The wallpaper was discoloured at the top and by the door a corner had been torn away. The pictures on the wall were at different levels and they seemed to have been jumbled together randomly.

'Mrs Guralnick is very keen on art. You can see from the pictures.' I had never noticed that the large one opposite the living room door depicted a scene of evisceration. It was suddenly clear to me that this was not the abstract swirl of mists around pink forms I had admired out of politeness, but a body on a slab amid faceless surgeons.

Carol was not put off. 'Our own hallway . . .' she breathed.

Andrew paced the length of it. I opened the living room door and he followed me in.

He scrutinised the room carefully, taking in each picture, the contents of each shelf, each item of furniture, either giving approval or withholding it. 'What would you say is the value of these?' he said, pointing at some plain blue ceramics.

I was a little disturbed by the question. 'I shouldn't think they're worth anything, nothing significant anyway. She just likes things like that. Mrs Guralnick.'

'No, I don't mean financially. I mean what do they tell us? How do they communicate with us?'

Carol grabbed his arm and tried to pull him away.

'You'll need to talk to Esme about that. I don't think the pictures and knick-knacks are included in the price.'

'Take this one. It shows someone in a kind of mortal agony. Why would you have pain on your walls like that?'

Still he stared at the painting. 'I'm sure I can take it off the wall while we're here, if it's troubling you.'

'It's not troubling me.'

'Good.'

'I'm just interested. It intrigues me. The people that inhabit the place.'

59

'Well, I'm afraid that neither the occupants nor their pictures are included in the sale. Except by separate negotiation.'

He was thoughtful. He strode up and down what space there was, as if trying it for size, barely looking up. Carol's face radiated joy. 'I just can't believe how nice it is.'

Andrew walked over to the front bay window and looked at the glass in each pane. 'Interesting,' he said. He stared out of the back window, into the garden. 'The shed. That's good.' He came over to report to me. 'It's a nice room. I like it. Can we see the rest of the house?'

I took them into the kitchen. 'You'd probably want to change all this. It is a bit dated. Fine for now, though.'

'Change it? I wouldn't change it.' He ran his fingers along the surface of the counter.

'That's fine . . .'

He was peering inside the cupboards.

'These cupboards are made by a craftsman. You want us to rip them out to put a bit of chipboard in to replace it?'

'Only if you wanted to. A lot of people do. I think this place is made for you.'

'Or the other way round.'

'How do you mean?'

'It was here first. It was made for this house.'

'I'm glad you feel at home here.' I had a sudden desire to be homely and welcoming, to make them a pot of coffee and serve them biscuits on china plates with an art deco design arranged on a large tray made of ash.

Andy was looking out at the shed through the window that faced the garden. I opened the back door and we stepped out.

Carol walked up the path. 'It's a lovely garden. I never

thought we'd be able to afford a garden. We could grow lots of food. I can see it now. A row of aubergines along here. Then tomatoes. I'd love to be able to grow tomatoes'

I moved across to a tree. 'I believe this is a cherry tree,' I said, bluffing, hoping they didn't know any more than I did.

'I love cherries.'

Andrew had reached the side of the house. 'That's not a cherry tree. Can I have a look in the shed?'

'I don't know why I'm talking about trees. You need me to unlock it? I don't know where the key is. Can you not see enough through the glass?'

'I want to go inside.'

I went to search in the obvious places for the key. 'You might have to come back to see the shed, if it's important. I would ring the owner and ask where the key is, but he never has his phone switched on.'

Andrew sauntered across to a row of pots and lifted up the third one. Underneath it was the key. He unlocked the shed and stepped inside, his eyes half-closing.

'Have you been here before?'

He smiled. 'Have you ever seen a magician at work? When they ask you to pick numbers and you add them together and by some miracle they have written the answer on the back of someone's shaved head without him noticing? We are predictable. And desperately in need of miracles. We all choose the same numbers and hide our keys in the same place.' He tapped his temple. 'We're all the same underneath.'

I felt a shudder run through me. At that point I could not have been more certain that he and I were totally unlike each other.

He entered the shed and stood there, motionless, breathing

heavily as if practising yogic breathing. His shoulders tipped forward as he breathed in.

'Is it okay?'

He shrugged. 'It's a shed.'

I led them back into the house and we went upstairs.

It did strike me as odd, the way he wanted to see very specific things. He didn't seem to notice the general feel of the place in the way that you would have expected. He was like someone looking for clues to a past life.

Carol clutched his arm as we mounted the stairs to the main bedroom. 'I like this. Very light.'

He stood there, looking out of the bay window into the street, nodding silently, reading the details Mr. Guralnick had left for them. 'He ran out of steam a bit here, didn't he? For every other room there's lavish detail. Here, there's just the dimensions.'

'I think he probably hadn't got round to describing this room. He's very thorough.'

'That of which we cannot speak we must pass over in silence.'

I must have looked puzzled.

'It's an old army saying,' he said, by way of explanation. 'There is a lot of light coming in here.' He stood in front of the window, a black silhouette against the light. He scrutinised the details again, flicking through the pages.

'He liked to go into the nitty gritty.' Carol said, and smiled.

'He's a detail man, the vendor. He worked at our agency. This is his last ever sale. It meant a lot to him to get the paperwork right. All the detail.'

'Except for this room.'

'I'll have a word with him.'

'They like their reading, don't they?' Carol nodded towards the pile of books on Mrs Guralnick's bedside table.

'She reads a lot of philosophy.'

Carol shuddered. 'I prefer something a bit more relaxing at bedtime.'

'I find it interesting. I like to read . . . Spinoza.'

Andrew looked at me as if showing he could sniff out a lie.

'What are you reading?' I noticed Carol had a book clutched under her arm.

'Frankenstein. It's for a project. It's much more interesting than you would imagine. The tragedy of having too much knowledge and too little wisdom. That's what it says in the education pack, anyway.' She laughed.

We drifted downstairs, leaving Andy in the bedroom.

'I teach in the primary school just up the hill, so this is perfect for me. Just a short walk to work from here.'

Suddenly Andrew was there. I got the feeling he didn't like us talking unless he could listen in.

'Can you guess what Andrew does?'

'I couldn't even begin to guess. A dentist? A lawyer?'

'You're just throwing out jobs. Try a proper guess.'

'An estate agent?'

He smiled at me and nodded. 'Close. Closer than you think. I'm a life coach.'

'I'm not sure I've come across one of those. What exactly do you do? In practice, I mean?'

There was a certain menace in his manner as he leaned towards me. 'I teach you how to live.'

'Right . . .'

'Some people will teach you how to live their way. I teach you how to live your way. I teach you to discover what your way is.' He was looking right at me, as if analysing how I lived, seeing the sadness in my journey back to an empty flat each evening, in the snatched takeaways and obsessive working late into the evening; the waking at two in the morning in front of the television, trying to understand where I was and what I was watching.

I'm pretty cynical about most new age ideas, but I did feel a frisson of excitement at his words.

'Like discovering what you want in life?'

'Like deliverance. Clarity of thought leads to deliverance.'

Carol came over and joined us. 'It means helping with the impossible problems in your life. He helps you sort them out.'

'Don't most people have families to do that?'

'No, families mostly create the problems.' He smiled again, as if he could see my family in his mind's eye.

'Is it expensive?'

'People will pay for something when they can see the value of it. Money is not a problem for me.'

It was going well. I didn't want to rush them. It was always good to let viewers relax in a house, feel like they belonged.

'I'll leave you two alone. Make yourselves at home. I need to make a few calls.'

I went out into the hall. As I flicked though the messages on my phone, I could hear them whispering to each other. A whisper always draws you in. I heard the chink of glass.

I sent my sister another text confirming that, yes, I would be at the party. 'Remember, it is her seventieth,' she added, accompanying the words with a smiley face and a picture of a birthday cake.

It was amazing, the stuff that the Guralnicks had accumulated over the years, the pictures that I'm sure they hardly noticed any more, the little objets d'art on the shelves above radiators and in alcoves, the wall still bearing the pencil marks of David's precise marking out. A bronze Ganesh and Shiva rubbed shoulders with blobs of glass and amber containing beetles and butterflies frozen in time. My parents' house was like that, too: every object that had caught my mother's attention in previous years was now an object of pain because my father had gone. My sisters reinforced her misery; at every family gathering they would remind her of my father, referencing his behaviour and rubbing it in, making the point that most men behaved as badly.

The phone in the hall began ringing. I ignored it. It was an old-fashioned black Bakelite phone with a dial and a proper bell. Esme had told me a local curry house had printed thousands leaflets with the digits on the phone number transposed, so people would call to order food. On my last visit Esme had answered wrong numbers six times. I could hear her trying to explain as one caller barked an order for a number 26 extra-hot, with nan and ten poppadoms.

I was determined to make that cake. How difficult could it be? It would take some self-belief. I would not be able to bear having to endure my sisters' feigned sympathy as they chewed with relish, mocking my failure, in front of their constructions of meringue, cream and cream. I was going to bake an orange and almond cake to David's recipe. I would get David to teach me to bake it. He would love that, the opportunity to explain each step methodically. He had time on his hands: I was selling his house to a cash buyer.

It was time to disturb the lovers. 'What do you think?'

Carol was smiling. 'We love it.'

Andrew was holding a tumbler into which he had poured

sizeable shot of whisky. I was surprised to see he had located a little silver tray on which a decanter containing scotch and some glasses had been set.

'It must feel like home already?' I said, giving the glass a pointed look.

Carol stretched herself out on the sofa.

'Are you thinking about making an offer?'

Andrew shook his head, pausing until I opened my mouth again. 'No.' He pushed away the glass of whisky.

'Okay.' I was taken aback. 'Do you need more time to think, then?'

'No. I don't want to make an offer. I want to buy it.'

'No offer?'

'They're asking a fair price. I'll pay it.'

It wasn't a fair price. David had overpriced the house to such an extent that I thought he didn't want to sell it. It was foolish for them to pay it. Still, why argue? 'That's, great. Thank you.'

'One more thing. The contents. I want everything in the house. All the furniture. Everything just as it is.'

'That's a separate negotiation. You want everything? Don't you have any of your own stuff?'

Carol gripped my arm, excited.

I noticed one of Andrew's eyes didn't quite focus on me. Maybe it was made of glass? How much compensation would someone get for losing an eye? Not enough to buy a house. Not even if you lost both eyes.

'Stuff? When I joined the army, I took lots of stuff. My parents gave me a tape player . . . a going-away present. One of those ghetto blasters with silver speaker horns. The first night I was unpacking and the sergeant came to inspect. We gathered in a nervous line, and he went over to my bunk and pointed his stick at my tape player. I still hadn't used it. He told his corporal to put it on the floor in front of me. "This soldier considers his personal property to be more important than preparing his bunk properly," he said.

'The corporal then smashed my tape player to pieces. He had a baseball bat I imagine he kept to mete out this type of punishment. They moved on to the other rookies' bunks and smashed up their stuff too. You can imagine how popular I was.

'Since then I've travelled light.'

As I poured the scotch back into the decanter and rinsed the glass, I tried to work out what made Andrew behave in the way that he had. I couldn't understand it: his obsession with small details, his desire to purchase the contents of the house, helping himself to the Guralnicks' drinks. And he hadn't actually sipped at the whisky. He'd poured it to make a point, but I had no clue what that was. And why would he and Carol be prepared to pay the full price with no attempt at negotiation? I wanted to grab them and say, 'Are you mad? Try bidding down a few thousand.'

I could feel my father lurking in spirit behind me, shaking his head in despair. He would never pay for anything without haggling. It could be an embarrassment, at the newsagent's for example. 'Forty pence? If my bread was as stale as this news I would never sell a loaf. Not a slice of a loaf.'

He and the newsagent would then banter, the newsagent saying he knew how rich my father was, despite which he was now trying to rob a poor honest tradesman and my father re-torting that if you added up the hours he worked and divided them by the money he made, he could prove he'd have been better off working at McDonald's.

'I'll warn them you're coming. They'll need to order a special uniform in your size.' And so it would go on.

The question that most haunted me about Andrew was why, if he had so much money, he was prepared to buy a run-down terrace in a dingy street in South London.

I dried the glass and replaced it in circle it had left in the dusty tray.

⚜

Later that day Andrew made the offer formally. I called David and told him about the offer. It didn't seem to make him any happier. 'So that's it, then.'

'It's good news isn't it, David?'

'Yes, yes.'

'David, you don't have to, you know.'

'What? I don't have to what?'

'You don't have to sell the house. You can stay there if you want to. Esme would understand. Do you want me to talk to her?'

He laughed. 'You think it's Esme wants to move?'

'Doesn't she?'

'We'll accept the offer. Thank you. You've checked them out? They seemed reliable?'

'They're cash buyers, offering the full price. What more do you want?'

He sounded envious. 'Cash buyers. You spend your life

paying for something and then some kid comes along and buys it for cash.'

'So you want to turn them down because they have the money?'

'No.'

'Great. I'll let them know, then. And, David, one other thing. I've got a favour to ask you. You know the cake you make?'

'Which cake?' he said, as though there was a large repertoire to select from.

'That one you used to bring in to the office on Fridays. The orange and almond cake.'

'Oh, that one. What about it?'

'Can you show me how to make it? I need to make a cake for my mother's birthday.'

'I thought you said it was a bit heavy.'

'I liked it. It was always my favourite cake.'

'I thought you were being polite.'

'Really?'

'It's very easy. You just boil the oranges in a sugar syrup . . . I can tell you everything over the phone.'

He was playing hard to get. 'Can't you show me how to make it?'

'It has to be unwaxed oranges. You must make sure of this. Seville oranges are the best.'

'Ok. I'll buy some.'

'You can't. It's not the season for them.'

'David, would you show me how?'

'You want a baking lesson?'

'Yes.'

He grunted and put the phone down.

I wasn't sure about the end of the conversation. Did he think we had finished or had he deliberately cut me off?

⁂

That was only a week ago. It is a shock to me to realise that it was only a week ago that David helped me with the cake for my mother's party.

He'd called me back an hour later, asking where I was. 'I thought we were supposed to be baking this afternoon?'

I had no recollection that this was what we had agreed, but the afternoon was proving quiet, so I visited the new Greek deli to buy the ingredients. I experienced a pang of disloyalty at not buying them from my father, even though his shop was long gone. As I inspected the shop's wares, I felt the urge to tell this shopkeeper, no, that's not how it's done. You can't have a Greek deli without fresh bread, without home-baked buns with fat black olives poking out and browned cubes of cheese and a big fold of herbs. You can't have all your pickles safely tucked away in jars. They need to breathe that London air, to mix in with smoke and diesel and grit. The herbs mustn't be packed in cellophane. They have to be in big bunches, waging a constant battle against limpness, doused in water each day and shaken out on the pavement, leaving lines of spray. That's how you run a deli. Even this man's moustache was wrong, clipped too short, so it never got the special attention, the rigorous combing required for a visit to the wholesaler's.

'So you liked the cake?' David was smiling.

'Hey, I'm Greek. I like anything heavy with a lot of sugar in it.'

'Then I'll take you on the Jewish assault course.'

'They didn't have any almonds. The man at the deli gave me ground almonds instead.'

He smiled as he led me into the kitchen and took out a kilo bag of almonds. He removed one and bit into it, gazing into the distance as he chewed, as if he could see them growing, far beyond the hills of South London. He cut a sheet of grease-proof paper to the exact size of his baking tray, trimming the surplus twice until he was sure there was no overhang, then tipped on to it half the bag of almonds, spreading them with his hand until they were evenly distributed. He knelt by the oven and turned on the gas, then lit a match. There was pop as the flame caught.

'Did your mother show you how to make this cake?'

He laughed. I could imagine him asking if he could try baking and his mother shooing him out of the kitchen. 'And did you show your son?'

He didn't answer. He took the almonds out of the oven and banged them on the table.

He seized a large knife and ran it up and down a steel a few times, holding it up to the light, narrowing his eye as he checked the blade. He gave it a few more strokes of the steel, tipped the nuts on to a board and began to chop them, running the knife backwards and forwards over the chopping board, sweeping the coarse powder into a bowl after it had gathered in small piles.

'You can use a food processor if you want to. I like to do it by hand.'

'Is it OK to use ground almonds?'

'Yes. And you can also add cucumber pickled three different ways when you're baking it by yourself. When you're baking it with me we do it properly.'

71

Placing the almonds on his scales, he cut one in half to get the exact weight. Each teaspoon of the powder was measured precisely, and a knife run over the top to ensure that it didn't contain too much. When he poured the liquids into the mix, he would hold the jug aloft until it was emptied of every last drip.

'You never told me you had a son.'

'I have an aversion to hard-boiled eggs and offal. Have I told you that?'

'I have three sisters. You know that, don't you? I have a crazy mother who's been in mourning for her life since the age of forty. And a father whose life she tries to destroy because she can't bear the idea he might be happy. In fact, I'm not sure she wants any of us to be happy. I think she likes the idea of us all weeping together for the rest of our lives. I've told you all that. How come you never mentioned your son?'

He pushed the bowl over to me and began to chop the nuts for the second half of the cake. He'd heaped another pile of nuts on the chopping board and was rocking the knife in great sweeping movements, creating another pile of the creamy chopped almond.

'Are you going to stir or talk?'

I stirred.

Watching my mother cook was quite a different experience. She would throw in every ingredient with abandon, and whatever the measure was she would put in an extra bit for luck, as if such generosity would ensure a good result. Often this was not as good as she'd hoped, causing regret: 'If only I'd put a bit less salt in, a bit more flour . . .'

We boiled the oranges and mashed the mixture with the

almonds and sugar. He left me to stir it. 'Don't stop for a moment or it will catch.'

It was a curious reversal of our customary positions. His quiet patience gave me a sudden pang of guilt. I couldn't help thinking back to all my moments of impatience, the times when I'd sighed with frustration, stared up to the skies and implored deliverance from his foibles.

'I know about him. Your son. She told me. Esme told me.'

He stiffened. The mound of nuts collapsed in the bowl and he sank over the board, his shoulders rounded. His pace of chopping had slowed almost to a standstill.

'Communication is different these days. He will be able to find you, if he wants to, even if you do move away. You can leave a forwarding address in the house or give it to us at the office.'

He grunted and let out a sudden gasp. There was a spluttering sound as he pulled away from the board. His hand was dripping blood, big drops falling to the floor and standing proud of the polished clay tiles.

'David . . . what have you done?'

There was a deep cut in his index finger which filled with blood each time I wiped it away. I held his hand, tearing off pieces of kitchen roll and wrapping his finger in them. The paper quickly turned red. David was deathly pale.

'I'll drive you to hospital.'

Esme came in, saw the blood and seemed about to faint. 'Oh my God.' She rushed off to find some bandages while I held David's finger tight in my fist. We stood in a clinch like two shy lovers exploring uncomfortable new territories.

'I'm sure it will stop. Soon.'

'She'll be back in a moment.'

73

Esme returned holding handfuls of lint, cotton wool and wadding. 'Look at you. I should have brought my camera. It's like a sixties art event. Meat joy. It wasn't a party then if you didn't spill some blood.'

We were still in our clinch as Esme strapped up his finger up. She wrapped the cut in a bundle of lint until it was securely bound. The trail of blood remained on the floor tiles, some drops smeared where we'd walked in them, others still domed and glistening.

'He's always doing that. He's not to be trusted with a knife.'

He shrugged and pulled his hand away, then watched as I ground the rest of the almonds in the food processor. I put the bloodied knife in the sink and rinsed the blade.

David said, 'It needs to be dried. To keep the edge.'

Esme and I shared a look.

David sat in the kitchen and issued instructions, still looking pale and shocked. I finished making the second half of the cake and slid both tins into the oven.

'What now?

We went for a walk as we waited for the halves of cake to bake. It was a warm evening, the late summer scents from bushes mixing with smoke from a distant bonfire. A car shot past end of the road, straining as the hill steepened, juddering then roaring as the driver changed gear.

It was a street in transition, half the houses gleaming with newly painted front doors, refurbished windows, old cracked mortar raked out and replaced. Others were dingy, awaiting their moment.

'It must be a strange feeling, knowing you're going to be leaving after living here for so many years.'

'It'll be good. You can spend too long in a place.'

'Can you? I rather like the idea of putting down roots. Perhaps I've moved around too much.'

'You can build up a history in a place. Then it's good to leave it behind.'

'I'll come and visit.'

'You won't. You couldn't make it outside the M25.'

'I will come. I can travel. I go outside London sometimes. Away from all this . . . When the madness gets too much.'

I waved a hand, as if there was some evidence of ferment hidden beneath the sedate streets. I noticed a sticking plaster someone had stuck down on the tarmac, pink healing on the grey.

'To leave it all . . . the memories, the troubles.'

I thought back. There had been odd moments when he'd come in late, having had to deal with some 'incident' he never explained. 'Have there been troubles?'

He moved on, slightly ahead of me. He was a fast walker. 'Nothing a slice of cake and a gin and tonic can't fix.'

'What troubles?'

He kept walking. I grabbed his arm and slowed him down. 'Tell me.'

'It's just random stuff. The kind of stuff you get in South London. Things just happen. Broken windows. Graffiti. Rubbish through the letterbox. It's just how things are.'

We stopped. We could see far across the common: a child trying to fly his kite although there was no wind; a dog running for the ball that his owner had pretended to throw; a boy doing a moonwalk with a purple bowler for an imaginary audience.

'Is that how things are?'

'It's how things are.'

'Should we be warning the new owners that this is what they should expect?'

'I think Esme and I might have been unlucky. Who knows why it was? Anti-Semitic? Anti-military? Personal? It would be good to know why people hated you.'

'David . . .' I felt frustrated, but what could I say? They were going. Leaving it all behind.

'We've put an offer in on a house by the sea. It's been accepted.'

'That's great news! But why didn't you tell me? Why do I have to force everything out of you?'

He asked about my plans. I told him what I was thinking of doing with the estate agency. Then I wondered if he was actually asking about something else; something more personal.

'You are so lucky, David, to have this chance, to be able to start all over again, with no money worries. No work worries. Free to do what you want.'

He was smiling, a private joke.

'Do you think Esme seems a little reluctant to go, though?'

'Esme? No, she's always wanted to have money. And she's desperate to move.'

We carried on walking. We both noticed a large lump of wood in the road. I guess it had fallen from a tree surgeon's truck. I helped David pull it to the kerb. I thought he would leave it there, but he didn't let go of it: he seemed to want to keep it. I didn't ask why straight away, but helped him as we turned to drag it all the way back to his house.

'What do you want it for?'

He was lost in concentration, looking at it from different angles, seeing something in it I couldn't see.

'We need to go in. The cakes . . .'

When I took the cakes out of the oven, I wanted to immerse myself in that heady perfume forever.

'So there they are.'

'You really made this yourself?' said Esme, as I cut a slice for her. It was still warm.

'David helped me a lot; but I'm going to bake it again. Next week. By myself.'

'You can call me if you get stuck,' David said.

'Yes,' said Esme. 'If you need someone to drip blood over your floor.'

'We should have let it cool properly. The beauty of this cake is it gets better as it gets older. In three or four days it'll be ready. In a week it'll be perfect.'

⁂

It is late when I finish washing the glasses from our party and clearing away the food. I lock up the office and walk home. A group of kids huddles outside the off-licence whose interior is lined with Makrolon panelling and reinforced with wire mesh. I go there in times of desperation. You point to what you have selected and the assistant manoeuvres his way silently behind the panelling to the appropriate shelf, pointing to each item, a mime artist awaiting a nod of approval. After you've paid through the hole with extra wire mesh he passes across the bottle, offering it a momentary reverence, as if it is a fine rare vintage. Girls in short skirts approach men to negotiate a purchase by proxy with flirtatious smiles. A freckle-faced boy looks at me, about to plead his case, then looks away. I feel a little offended he doesn't try.

He picks the wrong bottle of wine but I don't protest.

Next stop the corner shop to find something to eat. 'Bush meat pie,' the owner says with a big smile, 'Lovely-hot.'

'What's it got in it?'

The shelves are lined with tins of vegetable, callaloo and hearts of palm, and dried packs of noodles (with real shrimp). There are blocks of creamed coconut and scotch bonnet chillies, now soft and wrinkling. I can't see anything I want, but it is too late to cook.

'Lovely-good bush meat. Free-range. Organic. From the bush.'

He spreads his hands wide to illustrate the expanse the creature had to wander in, the size of the bush. I continue my pursuit of something edible. The rows of tins bear crude illustrations of their unwholesome contents as ominous as the description of the ingredients.

'What kind of animal was it?'

'Good meat. From the bush.'

I am too tired to pursue this. I tuck the warm greasy bag under my arm.

The flat feels cold and empty. I'd operated the override on the heating because I knew I'd be late, but now I am regretting it.

The pie is still hot and I eat it with the plastic fork the shopkeeper supplied.

The pastry is rich and soft, and the meat has a depth of flavour that makes me wonder about its provenance. It is only when I am half way through my dinner that I check on my laptop and discover I am eating primate. I finish it anyway.

I lie back, luxuriating on my sofa, thinking that this is

going to be my last evening alone for a while. I check on the cake in the fridge. It has settled a bit, even more solid than when it was baked, but it still looks okay.

So that was it. Nearly a week since we'd made the cake together and there it is in the fridge, a grey parcel wrapped in string. Now it makes more sense, David's moment of shock. The mention of his son being enough to cause the shedding of blood.

Four answerphone messages from Helena, one from Susanna, both checking I am still on course for Sunday, and one from Anna confirming her time of arrival tomorrow. A sisterly onslaught.

I am still thinking through possible excuses, mentally rehearsing them, but I know now there's no escape. I'll have Anna here, supervising me. And I have the cake.

The cake: a strange memorial to a fleeting friendship.

It is my last evening alone. No more sitting in the quiet: Anna is never calm. I look around the room, suddenly aware I should have made it more like home, perhaps by strewing it with scented candles, cushions and photographs of the family.

I will come home every evening and she will be there, perpetually talking to me, wanting me to chat when I just want silence. Maybe there is something wrong with me. Maybe that is why I am alone: because it is what I want. People can sense that underneath that is what I need.

Maybe having her here won't be too bad. I can hide in my bedroom. At least she will turn the heating on when it's cold and won't give me food that contains primate. And once she has some money, I can start charging her rent.

I need to go through the figures again. I feel guilty for the thought that they've improved because David has gone, but I know they're still a disaster.

Like my life. A misplaced tragedy. Put on hold to make some point I have forgotten to people who are too busy with their own lives.

❧

The next morning the office is already unlocked when I arrive and there is a bag containing a croissant on my desk. Someone has made me a coffee. They haven't noticed I don't like milk, and they've used my Greek coffee, stirring a couple of spoonsful into the cup as if it is Nescafé. I smile and wave to Beth, who is watching anxiously.

'Thanks, Beth.'

Terry nods proudly. Her collaborator.

Eventually I can't face the grit on my teeth anymore and discreetly pour it down the sink.

I check my diary. I have a lunch appointment with my father. He comes every couple of weeks to make a nominal check on the business, but he has never examined the figures in any detail. He just likes to meet for lunch, always at the same Italian café, where he complains about the food, comparing it unfavourably to Greek food, and flirts with the same waitress he has been flirting with for the last twenty years. He has long since lost his power to embarrass me.

There is a message from him, confirming the time to meet, as if it ever changes.

I wish I could cancel the lunch: monkey doesn't agree with me. My stomach is still churning, but he would be so hurt that I can't bring myself to call him. And I need him to give me more time for this month's repayment.

There used to be so many nights when I couldn't sleep. I would get out of bed and go downstairs and sit with my father. The same glass of Metaxa would last him for three hours. Sometimes he had a notebook in front of him and would sit rigidly still most of the time, then launch into bursts of frantic scribbling.

Sometimes I would ask to see what he was writing. He would react with mock horror. 'Would you like me to read your diary? Your private thoughts . . .'

'Mum does.'

'She does not understand. She thinks we're all plotting against her.'

'You can read my diary. It's not very interesting.'

He handed me his notebook. It was hard to make out his writing. Most of the words tailing off into a line after the first couple of letters. It detailed the businesses he was going to develop . . . a restaurant serving dishes made of aubergine a chain offering all-day English breakfasts. 'It's all about the turnover', he would say, pointing at his figures: this from a man who sat for three hours with a single coffee, then complained about rudeness if the waiting staff offered to get him something else.

Those schemes. I don't know if any developed further than scribble in that notebook, but he always seemed to have money. 'Investments. A bit here, a bit there.' He would tap his nose. He could sniff out a good investment.

When I meet him on the corner by the café he grabs my hands and kisses me as if he is desperate to see me, but he is also desperate to see 'my darling Lydia,' still wearing the same black waitress outfit, now stretching a little at the seams so the stitches bow out.

We sit in our usual cubicle. Behind us is the owner of the hairdresser's, sporting a bouffant of grey hair above his red shiny face. He is talking intently to one of his staff, a pretty girl in her early twenties who looks terrified.

'Let me tell you this, the company is definitely going to make money for you. It has to. I've put everything I can into it. More than I can. I've remortgaged. You know what? I've nearly doubled what I put in at first.'

My father explores his full range of facial contortions as he listens, mimicking by turn mock horror, joy and trepidation, although I can imagine myself sitting in that girl's place and hearing him utter the same words.

The young woman is hesitant. 'Does your wife not mind? What if it goes wrong?'

He laughs, uncomfortable at the mention of his wife. 'There's two types of people. There's people who take a chance and there's the also-rans. Believe me, you can't go wrong. You'll double your money. At least.'

I sometimes wonder what liberties my father has taken with my parents' finances. My mother's refusal to divorce means he still controls all the money, but it is impossible for him to discuss anything with her.

Lydia, the waitress, stands in front of us with her pen poised. When I was young she was an almost impossibly glamorous woman. I used to stare at her in awe, convinced that it was just a matter of time before she was snatched up to become a film star, but twenty-five years on she is still there taking orders, persuading us that the lasagne is the stuff dreams are made of, only surpassed by the tagliatelle carbonara.

The cook's waist has grown: the sequence of photographs on the wall plot his journey to corpulence, until now he looks like a sweaty Pavarotti, with only the smear of tomato on his brow and the grubby apron tight against his stomach to tell us he is not about to break into an aria. On with the motley.

'Lasagne. Lydia. You trying to kill me? At my age? Has someone told you I've left you everything in my will?'

'So it'll be a salad, will it? Listen mate, with Mr Moneybags in the kitchen over there, I wouldn't notice your little pile. You can't believe the luxury we live in. I only work here because I love the people.' She sighs, managing a sad, weary smile as she looks round at the collection of people occupying the tables.

'Yes, a salad. That's all. Got to watch my arteries. That's fine.'

'Shall I just put a little something on the side? Just to make it . . . look a bit more appetising?'

They go through this ritual each time and she will bring him lasagne with a lettuce leaf on the side and he pretends he is being virtuous.

'And your lovely daughter? What is she having?'

'Lydia . . . can you still not remember which one I am? After all these years?'

'Of course I can. Anna. How is your husband? Kids? Have you got a husband yet?' she says, looking down at my ring finger.

'I have three children. Three boys. They're all at wrestling school.'

'My God. What a family. So many. You should bring them in some day. Free food for them all. Well, perhaps I stick it on your father's bill.' She goes into the back area, shaking her head, and I hear her shouting at the cook. I wonder if they have finally married. She is shouting her frustration at seeing him smoking on the other side of the kitchen door.

Some days the cook puts opera on the little music player; the speakers crackle with the volume as he mouths the words silently, scowling in pain as if his entitlement to sing out loud has been robbed from him. Then he takes out an unlabelled bottle and pours the wine into tumblers and puts them unbidden on to all his customers' tables.

After telling Lydia about my imaginary family, I find I like the idea of it: just as something to tell people. It feels like an achievement you could share, like getting a degree from Oxford. I think maybe I should start visiting the café more often, picking up sandwiches while I build on the fiction. Maybe I'll change it each time, until I find a life that fits.

The financial advice issuing from the next table continues and the young woman speaks hesitantly. There is the money she's saved with her boyfriend for a deposit on a flat. 'He'll thank you. Believe me. I'll arrange it for you. Go in with everything you can. Get your family in as well. Believe me, in a couple of months you'll all be thanking me. In a year you'll be saying I'm the person who changed your life.'

My father is still chuckling to himself at this exchange. He indicates with his thumb his contempt for the man, make a gesture of scissors working their way across his throat. 'So how is Anna?'

'Funny you should ask that. She's moving in with me tonight.'

'Really? How has that happened?'

'It's just temporary.'

'Temporary? Everything is temporary. A lifetime is temporary.'

'She's sorting out things with her husband.' I laugh. 'The way you and Mum sorted things out.'

He sighs, on the brink of reciting the apology speech that always turns into counter-accusations, but then he lets it drop and shakes his head. 'I finally started reading some philosophy. Thales. We all come out of water and in the end we sink back into it, waving our arms and legs, desperately trying to breathe, trying to keep our head above that water, all tied together in one great mass. But living with Anna. Are you sure that's a good idea?'

'She's going to bring me cushions. She is going to cover every surface with decorative objects.'

'Lucky you. The happy family.'

'I always used to think you'd go back to live in Greece when you'd sold the deli, Dad.'

He laughs. 'My father had a café on the beach. Every season there would be women, tourists, he would get to know. For two weeks, a month. He learnt French, English, German. Especially German. Late evenings they would sit out in the café drinking and talking, all his friends, including a special lady, and he would open a big tin of fish, salted fish. He would pass that tin around and everyone would reach in and take a piece, the salted oil dripping down their chins. The special lady would always pull a face after being persuaded to taste it, but he would stand on one leg, energised by that fish, while someone started the tape and he would begin to dance.'

'Then I saw that same tin of fish down at the wholesaler's, the same pattern on the line, those circles of fish, anchovy eyes and thick lips. I bought it and when I opened the tin it was such revolting stuff I could not swallow one mouthful. Even after I'd thrown it away the smell was still there on my hands, seeping into my clothes. Everything seemed better than it really was in Greece . . . but maybe all this is a dream. My whole past is a dream.'

He looks at me and smiles, his focus shifting back to me. 'Anna. Are you sure?'

'How long is it since you've seen her?'

He sweeps his hands wide and shakes his head. 'That fish. Disgusting.'

The food comes, and as I eat the lumpy stodge I remember why I only visit the café with my father. He has a brief glance at the figures I've brought, grunts, and frowns.

'It's not so good, is it?'

He shrugs. 'It's still building . . .'

'I'm worried. I've just let one of the staff go. But still . . .'

He nods.

'I'm not sure getting rid of one person is enough. I can't give you the first repayment.'

He does his annoying head-shaking act, not quite saying anything, not agreeing or disagreeing.

'In fact, I might need to go the bank . . . to see about a loan . . . unless you can . . .'

He smiles. 'I am hitting a wall,' he says. 'Hitting a wall.'

I'm not sure what he means.

'Dad, I need some money. I'm worried the business is going to collapse. I don't think the bank will give me a loan and even if they agree it will take too long to sort out the details.'

He looks as if he is in great pain, turning his head from side to side. 'I'm hitting a wall,' he says again, and smacks a fist into his palm. Whatever he is offering, it is clear it isn't money.

I sometimes wonder if he ever really looked at those

figures. He won't look at them now because he can't help, whatever he may find.

'Anna . . .' I think back, to her sitting on the bed surrounded by the rows of fluffy toys that she refused to give up even in her teenage years. They are probably making their way to my flat right now.

'She can't face being on her own yet. And her husband controls the money. She can't get the funds to rent anywhere.'

'You, sharing with Anna. I cannot imagine that.'

He looks at his lasagne as if its weight is the weight in his heart. 'Family. We're all in that water together. You think you've got out . . . but . . .'

⁂

As I leave the café, a fight is about to break out in the street. Padraig is approaching. He regularly strides up and down the high street, swinging his white cane in a menacing arc in front of him and shouting, 'Get the fuck out of my way.' On some days his blank scary eyes rage at you when you meet him, seeming to focus on a point deep inside your skull, but without making any connection. On other days he walks past calmly, giving no hint that he can't see, sweeping his long greasy black hair back from his eyes.

A couple are just leaving my offices. They are frequent visitors. The man is white, in his seventies; he wears a wool suit thick enough to have its own sense of purpose, with a red carnation on his lapel. He carries a long cane topped with a carved ivory knob in the shape of an elephant's head. The woman is younger, with light Caribbean skin and tight braids. She wears Jamaican colours and speaks with a surprisingly haughty upper-class drawl. Each conducts a separate commentary on the world around them, each occasionally stopping to exchange a thought with the other. They visit the office regularly to work through all our properties. They comment on anything new that's come in since their last visit, always sharing aloud the reasons why it is unsuitable. Sometimes they will come in simply to stare at the details of a single property. We know better than to offer to help; they're probably just using us to get warm.

Today, as they are leaving, they step out into the path of Padraig.

The intermittently-blind Padraig is about to smash straight into the couple with his swinging stick, but miraculously his vision returns at the last minute and he swerves past them. He leaves a trail of abuse in his wake as he carries on his march and runs straight into a thin Rastafarian carrying a thick gnarled stick, waving it skyward. The Rasta inhabits that end of the high street, perpetually expounding his view of the world in an impenetrable patois that is punctuated by lewd gestures and whoops of 'Ras . . . blood claat'.

Padraig's stick clashes with the Rasta's and they both halt, momentarily silent.

The couple's commentary continues. 'What are you saying? What are you talking about? I don't understand a word of it.' The man turns to his partner and she shakes her head.

'I think it's some kind of curse. I think he may be cursing us.'

'Why would he curse us?'

'I don't think it's just us. It's everyone. He's angry with everyone.'

Padraig moves on, leaving the Rasta looking bewildered,

but soon he starts his jabbering again. I am grateful that I understand so little of what he says because what I do understand leaves me offended and disturbed. He berates a woman wearing a tight red patent mac and, rather obviously, little else. She has foundation caked on her pinched face. There is an inch of grey at the roots of her bleached straggly hair. She scowls back at him, surprised, before suddenly exploding into a stream of abuse.

At the end of the tirade he rights himself, points his cane into the sky and in a mock cockney voice says, 'Well I only asked . . .'

Now the couple notice me standing there. 'Have you got any decent houses? We had a look at your boards, but everything seems pokey. We like a bit of space.'

'I always keep the more exclusive properties off the boards so that you can look first. Just let me know when you're ready.'

'We'll be back soon. I just have to move some money around. It's all tied up in investments. I heard about the fire. Terrible business. Just shows though, doesn't it? Just shows.'

'What does it show? What does it show?' I want to chase after them, but instead I let them go and just ask myself the question. What does it show?

※

There were warning signs, but most things in life only make sense in retrospect. If we lived our lives from the end to the beginning it would be much easier to make the right choices

Mr Guralnick's call was a warning. He sounded a little breathless.

'It's about the surveyor.'

I'd tried to persuade David not to be there for the surveyor's visit.

'I think I should. I can explain a few things. These young chaps don't understand old houses.'

I felt sorry for the surveyor. I could just imagine him battling to carry out his measurements as Mr Guralnick explained mortar composition in the 1890s, earnestly making notes on his pad, offering explanations on top of explanations.

David had called, his voice urgent. 'That chap they sent round, he's not a surveyor.'

'Not a surveyor? He said he was. How do you know?'

'Registration. He's not registered. And he doesn't know what he's talking about.'

'Well, if they don't need a mortgage, they don't really need a surveyor.'

'So why send a fake one?'

'Maybe he's just someone they trust to advise them. Why worry? He's less likely to come up with problems.'

'There are no problems.'

'Good. So it doesn't matter then. They've saved some money and there are no problems.'

'But they should have a proper survey. And why say he was a surveyor?'

'Don't look for problems. Just think of the move. How is Broadstairs?'

I'd deliberately changed the subject and he knew it. He didn't answer.

I worry what Anna is going to do when she is in the flat on

her own all day, what changes she will make to prettify it, burning out her credit card before her husband cancels it on soft furnishings I don't want. She will convert all the rage she feels towards him to sweetness, turning it in on itself and directing it towards me. An onslaught of cushions, throws and candles.

I rush back, knowing I am late. She had called me earlier, panicking. She'd put the oven on to warm and a terrible smell had emanated from it. When she checked to see what it was, she realised the instruction manual was still inside, in its plastic wrapper. 'Have you never used your oven?'

She is baking something wholesome for me and I feel an urge to stay out late, to avoid her, so she can fling it in the bin in a rage. But meekly I head home.

Anna's transformation of the flat has begun: there are cushions everywhere, plush ones with tassels and every flat surface has a candle on it, as if there is an odour she needs to purge. The sofa is buried under cushions which I have to pile on the floor to get comfortable. The kitchen surfaces are clear, all the clutter now hidden away in cupboards, but I know I will have to search for the things that were previously right to hand. My world is slipping away from me.

I have to find a way to get her out.

I called Andrew, who was nonchalant. 'Everything's been put in place. Our solicitor has all the information he needs. He's just sorting out the last few details.'

'You wanted to buy the furniture. You said everything

in the house. Just as it is. I've called to let you know they're happy to negotiate.'

There was a long pause. 'Can you negotiate a price for us?'

'Not really. They would like to meet you, in any case.'

There was a silence at the other end of the phone. 'Is that okay? Shall I suggest tomorrow?'

I heard a grunt which I interpreted as assent. He told me he was giving a talk about life coaching at the local community hall. Would I like to attend?

It was the type of event I normally make a strenuous effort to avoid, but on impulse I decided to accept. I was interested in the plan that he had devised . . . I had a sense that it was beyond what was available from routine therapy or counselling. I was also curious to know how he could make a reasonable living from it.

⁂

The great furniture negotiation was about to begin.

I met Carol and Andrew as I walked up the hill. They were standing on the corner, waiting for me.

Andrew was quiet. He had assumed a mournful, dour manner and was looking intently down the road, as if seeing it for the first time.

'Are you ready, then? It'll be fine. They just want to meet you.'

I pressed the bell and Esme was there in a moment, holding wide the door.

I would like to say that with hindsight I recalled noticing something, some pointer of what was to come. Maybe I did experience the briefest moment of puzzlement, but to be honest I really didn't see much to alarm. Or did I? Because I would have expected them to show fear or apprehension. But if I noticed anything, it was suppressed elation.

Esme shook hands with Andrew and Carol. When she took Andrew's, she held it a fraction longer than was entirely necessary.

She invited us to sit down in the living room and went to make coffee. I followed her. 'Is something wrong?'

'Wrong, dear? Why?' Her grey suit jacket was bunched up at the back of her neck. I smoothed it down. 'We've got cake. David's gone into overdrive since you baked that cake together. Do you want to slice it?'

'You seem a bit . . . distracted.'

'I'm just tired. A bit of a headache.'

I carried in the tray. Carol smiled, clearing a space on the table for me to put it down.

'We love the house.'

'It's a place where you can spend many happy years . . .' Esme trailed off, as if there was more to say.

Then David came in. I knew something was wrong.

How do you characterise a look? It's easy to find meaning in retrospect. But at the time?

I wanted the meeting to be over. I wanted to be anywhere, doing anything: to be rebuilding my life in a community hall, to be buying coffee and cheeses for street people, to be taking financial advice from strangers and relationship advice from my father. Anywhere but there. I sensed an uncomfortable shift of mood in everyone present.

David shook hands with Carol and Andrew and sat down.

'We had your surveyor here yesterday.'

'He's a friend of mine. He's very focused.'

'No problems, then?'

Andrew got up and went over to the bay window. 'This pane. The glass is different. Did something happen to the original?'

I saw David's face screw up as he looked at me triumphantly.

'I told you people notice. It's in the details.'

'He noted a bit of damage here and there. Nothing more than the normal wear and tear of family life.'

'That all depends on the family.'

Esme came in. She looked round the room apprehensively as she poured the coffee. I distributed the cups.

'Could you remind me: what job is it you do?'

Andrew sat upright, as if at an interview. 'I'm a life coach.'

'You take on screwed-up people and make them normal?' Esme smiled at the idea.

He smiled. 'No. I do the opposite. I take the normality out of people. I bring out what is different about them.'

'Then what do you do? When you've brought it out?'

'We celebrate it.'

She passed round a plate of cantuccini.

Carol leaned forward to speak to her. 'You should come to one of his sessions. He's very good.'

'I've studied too much philosophy. My nature is so deeply critical I can't pay the milkman without engaging in dialectic.'

Carol smiled pleasantly, settling into the sofa. 'I do like this sofa. It is really comfortable.'

David was getting down to business. 'I understand you're interested in buying the furniture and appliances?'

'If you're happy to sell . . .'

'What exactly do you want?'

'I want everything. Just as it . . .' He stopped dead as David cut in.

'Everything? You want to buy everything. All this worthless stuff. It might have memories attached, but in monetary terms it's worthless.'

'All those happy . . .'

'What price did you have in mind?'

'You can name the price.'

'The price. What kind of price?' David stroked his chin.

I was anxious. Carol was startled, looking directly at me as if she expected me to provide the answer. Esme's face had undergone a terrible transformation. I saw her looking at David in a way I had never seen before. She was regarding him with pure loathing, and then as if she sensed what I was seeing, she dropped her gaze to an essay lying on the floor. She had drawn a red line diagonally through a whole paragraph. 'Wrong,' her comment said. 'Read the text.'

'What would be fair? Who wants second-hand furniture? Everyone wants new things.'

This was an interesting negotiating tactic, coming from David. No wonder his sales were always so low.

'There's the pictures. The art. Who can put a price on that? Half this stuff, we'd struggle to get a tenth what we paid for it.'

Esme had a puzzled expression, a little hurt.

'But there's something else. The happiness . . . the spirit of love . . . years of sitting together, moments of affection, love, an extrinsic value. How do you put a price on that?'

At this point I thought Andrew was going to give David some help, but he remained silent.

'It's worthless. So you can have it. All of it.'

'Everything in the house?'

'Every picture. Every cup. Every piece of paper. You buy the house. We move out and leave it all. Ready for you to move in. All intact.'

I looked at the two of them, trying to anticipate who would make the next move.

Carol was looking to me for reassurance, attempting a tremulous smile.

David marched across the room and stood in front of Andrew, too close. Andrew rose, pulled a ten-pound note from his pocket and dropped it on the table. He held out his hand. Were they going to shake on the deal?

David was shorter, so the top of his head only reached Andrew's nose, but he did not raise his eyes to meet Andrew's. Instead he stepped away and dropped his voice.

'You may be able to con the rest of the world, but you can't con me. Don't waste my time.'

Andrew displayed the traces of a smile around the corners of his lips. He nodded as if he had been expecting this.

'Forget about the furniture,' Carol wailed. 'I don't want the furniture.' I wanted to go over to comfort her, but I felt rooted to the spot.

Suddenly the impasse was broken. David shook his head. 'I'm sorry, Carol,' he said. 'I really am.'

Andrew strode across the room, his arms swinging as if he was about to attack David. Then he turned abruptly and marched out of the house, slamming the door behind him. I watched him standing outside in the street, looking back at the house. He looked up at the bedroom windows, then hurried away down the road.

Carol's face had collapsed, streaming with tears. 'What has just happened?' she asked, her voice cracking. 'I don't know understand.' I held her, noticing a smell of patchouli rising from her. Patchouli?

She wanted to rush out into the street to follow Andrew. I tried to hold her back but she broke away, running out of the door, looking first in one direction, then the other, walking at first, then running, changing her mind again and turning back to run in the opposite direction.

Esme sat down, shaking her head as I opened my mouth to speak to her.

I went into the kitchen. David was standing outside on the back step. His face shone with a triumphant glow. His sleeves were rolled up, and he was holding a large wooden mallet and a chisel. He'd started to carve the wooden block and I could see a horse's head beginning to emerge. He gave me one look and then continued to carve furiously, flecks of wood flying in all directions.

'When it's done I'm going to carbonise it. With a blow torch. Then it will be black. Charred.'

Esme came in with the coffee tray and put it on the kitchen table.

'There's still coffee. It's a bit cold.'

'What was it that just happened?'

She seemed surprised at my question, as though the answer was perfectly obvious. 'He is our son.'

An army of questions arose, competing, in my head, but I made myself wait for Esme and David to tell me more.

David shouted from outside, 'He was never going to amount to anything. Now he's amounted to less than nothing.'

'How do you know? How do you know?'

Esme closed the door and as we talked we could hear David carrying on with his sculpting outside. I could see him through the window, his face grim. It was clear Esme could not bring herself to look at him.

'He said he was going to take up carving when we moved. He has a natural sense of form, apparently. It seems he couldn't wait any longer.'

'It does look like a horse.'

'That's just what the world needs. More people carving horses' heads.' She smiled sadly.

'He's your son?'

She nodded.

'How could you not tell me? Right at the start?'

It seemed strange enough already, but when she pulled her legs underneath her and gripped her knees, and told me more, it seemed even stranger.

'How could I not say? That could be the motto of my whole life. How could she not say? It would break the spell.'

She nodded towards David, her face taut with fury, a knot of muscle rising in her cheek. 'It was always difficult between them. Men weren't involved in child care in those days. They were distant figures . . . it's easy for the mother . . . you spend all that time feeding them, changing them, the relationship is natural. Then this figure appears from out of the distance and starts getting involved . . . he did try, but whenever he helped it went wrong and . . . because he'd been excluded or excluded himself, there was no obvious way back in. I know he tried, to play football and things like that, but you know what he's like. He would trip over his feet and the ball would fly off in an unexpected direction and Andy watched mystified by the whole thing, unable to understand how he was supposed to relate to it.'

'But David's so personable . . .'

'Personable?' Esme looked surprised. 'David? They clashed from the start. In Andrew's teenage years, it got worse. He hated school. He said all the other boys hated him, but I think he made that up. Or he provoked it. When I saw him with other boys they seemed get on fine. He didn't look like the lonely, isolated figure he claimed to be.'

'David had a knack of doing the wrong thing. When he spoke it was always a shade too soon. He always interrupted Andrew, but sometimes it seemed as if Andrew engineered these verbal clashes. Mostly Andrew subsided into a silent sulk when David was there.

'They would have huge rows. He skipped school, and failed exams. David would berate him about wasting his life, and Andrew would stand his ground and sneer.'

I shook my head: any semblance of a coherent picture was slipping away from me as I tried to fix what had happened in my head, tried to relate it to my own family arguments.

'Then there was one final row and Andrew disappeared, rushed out of the house. We had no idea where he'd gone. "He'll be back," said David. "When he's ready."

'I sat up all night waiting for him, but he didn't come back. The next day I went out into the garden, dazed from lack of sleep. There was an early spring frost and everything looked beautiful, coated with spiky ice-crystals. I felt a sudden desire to trim the holly bush and went into the old shed we called the summerhouse for the clippers, but the door wouldn't open. I pushed it hard and realised that there was someone asleep there on the floor. Andrew.

'I fetched a blanket and gave him some coffee and toast. His teeth were chattering. We barely spoke. We just sat there, trapped in that moment, knowing this was part of a journey he had to take.'

I looked out at David, alternately banging away at the horse's head then twisting the chisel round, to bring out the flare of the nostrils.

'Did David not know?'

She shook her head. Her voice had fallen: it was soft now, just above a whisper. I moved so that I could sit next to her.

'For three days he lived in that shed. I left him food and hot drinks. I kept the back door unlocked so he could come back in as soon as he wanted to. David has an instinct for an unlocked door and kept on coming back downstairs to lock it after we'd gone to bed. I'd make myself stay awake, and I'd wait until his heavy breathing began, that rumbling on the brink of a snore. Then I'd get up and unlock the door again.

'Three nights?'

'Three nights.'

'And then?'

She assumed an apologetic smile. 'Each night I lay on the brink of sleep, hoping to hear the sound of him coming in. On the third night I was so exhausted I dropped into a deep sleep. I don't know what happened. What happens in families?'

She grabbed my hand, her eyes fixed on mine as if she expected me to provide an answer. 'Maybe it was the cold. Maybe it was living in a shed with his own excrement, with those unlabelled jars of neurotoxin pesticides, with the can of petrol for the lawnmower. I hated that lawnmower. It always took David ten minutes to get it started and then it would stall after two minutes and he'd begin the whole process over again.'

She smiled as if she had made a little joke.

'"I understand conflagration." David once said that to me. Can you imagine? I couldn't think what he meant.'

'I woke from my sleep and saw Andrew standing in our bedroom. I felt a wave of relief come over me. I pulled the cover up over me, feeling a cold breeze as if he'd left the back door open, and sank back into my dream. Then there was an overwhelming smell of petrol and the whole room erupted into orange light. As if the world was ending. Again.'

Coffee. I hate that bitter Italian coffee. Give me the Greek stuff with a bit of sludge, and a lot of sugar. I drank too much in that mouthful. I think I was crying. So was Esme. Before that day, I could never have imagined her crying.

'The firemen said we were lucky. The petrol can was nearly empty. And the covers absorbed it. The fire burned above us. A blanket of fire burned above us.'

'Can you imagine trying to explain these things to the police? David told them Andrew was sleep-walking. I could see the half-closed sceptical eye of the copper scrutinising us, but round here there's always bigger fish to fry. The angst of a middle-class family and a wayward son doesn't count for very much. We agreed to attend family counselling sessions and that was it.'

'Do you think he was sleep-walking?'

'We sleep-walk through most of our lives. Moments of insight . . . decisions . . . are rare . . . fleeting.'

'I can't imagine David joining in those sessions. Did he agree to go?'

'David saw counselling as a personal attack, not a possible source of help. He tried to tell us what to say. What not to say.'

'I bet you loved that.'

'I went in determined to tell the counsellor everything, but in that first session I felt only a sinking despair. She was wrapped in a fluffy green cardigan and spoke in generalities. Homilies. There was a carriage clock on the mantlepiece and pictures of a child smiling earnestly and behind it a family group embracing in a big hug. Whatever she asked us, whatever we replied, she would say, that's normal, that's quite normal. We had joint sessions and individual sessions and I began to make up outrageous replies to her questions, just to hear her say the same old thing. Yes, I frequently fantasised about killing David, Andrew, both of them together. Yes, in very painful ways. The more painful the better. "Rage is normal, absolutely normal," she would say.'

'So that was it. Eight sessions and we were completely normal.

'Despite this, we could not return to life as it had been before. Andrew signed on with the army. David suggested it. I don't think Andrew wanted to be a soldier, but he wanted to get out . . . and that was a way out.

'Before he went I got some cassettes and made some recordings on them. God knows what I said. I gave him the benefit of my knowledge and experience . . . but who ever really has anything useful to offer? I tried to tell him how to rebuild his life. And when he left I gave them to him.

'In the nights after he'd gone, my only comfort was the thought of him listening to them, maybe finding something in them that could help him. I also wrote to him. I would spend hours writing about anything and everything, but he never replied. Then, after two years, I received a package. Inside were my letters unopened.

'We didn't hear from him again. Not until now. The home-coming.' She sighed. 'The homecoming.' Her eyes blurred with tears. 'What am I going to do? Alice? What am I going to do?'

I wasn't sure what she was actually asking me. I gripped her hand.

Now I realise what she was asking. She was asking how she could avoid moving. How she could escape moving away with David.

What should I have told her?

Get away. Get away now.

⚘

I made my way to the community hall, wondering if Andrew's talk was still on. I thought he might have cancelled it, but I saw that people were gathering around the sad little community hall with its guttering falling off and the black stains of damp down the brickwork. There was competition – the building stood opposite the Spiritualist Church and Friday night was psychic reading night there.

The entrance of the hall smelt of floor polish. Beyond that, the odour of years of accumulated human decay hung around the place. The noticeboard advertised kosher lunches, tea dances, diet clubs and a beetle drive.

Carol greeted me, gripping my arm. 'He's just about to start.' She was still holding on to me. I thought she was going to hug me. 'I need to talk to you. After. Don't go.'

I took a seat at the back, in case I decided to make a discreet escape, despite my promise that I would stay.

A man in a check jacket nipped in at the waist was standing

on the stage and comforting a distressed woman. 'But you're not listening. You're not listening to me.'

She was dabbing her eye with a long multi-coloured scarf, some of the threads hanging off it.

He led her to a seat at the front. I looked at Carol. She smiled back at me, apprehensively. A group of older men clutching cans of lager formed a line in the seats behind me. Most of them had fallen asleep.

The crowd was hard to classify. Some people seemed to be there because they had nowhere else to spend the evening, solitary faces happy to be in company. Others were grouped in social clusters, helping themselves to tea and biscuits and chattering to each other. No one looked as if he or she might be a potential client for Andrew.

A buck-toothed man with thick glasses came on to the stage, feeling his way along the front of the table. The murmuring of the audience stopped when he raised his hand. 'I'd like to introduce someone to you whom I only met recently. When I heard him speak, I was impressed and it made me think that you'd like to hear him, too. So here he is, and he is going to talk to you about . . .' He looked down at his bit of paper. 'Well-being.'

The woman with the scarf clapped frantically, and a few others joined in, the applause growing until a steady ripple rang through the room.

Andrew took the stage. Someone clicked off the lights, except for the single spotlight which was fixed on his face, creating the impression of a disembodied head floating in the gloom.

He began to speak. 'Imagine yourself jumping out of a plane. You've parachuted before . . . but as you're falling, someone bumps into you . . . you're winded . . . your counting stops . . . four . . . four . . . four . . . four, you keep saying. Your chute opens, but it's twisted, and you're spinning, heading towards the ground too fast. When you hit the ground, the pain blocks out everything.

'When people say I'm going to talk about well-being I feel concerned. I don't like that term. I talk about being. The "well" bit . . .' He spat the words out, as if they represented something unpleasant and threatening.

'I'm here to help you stop listening to what the world is telling you and to listen to the frightened child in the dark, listen to what it is asking for. That child lives in terror. You need to hear it. First, I need to take you back. A long way.'

I wish I could remember more of what he spoke about. The police visited the office this morning and asked me lots of questions about Andrew, including this session and what it was all about.

When I tried to explain, they were obviously baffled. 'So was it an investment scheme?'

'No. It wasn't a financial thing. It was more a kind of spiritual thing.'

'What, religious?'

'Not exactly.'

They still seemed confused but didn't press me further.

'Do you think it was him? Do you think he started the fire?' I asked them.

They wouldn't answer, but somehow I knew they had no other theories about how the fire had happened.

I felt embarrassed when I was talking about Andrew. It was as if I was idolising him. I stopped talking.

'What did you make of what he was up to?'

I couldn't say. There was something mesmeric about his delivery: I don't just mean the illusion of the disembodied head floating in the darkness of the stage. He used words in an unusual way, applying them to situations they didn't quite fit. He talked about the lostness of childhood, the slipping away, the silence and desperation of realising you are truly alone, and how the only sanctuary resides not in other people, but in finding places of significance to you and inhabiting them, building your character around them.

'One thing he was clear about was home, how home is a key concept . . . it is the most important thing in our lives. We constantly flee from it, but it is the one thing we can never escape.'

They nodded as if that made perfect sense. It was hard to understand what that sense was. I have no doubt they remained unconvinced by Andrew's philosophy, at least as I had described it.

No-one had walked out of that hall while he was talking. Some slept through the whole thing. A few looked intimidated, as if they wanted to leave, but were scared that he would see them. Was what he said threatening? Did I feel threatened? No. I feel threatened by my family, not by someone shouting at me in a community hall.

There was one point he made that cut right through my cynicism.

'You may think you know what you want in life . . . but do you? And if you do, do you have a plan for how to get it? We live in a sea of discontent. We wake from a troubled sleep with anxiety banging away in our chests. We don't take the time to step back and look . . . to say, what do I want in my life? Do not be afraid to speak the words. People will stamp on the words, your desires, your dreams. But once out they will always be with you. Without taking that step, you will not even begin to achieve.'

Was this a form of religion? Although he did not mention of God, I felt as if I was listening to a dangerous prayer.

❧

I left the hall early, trying to get out before the crowd blocked me. As I stepped into the night air I heard someone calling. I turned and saw Carol running after me. I had forgotten about my promise to her.

'Alice . . . we need to talk.' She stood in front of me, panting, trying to speak, gulping as she tried to catch her breath. 'I want to say . . . to apologise . . . I'm so upset . . . I don't understand what happened.'

I took her into the lobby of the spiritualist church opposite.

'He told you about the owners of the house? That they are his parents?'

'I just want everything to go back to how it was yesterday.'

'Yesterday might have seemed different, but it wasn't. The situation was always going to blow up in our faces.'

She was distraught; her head was beginning to shake.

'Carol, there's lots of other places. That one wasn't so special.'

'But it was for him. He is an unusual person.'

'I can see that.'

Her tears came again, fast; her shoulders were rocking. 'I feel lost. He's slipping away from me.'

'He'll get over it.'

'What I don't understand is what he was trying to achieve.

Why does he want to go back there? Who wants to live in their parents' house? Even if they've had an idyllic childhood,' Carol said. She looked at me, pleading. 'But that's why he has to go back. Can you persuade them? Go back and talk to them.'

'I'll see what I can do. But Carol . . . think seriously about this. If he's not telling you important stuff now, what will he be like in five years' time?'

She nodded. The crowd had drifted away now. 'He can believe in a certain thing so intently that it takes over his mind and blocks everything else out. When the world intrudes on this thought, he's overtaken by crisis.'

'Tell him you want somewhere else. A different house. If you can't discuss it there can be no future for you together.'

She was already turning back, looking towards the hall. 'I've got to go and help him clear up,' she said. 'You really should think about what he spoke about. It is . . . important.' She pressed a booklet into my hand.

'I will think about it,' I said. 'Or I will try to. But you really should . . .' I didn't finish the sentence because I didn't really know what she should do and I knew she wouldn't do it anyway. She gripped my hand, let it go and went rushing back to the hall.

⁂

Anna is holding the leaflet from the church when I arrive home. They put a bunch of them through my letterbox two or three times a week, as if a single one would not persuade me but a bundle might.

'What is that noise? I've made your dinner.'

I can smell pasticcio. I want to tell her I can't face it, but she is so pleased that she's cooked for me, so fired with enthusiasm. There is an open bottle of wine on the table.

'Do you always work this late?'

'It varies. I had stuff to sort out.'

I sink into the heap of cushions she has arranged on the sofa.

'More cushions. Lovely. Where did they come from?'

'Come from?' Anna smiles sweetly, as if she has no idea what I am talking about. 'Oh, I just picked up a few more things. Just to make it . . . softer. I know you're busy. I just wanted to say thank you.'

Rows of scented candles line the mantlepiece, filling the air with the heavy tang of coconut and lime. She has installed two silver frames containing photographs of the family group. Four sisters, our mother scowling from the centre, caught saying something, mid-word; the rest of us smiling with gritted teeth.

'Thanks. It's lovely.'

She smiles, gratified. 'I know you don't really have time to notice these things, but I do at the moment, and I just wanted to make it a bit more homely.'

'I guess I'm not a decorative person. I'm more . . . minimalist.'

'It felt a bit cold. Stark. What harm can a few cushions do?'

'That's what they'll be asking at the inquest when I smother you with them.'

I throw one at her and she laughs. All good fun.

Stark. I liked the starkness at David and Esme's house. They had avoided much embellishment. They kept it bare. Except for the artworks, but they were not there for decoration.

They had been objects of contemplation. Now they were black cracked frames, charred memories.

'What did you do today?'

Is this how couples talk in the evening? What new things do they find to inject into this moment? 'I saw Dad for lunch.'

Abruptly she gets up and goes into the kitchen. There is the hint of a slam as she plonks the pasticcio on the table. A shockwave runs through the contents of the dish, a gasp, and a bubble of tomato sauce pops out on to the table.

'I needed to talk to him about money. He always had plenty of money. Now he doesn't. It seems he's run out of it.'

She ignores me, pretending I haven't spoken. She scrapes some pasticcio on to a plate, an elaborate process requiring a pair of spoons. She scrapes first one clean, then the other. She puts out salad and pours us each a glass of water.

'Well, that's what *he* says.'

'Yes, but it's a matter of pride for him to have money. He used to complain that he was poor, but he always had lots of money . . . wads of cash in his pocket. Now he only pretends that he has money: it's all gone.'

'The bastard. He's hidden it.'

'Perhaps; but maybe it really has gone. Maybe he was never the great business man we thought he was.'

She looks shocked. 'What's Mum going to do?'

'She's been living in her own world, one where she still has a husband. He's been living in his own deluded world, too, where all his investments bring him more money. It's all crashed for now, but it won't be the end. Eventually they'll both hit another crisis.'

She nods and we eat in silence for a while.

'This is good. Thank you.'

'I was sorry to hear about the couple who died in the fire. He worked with you, didn't he? Do they know what happened?'

'Families. That's what happened.'

She looks puzzled and squelches out another lump of the pasta and mince onto my plate without consulting me. Coils of steam rise as it collapses. I pierce it with my fork. 'Mm. This is lovely. But I don't know how I'm going to get through it.'

'You just start. Then you keep going.'

⁂

I stir from sleep to hear Anna snoring; she likes to leave her bedroom door open and the sound is filling the flat. In the background I can hear noises coming from the African church. I've got used to the fact that every Friday night, after day-long fasting, possession of tongues begins, followed by fulfilment of wishes, wilderness shouting, and the voices of serpents. The sounds reach into my dreams and shake me awake. It is a cacophony of the wailing of demons, children crying, the preacher shouting, the pulse of the crowd as they all rise to a frenzy, sometimes accompanied by the sounds of animals baaing, braying, howling. Maybe what I'm hearing are the dogs in the cars parked all around, waiting to be let out, chasing the spirits that have been released. Sometimes there's a drum beat, slow, painfully slow. Then, when you can hardly bear the anticipation of the next stroke, moving just slightly faster. We have all night. We have forever.

I stand at the window, staring onto the metal roof of the church, which used to be a warehouse for storing car-parts.

There are cardboard boxes from alternators mushed into the corrugated board of the roof. Sometimes you can see the board shudder when the power of a spirit reaches a high point, and wisps of the light dance through the gaps the movement makes.

A fox strides by, stopping to recover a chicken bone, stretching out its spine; it looks back at the church, unimpressed, and continues its journey. A minicab pulls over, sounds its horn a couple of times. The driver smokes the second half of his cigarette and drives off, his radio jabbering the whole time in Jamaican patois. A distant screaming rises to orgasmic pitch, then relaxes into laughter.

As the shouts of approval in the church turn into a roar, I try to imagine the scene inside. In the past I have caught brief glimpses when the doors were open. The lights consist of harsh rows of fluorescent tubes. There is no hiding place for demons.

I try to imagine the frenzy in there, but all I can think of is the fire, those flames curling over the Guralnicks, blocking their exit, David perhaps trying to squeeze through the window. I had attempted to persuade David to take the security bars off the windows.

'It's going to put people off. They're going to feel like it's under threat.'

'If they don't want them, they can take them down.'

He knew the score. He understood the poor impression the bars made, but he could not bring himself to remove them. They made him feel safe.

Anna stands behind me and puts a hand on my shoulder. 'You're cold. Are that lot disturbing you?'

'No. No, it's not them. I'm used to them. Except when

they slam the car doors at dawn. I was just thinking . . . about families.'

'About our family?'

'No. In general.'

She nods.

'About how everything's built on expectation. It's all about the promise of a job or partner or a child. That's what sustains it. You take the promise away and it collapses. It's a pact of expectation, but life's so fragile. Look at what can happen to it.'

'Are you thinking about that fire?'

'It felt wrong. There was something wrong about it.'

'Do they know what happened?'

'Something exploded.'

She nods. 'It was an accident, then.'

A car alarm goes off. 'I'm going to complain to the council tomorrow. They shouldn't be allowed to disturb people like this.'

Through a gap between the blocks of flats the blue of dawn is opening out. The door of the church bangs open and groups of men in smart suits emerge, carrying sleeping children dressed in white robes. They shake hands and embrace each other, then put the children in their cars and wait.

'Have you heard anything . . . ?'

She shakes her head. 'I hate to ask . . . but can you lend me some money? For Mum's birthday present. He's blocked my credit card.'

I look at the cushions and other useless items that are now covering every surface.

'Why do we do it? Why do we have these relationships?'

'I don't know,' she says, her eyes filling with tears. 'But at least we still have family.' She holds me to her. 'You're so cold.'

She's right. I am cold.

⚜

The final car door slams. Anna has gone back to bed. I hear her steady breathing.

I look at all the ways in which she's prettified my living room. If she was a vendor, I'd be congratulating her on her efforts. Why do I resent them so much?

The kebab shop has closed now and the mini-cab office is quiet. Someone is watching a Bollywood film, the high-pitched shouting turning into song, rattling on a tinny TV speaker. From a car radio issue the sounds of a football game commentary in Portuguese, great swooping vowels of excitement and bursting fricative attacks.

'When our desires are revealed, the world has no power to resist. It opens itself up. Its riches and pleasures are there for the taking.' I had felt a little surge of energy when Andrew had said that.

Where had it all gone wrong?

I feel exhaustion pulling at me, but if I lie down my mind races.

Usually when I felt like this I would switch on the radio and flick around until I found something interesting, maybe that throaty Lebanese singer I'd discovered once before. But Anna's presence makes me cautious; I don't want to disturb her, not so much out of consideration as to avoid her getting up again, talking, always talking and asking questions.

As a child I had a little radio with an earpiece so I could put my head under the pillow and listen to the shortwave stations, sounds bouncing off the ionosphere, the distant voices, the earnest shouting. When the voices were in Greek, I would become more awake, concentrating, picking out the words I knew, imagining that I understood it. It might be an interview with the crazy man of the village who always had a different viewpoint, whatever the subject. Or the wildly interrupting interviewer who jumped in whenever the other person spoke, cutting them off and ridiculing them. Or the newslady who reported slowly the unfolding drama in a tragic measured tone.

The sounds drifted, by turns quieter or louder as the atmosphere shifted. There was nothing like the solid reliable signals of today: you tuned in on the same wavelength the next night and there would be nothing there. The lady had gone. The crazy jabbering was silenced.

Is Anna right? Do I feel a need to side with my father because he betrayed the family? Is my emulation of him an escape route? What would I do if I wasn't running the estate agent's? Waiting for someone to cut off my credit cards, take my home from me?

Things become clear in the night, freed from the clutter of the day, the jabbering, the madness, the desperation that blocks out thought.

❧

In the morning I get sweet cheese buns from the Greek bakery, soft with fat raisins and moist and heavy with the creamy cheese and I make coffee for us both. I send a text to the office to say I'm taking the day off.

Then I fetch the ingredients to make the cake.

I have a feeling that if I break the rules David will materialise, his urge to correct me will be so strong. 'No, take those almonds out . . . two minutes ago . . . it's a light roast, you're not cremating them. Those oranges . . . are you sure they're unwaxed? Rub them on a bit of brown paper and see. That sugar syrup, keep stirring it. With a dry wooden spoon. Dry it in the oven for a few minutes to be sure.'

I feel lost. I have the instructions written out, every detail, but questions keep occurring to me. None of it makes as much sense as it did when he was standing beside me, supervising.

'Wow. You're baking?' Anna stands in front of me in a long black night gown, her hair tied up. She has make-up around her eyes. Surely she can't have put that on already? 'Things *have* changed here.'

She carves off half of a cheese bun and chews it. 'Do you remember the buns Dad made? I'm going to have to move out now you've discovered that bakery across the road. Otherwise I'll be like one of those people for whom they have to knock out part of the wall and use a crane to get them to hospital.'

'I'm fattening you up for the kill.'

'Mum stays thin whatever she eats. Just my luck to get Dad's fat gene.'

'She burns it all off with her rage and resentment.'

Anna smiles. 'I'm working on it.' She points at the baking tin. 'So that's for tomorrow?'

Do I sense a note of disapproval?

'Can you leave the oven on? I'll do mine when you're finished.'

❧

By late afternoon I am regarding my solid, orange and almond loaf with a sense of disappointment. I can sense David behind me, shaking his head sadly, saying, 'You know that's not right.' Later I will decorate it with icing sugar and a few orange leaves. But it will still be a heavy, unspectacular lump, sitting sadly in the cake parade, unequal to the baroque creations my sisters will have produced.

'It's lovely you could bake something,' Anna says, in the same tone she used when she appraised my make-up when I was going out as a teenager. She would haul me back inside to apply another layer and I would spend the evening with my eyes streaming from the unaccustomed density of clogging mascara and eyeliner.

As I try to remove the cake I see I haven't lined the tin properly: one side of it is stuck. But I have a replacement: the cake I baked with David, still tied up in parchment and twine, sitting at the bottom of the fridge. I can decorate that. The memorial cake.

⚜

I had been sitting in the office, staring out across the road, when the police arrived on the Sunday following the fire. It wasn't open for business but I'd gone in to sort a few things out.

They came in and told me the news. I could see they were shocked by the way I reacted. I was shocked to the core myself. They told me to take my time. The policewoman made me tea.

'Both of them, dead?'

'Three of them. Do you know who the third person could be?'

I didn't want to say it. I didn't want to say anything. 'They have a son. There was a history . . .'

She nodded. 'That would fit.'

They kept asking questions, skirting round what I knew, probing without making headway.

I asked them, 'Do you think he did it? Do you think the son did it?'

They didn't want to answer. They looked at each other, but not at me. 'We're considering all possibilities at the moment.'

❧

Despite my multiple assurances to my sisters, I still feel an urge to back out of my mother's party. As morning dawns, I burrow deeper into the bed, covering my head. Anna's presence in my flat ensures I can't escape. I can hear her as she cleans her teeth and boils the kettle. Although I have buried my head in the pillow, I can still hear her banging on my door.

'Only three hours to go,' I want to say. 'What do you expect me to do for the next three hours?'

I get up to watch her apply her make up. It's a work of art in process.

'I'll be done in a moment,' she says, making a few more deft strokes. 'Just a couple more things.'

Always two other things. Never just one.

'It's all right. No hurry.'

I take the cake out of the wrapping and put it on a plate, sprinkling icing sugar over it together with a few orange leaves.

'Do we need some other food? Some savoury stuff?'

Anna shakes her head. 'You know what she likes.'

I know what she likes.

❧

My sisters are surprised to see me.

'Look. Alice is here. And she's brought a cake.' This is relayed from room to room. 'Alice . . . and a cake . . . and Anna.'

My mother raises her hands, overplaying the miracle of my appearance. 'The whole family,' she says. 'The whole family.' She seems to shrivel a little more every time I see her.

'Why? Is Dad coming?' I want to say, but do not dare.

I sit next to her and she gives me the rundown of the progress of her physical complaints and chides me for not remembering what's wrong with her. Her voice has become croaky, as if she's in the process of adopting the persona of a feeble crone.

'Mum, even your GP can't remember them all and she has the notes in front of her.'

My cake is put on the table. They clear a space in the centre between the others, which are all presented on cake stands. It is a competition in which I haven't engaged properly. My cake suddenly descends from being an object of pride to a sad, plain amateur effort. It is a squashed brown lump, fooling no-one with its sprinkle of icing sugar and the few leaves strewn across the top.

In the kitchen a bowl is piled high with dolmades. I know Helena will have been up early, blanching vine leaves and wrapping the rice. She will have been at the fishmongers when it opened yesterday, buying cod's roe to whip into tarama and filleting mullet and chopping lamb, until her kitchen was a scene of carnage. She has baked rolls to my father's recipe.

My father always picked over a new batch of buns, selecting the ones which had burst open and putting them in a bag for the family, but we didn't mind. We preferred the exploded buns with the cheese baked dark and crisp on the outside and the black juicy olives lurking within, surprising the tongue with their mix of sour and salt.

'So still working all hours?' Helena asks, fishing more food out of her bag. 'It's not good for you, you know. You're going to find your life has slipped by and what will you have to show for it? A shop on the high street selling houses. You going to decorate your mantlepiece with pictures of your favourite houses?' She has adopted a superior authority over us now, because she has four children and a husband who still spends most of his nights at home.

'People always want houses,' my mother says. 'At least she'll have money. The rest of us will get swept away as everything collapses. Pfff. Houses are safe . . . what's that saying? That English one?' She behaves as if she has only recently learnt English, her accent getting thicker, increasingly fogging over the meaning of her words.

'Safe as houses. But most people die in their houses.'

'I've got good locks.'

'Most people who are killed, are killed by members of their own family.'

We are approaching dangerous territory. She raises her hands in horror. 'What about that one the other day? In Herne Hill. Just down the road. Did you read about it? Three people. Burnt to a crisp.'

'Mum . . .' Helena steps in. 'The man worked with Alice.'

'Did you know him? You knew him?' She shudders, as if my knowing David brought the danger even closer.

'It's all right, Helena. Yes, Mum, I knew them. David worked with us until very recently. I knew his wife, too.'

'Dreadful business. Good locks. That's the one investment that will always repay you.'

'I don't think locks would have helped.'

Susanna has some cream stuck on the end of her nose. 'Did you know him well?'

I was going to mention how he had baked the cake with me, but I thought that would put them off it. It was going to be hard enough to get them to eat it anyway.

'I knew them both. Quite well.'

'My friend, she works for the police. She said it was definitely the son that did it. He got them trapped and torched the place. But he got it wrong. Fire takes over fast. People underestimate fire. She said she's seen it all. You think criminals are clever, but they always make the same mistakes. She says she goes into a place and she sees straight away what's happened. That's where books get it wrong. There's never any mystery.'

Helena puts her hands together, satisfied she knows the truth.

'How terrible. How can these things happen? What goes on in families to stir up so much anger?'

'It's hard to imagine.' I catch Anna sniggering under her breath.

'I think your friend might be wrong.' I say.

'You know more than she does?'

'Maybe. Listen, you head down the high street, you can hear ten people who all know everything. They know the answer is a Marxist revolution or purging the immigrants or more Jesus in our lives. The only thing I know is that I don't trust certainty. About anything. Even about what I want. That's all I know.'

'About anything?'

'Anything.'

My mother stirs her coffee. 'I'll tell you one thing that's certain. That's your father . . . that he was a cheating . . .'

'Mum, please.'

'To burn your parents alive like that . . .'

I look at her, trying to imagine what that rage must feel like. She is tipping her plate sideways and a dolmade rolls off onto the floor. I pick it up.

She shrugs. 'Did you meet the son?' She crams a kofte into her mouth, followed by a sliver of cucumber.

I contemplate this. 'No. I never met the son.' Why did I say this? As I watch her chewing, silenced by the mass of minced lamb in her mouth, I know I have made the right decision.

'Thank you, God, that I never had a son. Enough trouble with daughters. A son. Burnt alive. Roasted like a dinner.'

Helena serves cake, even though no-one gives any sign of wanting it. 'That's the power of money.'

'You think he did it for money?'

'What else?' She often asserts that the only driver that counts is the financial one. Does this mean that because of her wealthy husband she has no drivers . . . that her existence is reduced to receiving the funds he provides?

'But what good is it if all you have is a lot of money? You going to curl up at night with your bank statement?' I realise Susanna is looking at me.

Mum hunches forward to raise an angry finger. 'At least it's her money. Alice doesn't have to worry about a husband squandering it . . . spending it on fancy shoes for his fancy girlfriend.'

'Mum, I've told you, get a divorce. He's the winner at the

moment. He's got the life he wants and he doesn't have to pay you anything.'

'That's what he wants, so that's what he's not going to get. Can we stop talking about him? It's my birthday.'

'Seventy, Mum. Have you written a bucket list?'

She crinkles her forehead. 'Bucket list?'

'You know. All the things you're going to before . . . things you're going to do while you can. Take a young lover. Swim the Channel. Become a champion limbo dancer.'

'Swim? If I'm going to swim it will be in a warm sea. Not here. It would kill you . . . swimming in the sea here.' She looks at me sadly and I get a fleeting glimpse of the gentler woman I remember from the past, or want to believe I remember. 'We used to go swimming, in a little bay. At home. All the girls in the family. The sea was calm there, no waves like here, always crashing. My costume . . . so modest.

'I hit my foot on a sea urchin. I had spines in my foot for days. I never swam again after that. Bucket list. A bucket on the beach. I have a bucket list. I want to go back and marry the boy who helped pick the spines out, then put his arm round me, helped me limp back to my house. My father shouted at him, he thought he'd hurt me.

'We danced together that Saturday, and I could not dance properly because of my foot. I could not put it down flat. I wore a big purple dress with ruffles everywhere and he helped me, moved me gently so I glided, took my weight. But my father told me I couldn't see him again, that we were cousins. Which I couldn't understand. The family was complicated, but I could not understand how he could be my cousin.'

Anna nods. 'It's all of them . . .'

'Now he's a wealthy man. Not a cheat like your father. A

proper businessman. If I had married him . . . we would have houses everywhere with their own beaches.'

'Just as well you didn't. You'd have to go swimming.'

'I could sit on the beach.

'None of us would have been here.'

She shrugs. The family she actually has is a sacrifice she is clearly prepared to make to obtain this imaginary new life.

'I would have had none of your father's lies. Now you get to listen to them. Lucky you.'

Helena gives her a plate piled high with food, and a glass of sherry, hoping to stop the talking. 'All these years. Listening and not speaking. Now you get to listen forever. Swswsw. In your ear.'

'Rumours. Gossip.'

'Rumours. Is it gossip that he's gone? A rumour. I won't listen to gossip. He's wrecked my life and your lives, but . . .' She puts her hands over her ears.

'How's he wrecked our lives?' I ask.

She shrugs, reluctant to say.

'Tell me.'

She will tell me, but she always speaks without much persuasion. 'You all . . . scared of having families. Because of his example. You waste your money. Then you can't afford children. No children. And no God. He took that from you. When I go, I'll be alone. Looking down on my family. Burning below.' She puts her hands together and looks up to heaven.

Helena takes me into the kitchen for a confidential talk. I am not prepared for this, and she draws me in, pungent with perfume, a rich Arabic scent, heady. 'It's good of you to put Anna up. We're not telling Mum anything about what's happened yet.'

'I can't tell Mum anything because Anna's not told me anything.'

'What, you've not talked?'

'We've not had the right moment. It's all been . . .'

She acts as if shocked, but I know Helena loves to be able to share a secret. She comes close, speaking into my ear, her belly pressing against me, tight in her purple dress. That scent is powerful, dragging me back to school days when we emptied scent samples over our necks until the smell made our heads spin. 'You know what her husband's like, well, maybe you don't. For a while he's been making unreasonable demands, and then the other day he hit her. She wouldn't let me tell you . . . but the thing is she's got no money and she can't contact him to sort things out. He's cut off her phone and he's emptied their shared account.'

I am intrigued to know what unreasonable demands he was making, too intrigued to realise that Helen is telling me Anna could be staying with me forever.

Back in the living room, Anna whispers into Susanna's ear.

'SwSwSwSwS,' our mother says.

'Mum, you don't want to hear this.'

'So don't say it.'

'I don't believe it,' Susanna says. 'Men are such bastards. You give them an inch . . .'

'They give you an inch. If you're lucky.' Helena strides in. 'You've seen him naked, have you?'

They explode into giggles, our mother laughing too, but looking perplexed.

'It's a slippery slope . . .' More giggles.

'So that's what you call it now?'

They carry on with this sister talk, the tattle that I always feel excluded from. Eventually things quieten down and Mother goes off to the toilet.

Helena turns to me. 'So, Alice, how do you like having a flatmate?'

Anna jumps in. 'It's great. It's like being girls again.'

'I can help you find somewhere more permanent. We've got stuff on the books . . .'

Anna shudders. 'No . . . I couldn't bear to be alone. I'd feel like I would be alone forever.'

'Wouldn't you be happier with your own place?'

'I don't know what will happen. I don't know what the future holds. Do you know what the future will bring?' She looks away, assuming her 'trying-to-be-brave' face.

Helena hands out cake.

'I've got no money,' Anna whispers to me. 'He's taken everything.'

She is still crying as my mother returns, carrying a plate.

Mum sits and stabs the cake and pushes a lump into her mouth. 'I know the future,' she says. 'I know the future.' She loves a cake that oozes cream. As she chews she turns towards me, firing a look of sudden hatred.

'You're a good estate agent. Very accommodating. Putting Anna. Up. Always putting people up. Helping them.'

Anna dives into a flurry of excuses. 'We're just having a difficult . . . it's just temporary.'

'Your father. He set the course. You put him up when he moved out, didn't you? He told me you made him very comfortable. He puts his head on one side when he says your name. "Alice," he says, like he's saying a little prayer. "Alice".'

Suddenly they are all glaring at me, their eyes filled with hatred. I had only put him up for three nights. He thought it more discreet than having him move straight into his girl-friend's place.

'He's a generous man, if you do what he wants . . .' Helena is leading the attack.

'He is a generous man. You refuse to talk to him. How can he be generous to you?'

'Generous? That's one way of putting it.'

The bickering goes on and I find myself sliding in and out of being able to follow the conversation. 'He would like to settle things, sort them out. But you won't let him.'

Some time later, Helena comes to sit next to me. 'I'm sorry about that fire. Your colleague. Were you close to him?'

'No. Not really.'

I just want them to eat the cake.

The prospect of Anna staying with me indefinitely makes my blood run cold. I barely speak the rest of the evening, zoning out, just trying to find a moment when I can leave without them turning on me before I'm through the door. Anna has begun sharing everything with me, gabbling confidences in my ear at every opportunity, still chewing her food as she does it. Sharing everything other than information about her husband's perverse demands.

I decide to extricate myself from the party. They can say what they like. I try to slip away without Anna noticing, but it's my mother who sees and begins to wail about how she never sees me and what a disappointment her whole life is.

I go to the table stacked with cakes and cut her a slice of mine, the memorial cake, sad, flat, shrunken, too long wrapped tightly in the fridge. I smother it with fruit and cream and take it over to her.

She pokes it with a fork, her face creased with disgust.

'You baked it yourself?'

I nod and she puts the fork to her lips, then drops it on the plate. 'Mmm. Very good.'

Susanna sits next to me. 'Tell me, Alice, if it wasn't the son, what do you think happened?'

Suddenly I feel myself put on the spot. 'I didn't say it wasn't the son. It probably was. I just think the police should consider other possibilities.'

Susanna is intrigued. 'So could it have been the father or the mother?'

'David, my colleague . . . I liked him a lot, but he was troubled. You could see it sometimes. You could see him brooding. Who knows if he could have done it? He was one of those people with an inner core, protected from the rest of the world. Concealed. You didn't know what it might contain, but you could imagine all his neighbours saying, I would never have thought it. Such a quiet, friendly man. And Esme, his wife. I loved Esme. She was smart, funny. She was acerbic but generous. Very generous. She was going to teach me philosophy. She was going to take me to the opera.'

'But weren't they were moving away? To the coast.'

'But she could have come back sometimes. Or for good. She was complicated.'

'She did it, then?'

'I'm not saying that. But there were moments when I saw a fury in her. The wrath of Phaedre. You can pick your Greek myths. There's one for every family. It could have been any of them. Or all of them.'

My mother shakes her head in despair at the cake.

'In a family . . . there is . . . this thing separate from any of member of it . . . a dynamic . . . that joins them . . . traps them together . . . any of the members of it and all of the members of it.'

Anna intones softly, 'Trapped together. Hard to imagine.' Her eyes light up with a distant fire.

Helena stacks food into plastic containers for us to take with us, although I have already told her we don't want it. 'That's for the two of you,' she says. 'You won't have to buy food for a week. I will need the containers back, though.'

As she passes me the heavy bag I realise she has been mouthing secret messages and making hand gestures which I've missed. She gives me a long hug and squeezes my hand. While she's holding me, I look over to the table and realise that my cake is still entirely intact, except for the sliver I cut off that my mother is now mashing into her plate.

❧

Back at the flat, Anna lies on her bed, fully dressed and snoring, while I sit in the kitchen and listen to a tape of Greek music, jangling away like my father's tape that broke, but oh so different, a tragic reminder of how easily a whole world can slip away.

The memorial cake has turned into a dense lump of sweetness. I can still see my mother's face, twisted with disgust, as she bit into it. 'You baked this? By yourself?' It is hard to explain the nature of her incredulity, since she despised the cake anyway.

I have a vivid memory of baking the cake together, then David bleeding on kitchen floor.

David hacking at that horse's head.

His rage.

Burning the carved wood with his blow lamp and then just keeping going.

My mother hissing, 'You're so lucky. Not to have been let down the way I have. Not to have your world ripped apart.'

Anna is behind me and puts her hands on my shoulders.

'Anna, he can only wreck your life if you let him. He can't do anything if you don't let him.'

She murmurs in my ear. 'What about you? Have you . . . ever let anyone . . . ?'

I realise how far apart we have drifted. All these years.

'Of course I have. I just don't let them take control of me.'

'Who?'

Who? It had been so long. I have always found intimacy difficult. I have always been drawn to handsome men who aren't attracted to me. I've found it hard to make the compromises most people make . . . joining that mental league table, where you find your division and you play within it. I must have a defect, or maybe I just accept that holding out for an ideal match will result in long periods of being alone. Ideal? Bearable.

I found him. Daniel, he was called. Suddenly I found myself staring at him at a party at college, and he smiled and we began talking, spending time together. More and more time, doing everything except having sex. We would go to the cinema, shopping, to cafés. Talking, always talking. I should have seen the signs.

We would lie down on a bed together and hold each other: we became so comfortable, just holding each other. Too comfortable. That final step was a long time coming. Too long. Eventually I took the initiative. It was a Saturday afternoon and we lay on his bed, wrapped around each other. I started to stroke him. He responded, but we struggled awkwardly at every stage. I moved his hand to help him explore new territories. His face looked young, gauche, and I felt I was forcing him into it. I was so focused on getting a response from him that I was hardly aware of what I was feeling myself. I was guiding him and if I hadn't done so, nothing would have happened. Then suddenly that shocking lump of flesh loomed in front of me. He lay back as I held him; a powerful twitching ran through his entire body. His finger explored, as if detecting a previously unimagined wonder, his eyes firmly closed. I pushed my pants aside and slipped that flesh inside me, as if tucking it away, out of trouble's way. He lay rigid, seemingly terrified to move, and when I began to rock my hips he shuddered and I felt him growing and his pelvic bone pushed against me hard. His breathing surged and suddenly it was over. There were tears in his eyes. Tears of joy, I hoped, although I didn't dare ask.

Was that all there was to it? No spark. No fire. Just a little sweat and some grunting.

It was a while before we repeated the experience. Excuses and reasons kept delaying it, but finally the time came. We were at a party and it was late. We headed back to his flat. I suddenly noticed his friend was with us, too. Daniel offered no explanation; the friend was just there. We were all drunk, and Daniel had left a bottle of Bison Grass vodka in the freezer. Suddenly we were kissing. We were all kissing, his friend joining in as well. Daniel was kissing him back. I felt fingers inside me. Not Daniel's. His friend's fingers, then there were other fingers, hooked around each other, and then tongues, as if united by the taste of me. We were lying down. Faces appear in unexpected places, then tongues lapping. One moment I was the main focus of activity, the next I was lying to one side, a mere spectator. Then I understood, but I didn't put a stop to it. We continued, the three of us in different combinations, until we all fell asleep.

It felt strangely freer with both of them than with Daniel alone. The presence of a third person dispelled his self-consciousness. Or so I thought. I was at liberty to roam around their bodies, kissing and licking, tasting, feeling them respond, pulling away, offering again, teasing. They would caress my tongue, their own tongues competing with each other.

I was happy at first, believing I had brought them together, united them in my body. But then I had to watch as they proceeded to make love without me, and I could see they were complete with just the two of them, Daniel's penis buried deep inside his friend.

Suddenly he remembered me and his face loomed towards me and he kissed me: I felt his tongue burrowing into my mouth, pushing against my teeth. I parted them, allowing his tongue in, soft, searching, then I snapped shut my teeth, biting down. I bit hard, neither knowing nor caring when I would stop. His eyes opened wide; they were watering. He was afraid that I might never let go.

Still I held on.

They shook together in a final spasm, and collapsed. When I released Daniel his eyes flooded with tears. So did mine. We held each other, our faces, our necks getting wet and cold. I reached over to put a hand on his shoulder and he looked at me, again with that fear in his eyes. I thought: he has forgotten who I am. He opened his mouth and touched his tongue gingerly with a finger. I could see the row of pink bloody marks I'd made.

In the morning I showered and left, knowing that it was over. Daniel asked me to stay for breakfast, for coffee, just to sit down for a few moments, but I wouldn't: we both knew that it was over.

※

'So does that count as unreasonable behaviour Anna?'

She laughs. 'Whatever they do is unreasonable behaviour.'

She drains her glass and reaches for the bottle. It is empty, but she tips it up anyway, finding another little trickle.

'So that's it? You're off men?'

'No. I'm just off compromise and disappointment.' She grimaces at the bitterness of the last dregs of the brandy. 'Perhaps therefore the answer is yes.'

We both sit there, two women on the brink of oblivion. I get up and go to turn over the tape.

'Don't,' she says. I sit next to her again and she grips my hand. Her hair has fallen across her eyes. 'My life has fallen apart. Please help me.'

I am alone. Trapped here with her, but alone.

I try to sleep, with Anna still sitting on my bed, her arm around me. Her face is running with mascara-laden tears. I use the corner of the sheet to wipe it and look down at the black smear the make-up has left. A shout in the wilderness.

Something about that black stain makes her laugh, and soon we are both laughing, not knowing why, just laughing and drinking Metaxa long into the night, and then, as morning comes, we drink some more.

※

In the morning I rush to the office despite the pain in my head. I sit down at my desk for a few minutes, then look up to see Beth trying to attract my attention. The police have returned.

As they approach my desk, Beth disappears into the kitchen with Terry. He pushes the door closed.

'We just wanted to check on a few details. It won't take long. Is now a good time?'

I can hear subdued voices and then silence.

'Let me get you some coffee . . .'

'No, I'm fine . . . How long did you say Mr Guralnick worked for you?'

They are kissing in the kitchen. I can hear them.

'I'll get you a coffee. I was just making one.' I pull the kitchen door wide open.

I take the police through to the back office. As I put the mugs down on the desk, I see they are watching me. I have become fascinating, in my delicate state. The policewoman sits at an angle to my desk. She needs to be watching something else, something outside in the back, even if she's just looking at a yard overlooking someone else's yard.

'So you didn't know Andrew was their son?' The police-woman says it as if in passing. She has been called out here a few times when we've had trouble removing people, but until now has always shown a bored, contemptuous expression, as if she thinks I am wasting her time. I get a whiff of her scent – 'Charlie' – and suddenly think of those teen magazines my sisters used to read, the free gift scent samples whose odour permeated their bedrooms. Does she wear it for work because it is cheap? Maybe she finds it repels all but the most determined attacker, and at night she transforms herself with a more sophisticated perfume...

'He forgot to mention it. He used a different name when he registered here. I would certainly have noticed if his name had been Guralnick.'

'Could you just tell me again about the time he and his girlfriend visited the house?'

I tell the story in such meticulous detail that it makes me suspicious of myself.

'Do you think Andrew killed them? And himself, of course.'

'It's one of the possibilities we're considering.' Her colleague has a thick neck. I can imagine him on the attack, head down, fists flying. Ginger hair curls in hoops around his neck, as if he has shaved his head himself and can't reach the back of his head.

'How well did you know Mr. Guralnick?'

What do I say? I feel that I'd known him forever, that I knew him better than my own father. But also that I didn't know him at all.

When the policewoman and policeman have left, I call Beth into the office. She is nervous: she knows what is coming. There is something about her blonde tremulous prettiness that infuriates me. I would like to get rid of Terry, too, but I need him for the time being. Beth is expendable, but even more than that she's perpetually annoying: it's the way she looks up with those doe eyes, trying to be appealing.

'Beth, today is the day we said we'd review your probationary period. How do you think you're doing?'

I catch a waft of her scent. I would dislike her less if she wore cheap, nasty scent, like the policewoman, but hers is sophisticated, delicate. She keeps her eyes down. Behind her, I see the sunlight growing brighter as a cloud blows away. 'I know you're annoyed that I came in here with Terry earlier. It was nothing. He was just . . . getting something out of my eye.'

I nod. 'It's not about that, Beth. It's just . . . I really don't think it's working out, Beth. I'm not sure this is the right job for you. I'm sorry.'

She sits still, as if paralysed in shock. I move towards her, intending to pat her back lightly, and but then make an awkward retreat. 'Stay in here until you've got yourself together. Take your time.'

I leave her to it, backing out of the office, and go to find Yvonne. 'Beth's in the office. She might need . . . If you could look after her.'

Yvonne gets up, not sure what is expected of her. Beth is standing behind me at her desk, at David Guralnick's desk. She looks fierce, magnificent in her anger and sweeps everything off the desk in one mighty push, the computer, the piles of paper, the nameplate, all tossed into a heap on the floor. Then she storms out of the building. I won't see her again.

2

DAVID: THE DAY THAT
I DIE IS BETTER THAN
THE DAY I WAS BORN

I REACHED DOWN into the cupboard and pulled out the surveyor's measure in its well-worn brown leather case. Most surveyors used those digital things so the size was correct to the tenth of a millimetre, but then they still rounded it up. I'd seen them do it. Rounding up – another word for lying, in my book.

'It's twelve foot six.' I stretched out the old cloth tape on the carpet, pressing it on to the skirting board against the living room wall.

I ran my finger along the top, where it flattened off, leaving a line of grime on my finger and a patch of whiteness running along the top of the skirting board. 'Twelve foot six,' I said.

'Well, good to know it's not shrunk.' A thick vein of sarcasm ran through all Esme's comments now. These days whatever I said provoked a sarcastic reply. I used to like the edge to her, the clever barbs, but not anymore. And I can't bear the frenzy with which she attacks her books, flicking urgently from page to page, as if the answer to a philosophical problem would vanish from a book written three hundred years ago if you didn't get to it fast. Finding the answer to questions no-one cared about.

'That is the point. It has shrunk. They said it was thirteen foot when we bought it.' I could still picture that sales sheet, its crude high-contrast photograph turning the place into a gothic house of horror.

'Six inches. It's not bad for thirty years' wear and tear. Most of us get bigger.' Esme's tone was bored. It was too mundane for her to talk about.

'I can't believe I didn't check at the time. I think it must always have been this size.'

'That was the wild frivolous times of our youth.'

That smile again. I wished she wouldn't keep showing me that all-knowing smile.

I opened the cupboard to dig out the papers. It used to amaze me when I visited houses to prepare sales details and I asked the owners about utilities. They would shove at me a carrier bag containing bundles of screwed-up documents which had been randomly stuffed in there: utility bills, insurance policies, bank statements. You asked them for something specific and they'd assume a worried look. 'Oh, OK,' they'd say, and you would watch for twenty minutes as they scrabbled through the bundle. 'I'm sure it's here.'

I have sorted everything in date order and put our documents in a fireproof metal box in the cupboard. Fireproof for a certain period, anyway. 'How long will it resist the flames?' I'd asked, when I bought it.

'Depends. How big is your fire?' The man in the hardware responded to my request with his own question.

'A typical fire.'

'That's the thing. There's never a typical fire. Each one is different. Like families.'

I bought the box anyway, from the hardware store on the high street. The proprietor kept all his goods behind the counter in wooden drawers, unlabelled, or if they did have a label it was from twenty years ago and for something other than what was there now. The real labels existed in his head. Cotter pins. Clevises. Linch pins. Whatever you asked him for, he would open the correct drawer and there it was. 'Eye surgery scalpels? Do you want the full set with luxury handles or just the basic range? Are you going to need the cornea-lifting forceps to go with them? They have a special bowed tip . . .'

He had paraded his selection of metal boxes in front of me and I'd carried the item I'd selected up the hill. It was heavy: I'd had to stop and rest every fifty yards.

The cupboard was the same one in which we kept our drinks. Spirits. Liqueurs. A bottle of crème-de-menthe that was probably twenty years old. No evening had been desperate enough to induce us to drink it, although some had been close. I remembered heaving all that stuff out to get to the papers and the fireman tripping over the box and suddenly there was broken glass and spirits everywhere. He was shouting at me: he didn't seem to realise what it meant if my box of papers went up in flames.

'While you're down there, can you see if there's another bottle of gin in the cupboard? There's only a trickle left in this one.' Esme was starting the booze early: it wasn't even 5 pm. I ignored her and pulled out the metal box, taking from it the beige folder marked 'House Purchase'. All our married life was documented in that box. I took pleasure in the order

I had maintained. I could find a document from thirty years back in a couple of minutes . . . it was impressive. You can create order over many years (but you can destroy it in a few seconds).

Esme found my well-organised habits annoying, preferring the sort of chaos exhibited in one of those art installations where someone empties the contents of their bins out on the gallery floor as a critique of the consumer society.

I pulled out the sales record from thirty-five years ago with a triumphant flourish.

'Here it is. Look, I was right. I can't believe I took it all on trust.'

'Especially when you know what sharks estate agents are.'

I ignored the dig. 'At least we believe there are things in the world we can measure . . .'

Esme half-closed her eyes, about to defend Spinoza. 'You are wrong on so many counts . . .' She decided to stop there. She stared at the long-forgotten sales details, shaking her head sadly.

I had once thought there was something admirable about the life of the mind but now it infuriated me, an indulgence, like men who give up work to study the Torah and the Talmud, bringing up families on handouts just so they can read Rabbinical arguments that have no conclusion. Why do they do it? To enable them also to argue without conclusion?

'I know you think studying a seventeenth-century philosopher is pointless. I do ask myself the question, too: why do I study him? The truth is, I have no choice, which you would understand if you read more Spinoza.' She fixed me with her intense look, as if I would understand if only I paid enough attention. But I gave up attempting to understand a long time ago.

I took the bill of sale from Esme and made a few additions to my draft.

'What's Alice going to say when she sees that lot?' she asked, as she looked at my notes. 'How many pages have you prepared now?'

'She can say what she likes. This is my sale. She won't interfere.'

She smiled. 'So be it. Are you ready yet?'

'Ready?'

'Ready. To pass your masterpiece to her. She said some people were interested.'

'She said that? When did you speak to her?' I didn't like Esme and Alice having private conversations.

'She called yesterday. You were . . . I can't remember where. She's going to pop round later and take some photos.'

'I want proper photos, not something she's taken on her phone.'

'It's a stop-gap until the photographer can come.'

'I know Alice. She'll think, "Oh, these are all right, and besides there's no commission," so she'll decide hers'll do.'

There was an art to writing details. It was not a straight-forward matter of description. What you presented was a framework that the new owner could build on.

I could look at our house objectively. It was a neat house, solid, well-made. Whoever bought it would have nothing to complain about. There were a few cracks in the front eleva-tion: I could already hear the surveyor, some sharp-suited lad with the ink still wet on his certificate in surveying and golf course management, talking about subsidence. I would let him talk. Then there would be a dramatic pause as I nodded and I would pull out the picture of the bomb crater forty yards away. 'Ever heard of settlement?' I would say. He would look mystified, embarrassed and finger the phone in his pocket, wishing he could check what I'd told him on the internet.

Settlement. Things can take years to recover after a shock like that. The earth rediscovers itself eventually, but the lines of force are still there. Paths of strain running through the structure, running down deep.

For so many years I'd been creating these pictures, constructing others' dreams, in short, stark prose. When I came to write the details of my own property, I could wax lyrical at last. Thirteen pages. There was so much pent up . . . my whole career had led to this point.

⊱❦⊰

Esme took the sheets of paper from me. 'Shall I call Alice and tell her you're ready?'

'I'll call her.'

'You won't, though.'

'We'll go and view some properties at the coast. Unless you don't want to move . . .'

'I do want to.'

'You seem reluctant.'

'Let's go. Tomorrow.'

She resumed her essay marking. I saw that she was smiling, as if triumphant. She allowed herself to read for a bit after every third essay she marked, which is why the pile took forever to go down. She often sighed at the nonsense her students wrote; just occasionally, she nodded approval.

Esme talked about substance. She told me how in Spinoza's day two types of substance had been identified: Res Extensa and Res Cogitans. The stuff of dimensions, the physical space, and the thoughts and ideas we put into that space. It struck me as a good description of an estate agent. Being through extension. Being through perception.

Alice hadn't wanted me to prepare the details. 'You're too close to it all,' she kept saying. 'You need the distance . . . you need some objectivity. Let me do them for you.' She was right. I should have let her do it and got it out of the way. But no, I had a final battle with myself: if I couldn't do this, what was any of it for? Pride wouldn't let me give way. I had been kicking around what I would write for weeks.

'Okay, but I might need to rework it a little. And David . . . ?' she presented me with what I'm sure she thought was a coquettish smile, 'when you reach twenty pages, stop.'

Esme watched me writing, looking up through those half-moon reading glasses. Her face creased a little. In that glance I saw two people at once: the person I first met, delicate, so beautiful I was afraid to look at her; and the woman she had become, the kind of woman people ignore, the grey hair drawn tight, draining the remaining beauty from her face. Past the age of any interest. At moments like that I realised my life had slipped by. What had I achieved? Suddenly it had all . . . faded. Her slow patient look . . . benign on the surface, but buried in there . . . when I unpicked it, an amused contempt that infuriated me.

Alice thought no potential buyer would take five minutes to read a few pages of A4. I'd been writing sales details for so many years, always struggling to get the key information correct. A full-service history. This was the first time I'd been confident that I was accurate. I knew everything about this house. The boiler. The plumbing. The electrics. I could sketch out how the ring mains were wired. I used to put a drop of oil on the main stopcock and move it back half a turn every year. I would inspect the roof and clear the gutters every six months. It was like a well-maintained ship, setting out on a journey, and I was guaranteeing its arrival.

'Do you want some coffee?'

Esme drank five strong cups a day: she was fired by coffee. Without it, she collapsed into a flaccid, motionless lump, an object of morbid rage capable of observing the world but not interacting with it.

She picked up my notes and stabbed indignantly with her finger. 'What is this? Sun loggia? Do we have a sun loggia?'

'It was in the details when we bought the house.'

'That's right. We asked them about it: it was a circle of stones in the corner of the garden, not a sun loggia at all.'

But what a circle of stones: at the right time, with the wind blowing in the right direction, from those stones we could catch the scent of the far distant gin distillery. Maybe we imagined this, but we didn't imagine the smoke from the fishmongers' smokehouse, percolating from the racks of salmon, haddock, mackerel and eel. I used to buy eel. I remember my horror once when the fishmonger chopped the head off and put the creature, still twitching, in a bag. As I carried it away, I could still feel it moving. It finally stopped when I deposited the bag on the kitchen table.

'I'm not cooking that,' Esme had said, so I cooked it, but

as I ate I couldn't forget the shudder of life that had still remained in that chopped, mutilated body.

'Anyway, we do have one now.'

'What . . . the shed?'

'It was a wedding present.'

'It's still a shed.'

'It's a summerhouse. Anyway, it doesn't matter. It's better if they don't know what a sun loggia is. The details have to include a licence to dream . . . a space that can turn into whatever you want it to be.'

'A licence to dream?'

'It's the most important part. No-one buys bricks and mortar. They buy a vision of the future.'

'I'm going to look at estate agents in a new light now . . .'

'You never sell the thing itself. When someone buys a mobile phone, no-one tells them ten pounds buys a phone with everything they need and a battery that lasts a month. A good salesman can convince them to spend four hundred pounds on a phone with a dodgy aerial and a battery that lasts half a day. Dreams can do everything, except deliver. Did Spinoza not mention that?'

'He wasn't big on dreams. His ethical compass didn't reach into the dream world. Thanks for asking, though.'

'My mother warned me . . . don't marry a clever woman . . . too much trouble, she always said.'

'You should have listened.'

'Oh, I listened. Then I ignored her.'

I still felt a shudder running down my spine when I thought of Andrew in that summerhouse and the smell of betrayal. All Esme's philosophy providing so many ways to avoid doing the bloody obvious. The traces of our son embedded in there, living like an animal for God knows how long. I cleared every trace of him out of that shed, but I couldn't get rid of the smell of him until I painted it with creosote, three coats, inside and out.

No-one would want to sit there now, in the sun loggia, whatever dreams it may have held.

Esme looked wistful. It wasn't like her to sit for so long without reading.

'When did she say that?'

'Sorry?'

'Your mother. When did she say that?'

'I don't know. When I was growing up?'

'When you were growing up. She just happened to say that. A bit of advice.'

'Why do you ask?'

'No reason.'

There was never no reason, only a reason that she wouldn't tell. She watched me, storing it all up: her ammunition.

I was going explain, but I had learnt the value of silence. Allowing there to be nothing.

'You do want to move, don't you?'

'I can read anywhere.' She picked up her book again and began to flick through it.

'It's going to be a bit different. Exhibitions will be . . . paintings of boats and seagulls. Model beach huts and hand-crafted silver jewellery. You'll hate it.'

'No more standing around drinking bad wine, trying to look interested.'

These days when she took me to exhibitions, the artists had begun to talk to me, and listened as though what I said counted for something. It made me imagine what it must be like to be wealthy. Even I was susceptible to a bit of unearned flattery.

'I've started to like some of them. That private view the other day: the Welsh sculptor with the red hair who had created those large forms around ready-made holes in the wood. I found myself drawn to what she was doing.'

'You talked to her for a long time. You even let her talk. It must have been serious.'

'She said I had a real feeling for form and texture.'

'I'm sure her perceptions weren't influenced by the prospect of a sale . . .'

She hated anyone saying anything nice about me.

'I'm going to take up sculpting. I can see it in my head: my first piece, a horse's head carved out of wood, carbonised wood, and the mane will turn up as if made of little flames. Flared nostrils.'

"Those nostrils always have to flare. You should have a go. You would get a lot out of it.'

'I can see just the spot where I would place it, out in the garden, where it would catch the setting sun as it dips between the two houses opposite.' I looked out at the back garden, at the circle of stones where we would sit late on a summer's evening and catch the last half hour of sun. I would read the paper and then start the crossword and she would read Spinoza and we would have a gin and tonic strong enough to lie to the doctor about. That seemed to me as close to paradise as anything you could get on this earth or beyond.

'But I thought we were moving . . .'

'We need to find somewhere with the right kind of spot to let us enjoy the setting sun.'

She nodded slowly, in a way that told me we could be preparing for a long battle.

⁂

I never had trouble sleeping. I would put my head down and that was it. Oblivion. I never had that experience of lying for hours trying to sleep. Which was just as well, because Esme was always slipping in and out of sleep. Often she would sit bolt upright, emerging from the middle of a deep sleep, and get up as though in a trance and go downstairs. More often than not if I woke in the night she had gone; and many mornings I would find her downstairs on the sofa, sometimes still awake and reading but mostly lying asleep, half-covered with a blanket.

This morning she was shivering, and she stirred as I came in, snatching up the book, not wanting me to know she had been dozing.

I had made some breakfast and brought it to her on a tray.

'Is it today?'

'What? Is what today?'

'The day we're going to look at houses?'

I put the tickets on the table. 'I'd like to get the 10:03. Can you be ready in time?'

She would have given me the same look of horror whatever time I had said.

She sat opposite me on the train. When she was angry she always sat opposite. Sometimes I would move to sit beside her, which either made her angrier or sometimes resulted in her forgetting why she was angry.

148

She watched the passing rows of south London terraces. 'I can't read another page of that novel,' she said. 'That irritating, knowing child should have been strangled as soon she began to speak. That's the trouble with novels these days. It's always the wrong people who get killed.'

'Like life.'

'Is it?'

I didn't really know. It just felt like an appropriate response.

The landscape got sadder and sadder, until we reached a sudden outbreak of green, followed by mud flats.

'What are we looking at?' she said with a weary voice. I passed some paperwork to her. She flicked through it without really looking.

'The one at the top looks interesting. The rest . . . well sometimes you can be surprised.'

'Whatever you think.'

'Whatever I think? You don't have a view?'

'You're the professional.'

I was puzzled. 'So whatever I choose, you'll just go along with it and not complain?'

'It's just a house. How wrong can it be?'

We began to catch glimpses of the sea.

'I'm going to like being by the sea. Big skies. You never feel like there's a sky in London. Even at the top of a hill it still feels like you're enclosed. It's like stripping off layers. Each town you pass is another layer.'

'I must come along on the next estate agents' summer outing. It could be more fun than it sounds.'

'Then you stand there on the beach, it's just you and the sea. I always think of the sea as crashing waves, but the last few times I've seen it, it's been calm.'

'Maybe you have a calming influence.'

'On the sea. Not on people.'

'You've not been upsetting Alice, have you? You need to finish those sales details. Just do what she wants. Don't try to fight a battle with her now, when it counts for nothing. Just let it go.'

'Is that what I should do? Things are fine with Alice. I was happy to leave the business.'

I found something more exciting about the estuary than open sea. You couldn't see the opposite shore of it at this point; it was obscured by the layer of grey mist that hung over the water. There must have been times when it was visible. Within that mist was the wreck of the Robert Armstrong, submerged, still containing thousands of tons of explosive, too dangerous to disturb.

Then we were there, tipped out on to the platform amongst all the families and their equipment. We struggled past them. A group of mothers had equipped their children with possessions that recreated a seaside visit from an earlier age. They carried tin buckets and wood and steel spades and were dressed in tasteful combinations of primaries and pastels. Even their sandwiches derived from an era before pesto and mozzarella and salami. It was an era that, probably, no-one had ever known. A false memory. But a good one.

Esme was snarling. She found outward signs of happiness disturbing.

I had worked out the route we needed to take. It was not the most direct one, but it had the advantage of avoiding a little art gallery containing watercolours of seaside scenes that would be bound to send her into a rage.

I could tell from my first glimpse of the details that this

house would be the one. There was nothing remarkable about it. It was a small terrace house with a tiered garden, but sometimes you just know a place will fit.

The woman showed us round quickly, a cursory tour. There was little to say. The rooms were chaotic, with piles of washing and toys everywhere. She let her desperation break through too many times . . . always a bad tactic. Some viewers would have used it to hammer down the price.

She took us into the garden, pointing at the crops regretfully, as if the move was so imminent that she would never get the chance to harvest them. Finger-sized courgettes with big crinkled leaves that were starting to turn dusty white. Clumps of green tomatoes, the occasional red one splitting its seeds, having been damaged by a recent onslaught of rain.

She led us to the top tier and pointed. 'From this corner of the garden you can see the sea.' She realised she'd forgotten something when we were doing the tour and led us back to the front bedroom. 'You can also see it from here, just about, in the gap between two houses opposite. Just a sliver.'

We looked where she had indicated, admiring the line of sea and sky that now appeared, speculating on where the one met the other.

'Thank you,' she said, as we left. 'You will . . .' she paused, 'give me a call if there's any questions.'

'You never asked her why she was moving. I thought you always asked that.'

'Do you want me to call her?'

She smiled. 'I know why she's moving.'

We walked back down to the town, and I forgot to avoid the art gallery. Esme did not pass judgement. Just a glance and she moved on. She did not say anything. Neither did I, but her look was one of acceptance; of a fate that could not be avoided, an inevitable course of events in which she was trapped.

We walked along the sea front and beyond. I was angry, marching ahead, driven by a rage. She had always undermined the moments of pleasure in my life, snatched away any potential joy. When there was something I wanted she would offer a comment laden with sarcasm, and I would feel the sting of her ridicule for having dreamt for a moment . . . needing permission to imagine that things could be the way I wanted.

The clouds were rolling in the wind, unfolding long-drawn-out bundles that trailed across the sky, then moving faster, as if the world had speeded up.

I was walking rapidly when I realised I had left Esme behind. Looking back, I could see only a man with a black Labrador that was running first towards the sea, then back to him, as if desperately trying to communicate something. What boy? You've got a message? Someone's lost in the sea? They're trapped? There's three of them? And a dog? No dog. I'll see what I can do.

Esme liked to dawdle. However slowly I walked, she walked slower. She liked to control the pace. I imagined the scene from afar: a distant man striding along the beach, his scarf flying around behind him in the wind. A squat man passing him, two people briefly cutting through the isolation as they crossed each other's paths. And far behind a dot that could be a person, just discernible, a person perhaps related to one of them. A distant dot with just a hint of human form.

When I saw her later in the café I was determined not to give any hint that I was angry, or any sign that her diversion away from the path without telling me was anything other than what was to be expected. I gave not a hint.

We went into the gallery at the back of the tea-shop. On a plinth was a large black head with golden rays emerging from it. Underneath there was a brass plate.

> 'Happier the night of my death
> than the day the earth light pulled me
> from my mother's womb'

'That's not for sale,' said a voice. A man approached: he had straggly black hair and a biker jacket.

'Okay,' I said, although I think I was supposed to plead with him. It was an ugly thing.

We went back into the café. 'There's a bit too much of his inner madness on show.'

'That's what I think art is. A safe place for us to release our inner madness.'

'Is that what you tell your students?'

'It's what they tell me.' She smiled. 'Do you remember those events in the sixties? People writhing in entrails . . . slaughtered animals . . . Hermann Nitsch . . . all that stuff. It was like an orgiastic explosion of inner drives that had to be let out.'

At the time I used to ask her why we had to go those events . . . so much debauched savagery. She would tell me it was important, that suppressing such drives would lead to disaster.

'We are the creatures who have survived through a million years of savagery and cruelty for this brief window when we have managed to acquire a veneer of civilisation. But that old history is not far from the surface: it doesn't take much to bring it out. The wonder is how rarely it actually emerges.'

The woman brought us lukewarm tea.

'I don't want to buy any of his stuff. However little he wants for it.'

'You want to buy the house, though, don't you?' she said to me.

I nodded.

Back in the town, we passed an old-fashioned butcher's shop, its curved windows displaying a small clay model of a butcher wielding an outsize knife above a perturbed pig on a slab. I caught his eye and he waved at us. Waved and smiled. Esme's lip curled with contempt. It was all too pleasant. She disliked many things that other people found attractive. Quaint Dickensianism caused her physical pain; she was happier in a market full of uncovered meat, flies buzzing around, blood dripping out into the gutter. She would prefer to see a butcher's shop with a bandsaw and flecks of meat and bone on the wall behind and a tray of severed skinned heads, with the bulging eyes staring out unseeing towards the separated halves of its body, than a traditional clean butcher's shop, its prepared joints rolled up and boned, all the unpleasant detritus hidden from view.

'I might need to take a trip. To help make up my mind.'

'Where are you going to go?'

She spoke softly. 'Sheerness.'

'Sheerness.'

She offered no explanation, and I knew better than to ask for one.

We sat in the garden, drinking a cup of tea. I no longer felt the inclination to pull out the weeds that fought their way through the gap in the stones. They would soon be someone else's problem.

'Do you remember when we first moved here? We knew everyone in the neighbouring houses. You couldn't just make a cup of tea for yourself if you were in the garden. I had to buy that ten-cup teapot.'

She smiled, nodding, and got up shakily, banging the book closed. 'It happens every time. They say it's an exciting new book that's going to change the way we think, and when I read it I find it's just forty-year-old ideas wrapped up in new language. It's the same with the essays: students playing tricks with syntax to present a mundane idea as if it's interesting and original.'

The odd assortment of fences that backed on to ours suddenly struck me. Seven different fences, each with its own style, each in a different state of collapse. 'We hardly know anyone now. I offered the man in number twenty-seven a cup of tea the other day and he looked at me as if I was mad. Even Brian's gone. I never thought he would move.'

Esme smiled. 'Do you remember how horrified you were when he moved in? "He's got tattoos. On his neck," you kept saying. You were terrified that the neighbourhood was taking a turn for the worse.'

'Well it did, even if it wasn't his fault. When that car blew up outside the house . . . I thought the end had come. Even when I'd pulled the curtain I could see the orange glow, and that heat . . . I have never felt such heat . . . even through the glass. It was as if someone had opened an oven door in the bay. I stood there thinking, so this is how the world ends.'

"I remember the fireman leading you away . . . saying the

petrol tank could explode at any moment. And you wanted to go back, to get stuff from the house.'

'I thought we were going to lose everything. Brian sat me on the wall and tried to distract me with his stupid jokes . . . and I started to shake. I think I was sick.'

'It was shock . . .'

'And I looked at his thick neck and his tattoos and I thought, what a strange turn of events that we were sitting there together and he was trying to comfort me.'

There was a rustling behind the fence. An Algerian family lived in Brian's house now and the entire garden was given over to mint and parsley. The woman saw me and smiled and gave me handfuls of the herbs.

I answered her in French and she giggled and ran inside.

I put the herbs on the table. 'Will you be able to use those later?'

She nodded. Her voice softened. 'It was nothing to do with Brian, though. I know you thought it was.'

'We never really found out who it was. An unanswered question.'

She waited for me to say something. Neither of us could say it, how something can be obscured in mystery then become clear, and how you preferred the mystery.

'Brian said it was all to do with the woman opposite, that she'd moved in with that younger man from the gym in number four with the three kids. It was too much for her ex, who was living just down the road. So he fire-bombed the car. I'm not saying it was justified. But it was hard on him.'

Esme had an expression she pulled when she immersed herself in the past. Her eyes narrow, her upper lip pouches, and her mouth opens a little in preparation for those ancient

voices made manifest through her own soft voice. 'A firebomb
. . . I remember Andrew staring at it . . . transfixed. I never
thought to lead him away. It seemed a natural thing for a
boy, a child, to be obsessed by fire.' Esme caught my eye and
I knew what she was thinking. She reached over, touched my
hand, gripped it, then let it go again.

'Is that when the damage was done? Or was it done
already?'

&

When it got darker we went inside and sat in the front room.
I could still see that car with its rear window smashed, the
flames blazing through it with a heat that made you gasp,
and the fireman leading us down the road, so far down the
road, all the time telling us how much worse it could have
been. He recounted stories of other fires he'd seen, but what
he was saying seemed to be at one remove, as though he was
never really there to tackle the fires. As if his role was to bear
witness and recount the horror to others.

Esme put down her book. 'Such anger. To make you do
something like that. I can't understand it. I don't think I've
ever felt that kind of rage. Conflagration.'

Watching her, I felt a pulse of excitement running up my
spine. 'I understand. I have felt it.'

She was a little startled, and got up, slightly unsteady.
'Did you buy more coffee? I asked you to buy some. From the
Algerian shop in Soho, not locally. Velluto Nero.'

I was entitled to my rage. She could get angry about coffee.
'When have you ever been angry like that? I don't think I've
ever seen you angry. You just sulk.'

I was angry. I just kept it all inside.

❧

When Andrew was three, I found myself getting angrier and angrier. The house was always a mess because Esme had started teaching. There was evidence of mounting chaos. Andrew was being looked after by her sister during the day; she had no control over him or her crazy sons. When he came home it took an hour to settle him down.

We argued all the time. Once the row hit a new level. It was a Saturday morning and I had cycled down to a deli in Streatham to fetch fresh bagels and pots of chopped herring and salmon and cream cheese. I don't know how it started, but I kept on thinking she could just have let me eat my bagel first. By the time I left for work there was a pit of emptiness in my stomach, reinforcing my wrath. I was really angry because of the lack of a heavy dough lining in my stomach.

I sat in the office with nothing to do. There were no customers and only one viewing had been booked. The owner emerged from his office every ten minutes, tutting with despair as he passed my desk. We were short of money. All the order had disappeared from our life. All the routine. The house was in chaos. And Andrew was a sickly baby, always grouching, unresponsive to whatever I did.

When I returned in the early evening, I was ready to apologise: I had been tired, insensitive. I had picked a fight for no reason. I had written out my apology on a notepad, rehearsed it while I drank my afternoon tea, then again as I waited to meet an elderly couple still deliberating whether to move into a purpose-built flat on the seventh floor of an ugly grey block.

I had folded the paper up and was keeping it in my pocket, running my fingers over it occasionally.

I returned to find the double lock secured and the house deserted. The bag of bagels was still on the kitchen table, untouched. I sat there, perfectly still, absorbing the smell of dough, unable to eat.

I took up the newspaper and read the same article again and again. It was about a couple who had gone camping in France. Thieves had pumped sleeping gas through the vent in their tent. The couple lay there powerless, watching as they were robbed, unable to tackle the thieves. Unable to do anything but watch a part of their lives being carried away from them.

Sleeping gas.

Somehow, nothing else in the paper could grab my interest after I'd read that story. My eyes would drift back to it. The sun dropped down lower until it was too dark to read and I could only see the glow of the page, the shape of the words. I was cold, shivering and hungry, but I could not move.

How could you do that? How could you pump in enough gas to paralyse them? To hold them in that suspended state?

She had gone, and taken Andrew with her.

I felt such rage. I felt the heat of that fire . . . the house was cold and dark but I could feel the flames exploding through that window. I wanted to burn the place down. To be powerless and watching as someone steals away your life . . .

'I have been angry.'

Esme looked up from her book, over her reading glasses. 'Oh, that time. I remember. I did leave you a note.'

'I thought you'd left me. And taken him, too.'

'I left a note on the table. You probably knocked it off. Or put your paper on it.'

'I thought you'd gone. I was in despair. My world collapsed. Or exploded.'

'You are such a fool sometimes. You think I would have gone . . . that I would have left? In an argument about bagels?'

She was shaking her head and laughing to herself in a way that made me angrier than I had been even then.

⁂

I fixed us both a gin and tonic. The lemon was past its best, soft and pasty, and the tonic flat, but the gin was okay. I thought she would notice the lemon and comment on it, but she said nothing.

She sipped the gin, seeming to grow a little from a power it gave her. 'Sometimes I think back at all the things we've seen . . . some of the stuff we took seriously . . . it just seems silly now . . . or corrupt. Where was the joy in it . . . the Dionysian joy they tried to create . . . all that blood and meat? It was just sad old men exploiting women.'

'And meat.'

'And meat. How was it we felt so optimistic? Maybe things were better then? It feels as if we're living in an age with the humanity sucked out of it now. They promised us we'd only have to work eight hours a week because of technology; our role would be to consume, not to produce. They didn't tell us we would only be paid for eight hours . . . and they would choose the hours. The myth we live by is that everything always gets better.'

'There's a lot of good things . . .'

'There's computers to think for us . . . to remember how it was . . . so we don't have to worry.'

'It'll be different when we're out of London. It'll be like stepping back in time.'

She was not convinced by this prospect. 'I rang the woman. We've agreed a price.'

'So, we're really moving?'

'We need to sell this place.' I drew the curtains. 'I said it was in an "up and coming neighbourhood". I noticed they used the same phrase in the sales details when we bought it. Can a place be up and coming for thirty-five years? Surely it must arrive at some point?'

'They should make a rule, if one area goes up, another has to go down. It seems only fair. Everyone would start moving out of Hampstead and Dulwich and coming here. Is there an opposite to up and coming?'

'There is no opposite. There is only a silence.'

I sipped my drink. I'd made it too strong, but I refused to add more tonic. I liked that fuzzy feeling.

It was quiet, considering we were in South London. Barely any traffic noise, no shouting, no aircraft. From the garden we could hear only a blackbird and the wind rustling the pods on the laburnum tree. I remembered warning Andrew about them, telling him they were poisonous. He would react by picking a pod and holding it to his lips as if it was the most delicious food.

'Do you remember the drug dealers in the rented house?'

'They never took up your invitation to attend the neighbourhood watch meeting.' She loved this story, never missing an opportunity to recount it, always with further embellishment. Now her picture was clearer than mine.

'We don't discriminate.'

'They didn't come though . . .'

'I remember as I stood there on the doorstep that he looked at me as if I was mad. He stared at me for a long time, with great concentration. What drug gives you such concentration? I thought he was planning to attack me, but felt paralysed by the range of options. In the end he just slammed the door without a word.'

'What a hero. Are you going to tell our prospective buyers about the memorial hump? The most notable feature of the area.' Esme thought that was so funny she was still laughing to herself a few minutes later (but it could have been relief at finishing the pile of essays at last).

At that time the drug dealer was battling with the police, spray-painting messages on the road. "PC452 is a child-molester" . . . that kind of thing. Then the council workmen would come along and dump tarmac on the abusive message. A few days later a new message would appear.

As the battle went on the hump got higher and higher, until it was as high as a speed bump; you could hear the car exhausts scraping along it. A different policeman, a different message, but the sentiment was constant.

One morning I was walking towards the common and noticed the door of the drug dealer's house was open. There were none of the usual signs of life: screaming children with faces smeared with every kind of grime, dogs disfigured by mange and injuries from fighting, women with long thin arms, bruised sad faces and greasy hair, their eyes staring intently ahead, registering nothing. The place was deserted.

I knocked on the door of the house opposite to summon

another member of the neighbourhood watch. We went in, warily at first, until we were sure the drug house really was empty. I was shocked by what we found . . . I did not understand how people could live like that.

'I should mention about the window. In the details.'

'What about the window?'

'About the glass having been broken . . . how it's not the original glass. People notice that type of thing these days.'

Esme looked aghast. 'What are you going to say? Up-and-coming area with just occasional anti-Semitic attacks?'

I could remember that moment clearly. The explosion of glass. The thud of the brick on the carpet. The silence. 'I thought you said it was because Andrew was in the army.'

'It could have been either reason.'

'Great. So now I've got two things to worry about. I was in the Merchant Navy. It could be because of that, as well.'

'There's lots of reasons to hate. It's just glass. Our replacement for what was there. The incident's forgotten.'

'That old glass catches light in a particular way. Modern glass is just flat, characterless.'

'You're worrying about the flatness of the glass?'

'Someone has to worry about the details.'

'Do they? I worry about how we will move away, finding the most important section of our lives gone. We will leave the house and they will rip everything out. Nothing will remain of what we did. No trace.'

I found it hard to believe she was getting sentimental about the house now.

'So good riddance to it.'

'No regrets?'

'Not one.' I could see myself closing the door one last time, feeling the surge of joy at leaving it all behind. 'All the stuff that's happened . . .'

'It's random. It's London.' She grimaced. 'Or maybe it'll follow us. What if someone wants to find us?'

'We'll be gone.' I held her, sitting on the corner of the chair. 'No-one wants to find us.'

⚜

'I've brought all the stuff.'

Alice was here, with her bag of ingredients. She had tied her hair back. I was surprised she was prepared to show her ears like this. She emptied the bag on to the kitchen table and put on her apron. It was the old-fashioned pinafore kind, and she wrapped it tight around her breasts.

She piled up bags of ground almonds. I had told her we needed to grind our own or the oil would be rancid. I turned over her bags of ground almonds.

'That was all he had. He said they would be just as good.'

In anticipation I had bought a kilo bag of whole almonds the previous day. I slapped the bag on to the table. It made a reassuring thud. I lifted the scales out of the cupboard, together with their stack of weights.

'It's going to be a shock when you move away, David. I feel as if I've always known you.'

'Always is only a week longer than everyone else's every day.'

I ground the almonds in the food processor and tipped them out into the bowl, batch by batch.

'It must be amazing . . . that feeling you are about to start your life over again.'

'You boil the oranges in the sugar syrup. It's a thick syrup, so they'll begin to float. A rolling boil. If they stick, give them a poke with a wooden spoon. Did you get organic oranges?'

She shook her head.

'Alice, I told you, they treat the peel with something that is poisonous when you heat it.'

She laughed. 'It's all right. The cake's for my family.'

'I'm not sure whether it would be a slow lingering death, or instant.'

'They're immune to all poisons.' She dropped the oranges into the pan with extra relish.

I felt suspended . . . suspended between two worlds, one slipping away fast. I stirred the pan, then passed the spoon to her. 'Keep stirring. Only until it shows the faintest hint of colour.'

'I'm envious of you, being able to leave. I would go away if I could.'

'What, leave the business? Where would you go? A Greek Island?'

'No.' She laughed. 'The opposite. I would go to Scotland. Orkney maybe. Or Iceland. Just to be alone. Away from the city.'

'That's even scarier than moving to Broadstairs.'

'If you're going to leave, you've got to do it properly.'

'Maybe you should move with Esme. She likes bleakness.'

She jumped a little at the roar of gas as I lit the oven. As you lit one side the gas built up on the other side, so a little ball of gas was bound to pop, however fast you were. People weren't so worried about health and safety when the cooker was made. Electric elements remained exposed, tempting you to touch them. Fires were left unguarded.

'Scarier than Broadstairs.' She ran a spatula over the top of the mixture. 'Are you okay?'

'Yes, I'm okay. The oven just needs to warm up a bit more.'

'I mean, are you okay about the move?'

I passed her the baking tins and some olive oil. 'Make sure you grease the pan really well and then put some ground almonds in it. Shake them all around. If you leave a patch uncovered, you'll never get the cake out whole.'

I thought she was going to hug me. I let her get close enough for me to catch a waft of her perfume, the heat from the glow of her skin, before I stepped back.

We poured the mixture into the baking tins, smoothing off the tops, then placed the tins in the oven. The oven door was satisfyingly solid, its blue-grey enamel bearing weight from another age.

'Of course.'

She pushed the kitchen door to. 'I don't think Esme wants to move.'

Sometimes she just talked for the sake of it.

'Now we'll leave the cakes to bake while we go for a walk.'

'The walk is important?'

'The walk is critical.'

I set the timer. 'We'll be back to check it after forty-five minutes.' I could not help thinking what it was like to be young, still discovering being with another person rather than shutting doors, shutting doors as if they would never be opened again.

I wished . . . out of all the things anyone could wish for . . . to be young again . . . to make my mistakes all over again. To take back my stolen life.

Outside on the air was borne that balmy stickiness that

could suddenly turn a few days of warm weather into a seemingly never-ending summer. The musky scent of tree pollen prickled my nostrils.

'I think she's really scared of moving away from London. All the art, the theatre. It's her life. She might end up hating you.'

Alice was so young.

'All my life we've struggled . . . with money . . . there were things we could never have . . . she never complained, but I always felt bad. We went to places and it always felt like we didn't belong. Maybe we tried too hard, but London is a place that belongs to other people . . . to the wealthy. She wanted private education for our son. She wanted to buy works from young struggling artists. But we were always struggling ourselves.'

'Now, by a quirk of fate our house is worth all this money. We can buy another house out on the coast and still do the things we missed out. It's all just a little bit too late. The artists have had to manage without us. Our son: well, he did what he did. But we will have some money. We can do some of the things we wanted to do.'

Alice took my hand, slowing me down as we waited to cross to the common. She spoke softly: I turned my head to catch her words with my good ear. 'I didn't even know you had a son.' There was a hurt note in her voice.

I thought . . . I was sure I must have mentioned him. Maybe he just never cropped up. During those days in the office there was a limited range of subjects you could touch on. 'I guess he doesn't mention me much, either.'

'Have you seen a house you like yet?

'We have seen somewhere, but it's too nice for Esme. She'd

rather stare out on a wasteland than a nice hillside. She'd rather look onto mudflats than a coast with sea and a beach and rocks and people enjoying themselves.'

Alice laughed. 'I can imagine her not liking a typical seaside town.'

'She believes in compensatory events. Cycles of punishment and reward. She thinks we still need to be punished.'

Alice's face creased, puzzled. 'Punished? What do you need to be punished for?'

'For every good thing, something bad happens. There's a balance.'

I saw a big lump of wood in the road. It had probably fallen from the back of a tree surgeon's truck. I moved it to the kerbside. I would come back later and heave it home. I could start my sculpting. I didn't need to wait until we moved.

'How does that work?'

'Ask Esme. But it does.'

'Punishment for good deeds. A screwed-up Karma.'

'It's the savings bank of fate. You build up, you cash in.'

She kept taking her mind off the matter in hand.'That suggests no matter how much good you spread, it will result in unhappiness. You have been happy, haven't you? You always seem happy, the two of you. You're my inspiration.'

'She thinks I am her punishment.'

She smiled, thinking I was joking, and that the sombre, miserable persona I had adopted was for comic effect.

'All families are screwed up. My sister keeps ringing me because she won't believe I'll be there for my mother's birthday. The more I insist I'm coming, the more she thinks I'm going to pull out. They really won't believe it when I turn up with a cake.'

I pulled the timer out of my pocket, even though I knew precisely how much longer the cake needed. 'We should start heading back.'

'I bet you're from a big family?'

I shrugged. 'Not so as you would notice.'

She smiled, maybe trying to imagine a household of genetic variants. 'The massed Guralnicks. A sight to behold.'

'We don't really do much massing. More a parting of the ways.'

'Do you not see your relatives at all?'

Walking along the edge of the common reminded me of how I used to walk there with Esme most evenings after we'd eaten. She had the idea that a walk was needed to settle the digestion and clear the mind.

'When I first met Esme, I couldn't believe she would even walk down the road with a strange-looking Jewish guy like me. I wanted everyone to see us together. Everyone except my family.

'I came home one evening, and it was as if someone had died, and, in a way, they had. I was no longer welcome at home. I left the house that evening.

'I returned the next day, to see if I could talk to them, get them to understand. It was a Wednesday; I could hear the bin lorry grinding its teeth in the distance. Dumped outside with the rubbish were all the props of my life: my clothes, my books, my bicycle. I watched as the lorry drew up and the bin men threw everything into the jaws of the crusher.'

I stopped. Did I expect her to question my story? We walked up the street in silence for a while, until she began to talk about property, marketing strategies.

When we got back we took out the cakes out. The one at

the front of the oven was overbaked, the one at the back a bit underdone. It was an eccentric oven.

After she had gone, I tried to drag the piece of wood with the hole in it into the house, feeling as I did so a pain searing through my back. I hauled and dragged the wood along the pavement and across the road, finally leaving it by our front door.

⚜

Suddenly I was wide awake, the smell of baking dragging me out of my sleep, and I rushed downstairs, convinced the oven was still on. After I'd checked it I knew I would not be able to sleep again. Esme was breathing steadily, her gentle rhythmic breathing accompanied by a faint whistle. The glow of moonlight caught her face, twisting it into the expression of someone about to ask a question.

I got up and made a cup of tea. There was no milk. As I sipped it, I watched a pair of slugs coil around each other on the window, their mating dance leaving a heart-shaped trail of slime. Their clay brown undersides offended me, and I felt a desire to go out and crush them, squash them to an essence of wet pulp, destroy them in the act of ecstasy.

I tried to read but I couldn't concentrate. My attention kept flicking away and I repeatedly lost my place in the book. I needed no thrillers in my life, with their tedious themes of violence and sex. Gratuitous descriptions that made me feel uncomfortable. I flicked through a few pages, then put the book down and tried a crossword, but I couldn't concentrate enough to solve the cryptic clues. Overcome by that state of emptiness.

I turned off the kitchen light and sat on the back step, smelling the mint and parsley, damp soil and decay. The sky was clear. I could see two planets and wished I knew what they were. How did people know what they were called from just looking? Was there a way to recognise them without plotting their track night after night? Without referencing some astronomical guide?

I dug the newspaper out from the bin. They were Jupiter and Mars, close and over the next few days getting closer. Best observation time 2 am to 3 am. That was always the best time to see anything: even the Isle of Sheppey. Especially the Isle of Sheppey.

Suddenly I knew what I needed. I needed carving tools. I needed a bit and brace.

I went to Andrew's old room and slipped a knife through the tape sealing the boxes we had filled with his stuff. We had been on the point of getting rid of it, then changed our minds. Throwing someone's life away was too final. One year I had bought Andrew woodworking tools, convincing myself I had detected a hint of interest in him. His reaction to the present was only puzzlement.

It had been difficult from the start with Andrew. There was always a distance between us that couldn't be bridged; often, I would wonder why. I sometimes thought he might be . . . if Esme might have . . . did the dates make sense? When I tried to work them out I could get no definitive answer, but there are questions that it's best not to ask: once you've asked the question, you can't un-know the answer. There is no going back.

Childcare was a problem. When I tried to help, Esme would give a sigh of exasperation and take over. It became clear this was her domain and nothing I could do would help her. When I changed his nappy, I never fitted it properly; no matter how many safety pins I applied, it still worked loose and left a trail of pee on the living room carpet. When I was with him it was as if he didn't trust me. He'd become unsettled, a long slow cry starting to build into hysteria, and Esme would look at me with a sad face, pitying me and herself. Did she pity herself, or did she really like the fact that she was the only one who could care for him?

As he got older, I would try to find toys that we might be able to play with together. I bought a train set. I bought miniature cars. I bought a house that you could build from miniature bricks, with pretend mortar.

'Look,' I said, as I mixed up the grey paste. It raised his interest, briefly. He put a few bricks on top of the ones I had already laid. 'No, not like that. They need to go . . .' He had stacked them directly above each other, so I showed him how bricklaying should be done. He lost interest.

He watched as I built the house myself. 'Do you want to do some?' I would say, but he withdrew his hand, tucking it behind his back.

'Do you think he might have a problem?' I asked Esme.

She looked at me for a long time without speaking. 'There is a problem . . .' she eventually said, in a slow, determined tone. 'You need to deal with him on his terms . . . at his level.'

It was a battle of wills that I did not want. I soaked that completed house in water and scraped off the mortar. I put the bricks in the oven to dry them off, then replaced them in the bag.

I left the whole kit in his bedroom, hoping one day he might build the house himself.

I would take a football when we went for our walk on Sunday mornings. I tried to get him to play, sometimes kicking the ball around, encouraging him to come and tackle me. But he would watch me and laugh, and I couldn't help seeing his was not the laughter of amusement. I'd throw the ball to him and he'd catch it a couple of times, but then he would decide the game was over and walk away. The ball bounced off and I had to run after it to stop it rolling down the hill.

Now I saw again that bag of bricks and the Build-a-House set, leaning against the waste bin in his bedroom.

We looked out across London. 'Do you see those buildings? Just to the side . . . that's East London. That's where my father lived. And my father's father. And before that the family lived in Poland. For hundreds of years they had to keep moving around, escaping trouble. Father of fathers. That long path leading to you. The Y chromosome. What makes you a boy and not a girl. It gets passed down from father to son unchanged. All the way back through generations, back to Moses, to Aaron. To the first Jews. And beyond. Generation to generation.'

He was crying. 'Is it so sad? Why does that make you sad?'

I found the tool box, the chisels strapped one side in rows in order of length, a brace and set of bits arranged on the other side. They were still covered with the cellophane from the shop. I like the solidity of hand tools. They make you feel as if you are working on the shoulders of craftsmen, as if they are watching and nodding approvingly.

As the dawn arrived, I dragged the lump of wood through the house and put it on the concrete in the back garden. I fitted the five-eighths bit and began to cut a hole. It was satisfying to see how fast the bit cut into the wood, sinking into the hole it was creating as fragments twitched and flicked out into a heap.

When I had finished I hammered the metal spike into it and skewered the ground with the other end of the spike. It went in deep, but still I hit it so it would go deeper. Then I realised I probably would not be able to get it out again when the time came to move.

I began to tap away with the chisels, just to get a sense of the form, taking control of it.

Later, I looked up and saw Esme standing there in her pyjamas decorated with pictures of famous buildings. Eiffel Towers, Statues of Liberty, the Empire State, Houses of Parliament, all snug in blue winceyette. She nursed a cup of coffee and held out tea for me, smiling.

⁂

I would have liked to say I was surprised by Andrew's visit. But I wasn't. In a way he had never left. He loomed as a presence in the house, always threatening to emerge from the darkness.

When Alice rang to tell me a couple had made an offer, I didn't really think it would be Andrew, but I couldn't imagine it was anyone else. His existence blocked out other possibilities. When he turned up, I was not shocked. Instead I experienced a collapse of hope, a failure of the promise that someone else would come to live in the house and purge what he had left behind.

I was in the loft sorting out boxes when I heard Esme answer the door. I recognised Andrew's voice straight away, even though I could only hear its rhythm and intonation. I didn't go to greet him. I bided my time.

When eventually I went downstairs, and saw them all gathered in the living room, I did not look at him or acknowledge him.

Alice gripped my hand and kissed me on the cheek. She had taken to doing that since my resignation.

'Carol,' the woman said, holding her hand out flat, smiling. She had short hair, and a pretty but earnest face. I wondered what he had told her . . . about us . . . whether he had told her anything . . . what he was planning. What did he expect would happen?

Did she hold my gaze a moment longer than necessary? Was her smile a touch warmer than might be expected? He must have told her.

Alice introduced him, and I gave him a nod. It was a brief nod, and I could sense Alice's unease. I pretended I hadn't heard the name and made her repeat it.

I couldn't see much change in him, though of course there was some. His features were more extreme, his cheeks more sunken, his eyes more fixed in their stare, his teeth more prominent. He wouldn't sit down, he was on edge, always fidgeting. It was as if he had become more himself . . . that his behaviour had fulfilled the destiny of his appearance.

Esme and I began to talk at the same time. We both stopped. She put out a hand to invite me to continue. I caught Andrew smiling. Vindication. The recurring battle, those clashes of us both speaking at once that he used to engineer, waiting until I spoke, he talking and then stopping in exasperation, finally dropping into a silent sulk.

I would not speak until it became necessary.

Alice did the talking for me. She was good at filling in,

providing that social padding of innocuous questions. All the time I was watching him. Watching and wondering what the plan was.

His presence was not benign. The one thing I could be sure of was that it would all end in trouble.

Esme. I could sense her scrutiny. As if she thought I was about to explode.

'Do you know . . .'

'We really . . . sorry . . .' Carol spoke just as I began. I noticed a flicker of satisfaction on Andrew's face. 'We really love the house.'

I nodded. 'Good. Buying a house is the biggest decision of your life . . .'

'Is it?' said Andrew.

Carol sat on the sofa opposite me while Esme disappeared to the kitchen to make coffee.

'Do you know the area?'

She nodded. 'I teach at St John's Primary.'

'I know it. It's a good school.'

'We do what we can. Sometimes it feels like you're trying to force the top on the jar that's fermenting.'

'Like sauerkraut?' I said.

She looked puzzled. Andrew's face screwed into a sneer.

'Sauerkraut ferments in the jar. As it pickles.'

'Yes, I suppose so, then. Does it explode?'

'It can do.'

Andrew was examining the window, checking the pane which had been replaced.

'The glass is different in that one. The window got smashed.' I could see Alice shaking her head as I said it.

'How did that happ . . .'

'It was just one of those things. Just one of those things. It's in the details.' I was beginning to be riled. I didn't want to play his game any longer.

'I'll get them typed up tomorrow,' Alice said. 'First thing.'

Esme came in and poured the coffee. 'Nice cups,' Carol said.

They were a garish orange colour, and featured a woman in a blue kimono, her white face in a too-broad smile as she poured tea from a pot.

'I like your pictures. Are you an art lover?'

Esme nodded. 'It's just as well we were never wealthy. I'd have filled the house with all sorts of nonsense.'

'But these are . . .'

'I find more and more that any pleasure I took from art has disappeared. It's no longer the skill that counts. It's been replaced by the obsessive drive to capture something in the world . . . the object itself is just the memory of that act of creation. I'm sorry, I do keep slipping into lecture mode.'

Carol laughed. 'The peril of being a teacher.'

I found myself admiring the way Andrew could face me without any embarrassment. 'What do you do to fill your days, Andrew? Or should I say, your pockets?'

His face screwed up, puzzled, as if he didn't understand.

Carol jumped in. 'He's a life coach.'

Esme looked cynical. 'How does that work?'

'He helps people find what they want in their lives. Then he shows them what blocks them from getting it. He's very good. He's giving a talk tomorrow. You should come and hear him.'

Esme flashed me a cynical smile. 'I'm not sure I need un-blocking. All my desires have been fulfilled.'

I had had enough. I pretended I needed to go to the toilet, then, instead of rejoining them, I went back to Andrew's room. There I could look down on to the shed where Andrew had hidden for so many days, Esme helping him. Weeks afterwards I could still smell his presence among the reek of oil and petrol.

The lump of wood is down there on its metal spike, the form gradually emerging from it, the shape that was captured within working to emerge, battling to achieve the final form, using me as its instrument to uncover the inner truth.

I pulled out the tape measure from the drawer and stood up. Andrew was behind me.

'She seems very nice.' I knew I sounded nervous. I wanted to be confident, indomitable.

'Carol? She is. Too nice.'

'I just hope she doesn't get hurt.'

He smiled as if he understood. 'Why should she get hurt?'

'When she finds out the truth.'

He came and stood next to me. 'We all get hurt by the truth.' He looked down at the shed. I shuddered. He was large and powerful. His just standing there felt like a physical threat. 'Have you taken up carving?'

I nodded. 'I was going to wait until we moved, but then I just started. I've been using your tools. Sorry – but I had no means of asking permission.'

He nodded. 'Mum's looking okay. Better than I'd have thought.'

'What did you expect?'

'Something different.'

'It must be very strange for you. Here again after all this time.'

'It feels like the most natural thing . . .'

'Natural is overrated.'

'One thing I've learnt over the years is the value of natural.'

'And to buy this place and move back here is a natural thing?'

He nodded. 'It's a thing. There's a quality about a place that you've lived in already. It has a presence . . . A place for my thoughts.'

'Some thoughts are best left behind.'

'Some thoughts can never be left behind. They aren't a flux that passes . . . that you can just dip into and out of. Your feet are always in that brine.'

'Home sweet home.'

'With the mezuzah on the door post.'

'Except it's not. I took it down.'

'Why did you do that?'

'Why would I want it? It's nothing to me.' It made me angry that he was asking. 'So you're a life coach now? How does that work?'

He stepped back from the window, and headed out of the room. 'You don't need to ask about it.'

'I'm glad it's providing a living for you.'

He turned around in the doorway. 'It's working.'

Esme had a respect for the natural. For me it was an excuse for all the worst instincts. Things that should have been constrained.

There were pigeons on the roof. I could hear their claws scratching on the slates. He reached into one of those boxes that contained the remnants of his childhood, taking up one of his books as if puzzled that he could have ever possessed it.

'I don't understand what it is. It sounds like something

driven by selfishness. Self-centredness,' I said.

'Where would you want the centre to be? If it wasn't based in the self?'

'My centre? Do I have a centre?'

After he had gone, I was still wondering about that. Did I have a centre? It felt as if any core I might have had was now somehow displaced.

Alice stood in the doorway. 'What's this? A secret negotiation?'

When we were downstairs again, I realised I'd had enough of this play-acting. Andrew sat next to Carol; she gripped his arm and they began talking. This time I had no scruples about interrupting. I had had enough of dishonesty and games.

They left, Carol weeping, Alice and Esme staring at me as if I had gone mad.

I let Esme explain to Alice while I went outside and began work on the horse's head.

After Alice had gone, Esme came out.

I didn't stop carving. I carved like fury.

'How could you do what you've just done? You can't bear to give him a chance, can you?'

I carried on carving, my rage spilling over. I shaved away far too much wood, repeatedly having to readjust my original concept of the form.

'He was never . . . never . . .'

'You know everything. You always know everything.'

I didn't want to retort, but on certain matters, yes, I do. I remember as a boy talking to my uncle, telling him how I was suffering a crisis of belief, how I didn't know if I really believed in God, or the course of the Jewish destiny.

He laughed. 'That's normal. Everyone has doubts. No-one

cares what you believe. It doesn't matter what is inside. How you behave is all that matters.'

It was a shock to me that people should opt for mass delusion because it was more comfortable. But the more my life progressed, the more truth there seemed to be in the idea. Even my wife, she who devoted so much time to philosophy, would listen to her son and be unable to discern the plain truth. She had chosen delusion and she was trying to drag me into it with her.

❧

A couple of days later I was walking by the office and saw Alice. She waved. I went in. My nameplate was still on my desk.

'You've still got my desk, then. I thought someone would have taken it by now.'

'You've not officially left yet.'

'Should I be turning up for work?'

'Just finish those details and bring them to me. I'll let you know if we need you to cover anything else.'

It seemed very quiet.

'It's good to see you.'

Alice got up and shut the folder she was looking at. 'Come on, David. Let's go for a drink.'

I was taken aback. I had never been out for a drink with her before. It was a surprising new step in our relationship.

She led the way to the pub at the junction. It had just reopened after a two-year closure, prior to which there had been constant brawls. The landlord had been arrested for attempted murder. The damp boards covering the windows had now been removed and the interior had been recrafted.

It was quiet: early evening. A couple of afternoon drinkers were hanging on in there, their gaggle of empties still uncollected. I bought the drinks. We sat at a table in a quiet corner, the only company a man sleeping on the bench opposite our end of the bar.

'There is something about a drink after work. I really enjoy that moment . . .'

'Are you getting into bad ways now I'm not around?'

'I don't go out with that lot. I wouldn't trust myself not to say something with a drink or two inside me.' She laughed.

'Really?'

'Come on. Have you never done that? Suddenly found your tongue loosened a little bit too much, and started telling a few home truths?'

'I've actually never been drunk.'

'Really? Never ever?'

'Well, not since I was fifteen. My father was never a drinker except on Christmas Eve. It was a Jewish thing, getting drunk that evening and playing cards, gambling, to ensure you weren't overcome by Christian piety. They would drink sweet kosher wine and eat salty nuts and spent more time arguing about the rules of the card game than they ever spent playing it. I heard him tell jokes that I could hardly believe had come from his lips; his laughing grew coarser and each joke competed to be cruder than the last.'

'He sounds just like my father. I don't think mine had to work hard at avoiding Christian piety, though.'

I told Alice how he had beckoned to me and given me a glass

of wine. I sipped at it, quite timidly. It made my face crease up at first, and my head began to spin. I wanted to avoid getting drunk, losing control. Then I found one of my father's friends was staring into my face as if he wanted to see into my head. He beckoned me over.

'Your father says you're good with numbers. Is that right?'
I nodded.

'Look,' my father had said. 'He got first prize for Mathematics, top of the school.' He produced the book that I'd won. The title was 'The Marvels of Modern Science'. It was embossed in gold and stamped with the school coat of arms.

'Mathematics. That's what drives the world. Mathematics and madness. Nothing else.'

The circle of joke-telling had reached me. They were all looking at me, all those beards and whiskers, waiting for me. I felt a sudden lurch in my stomach and ran to the toilet.

'Sorry Alice, I'm rambling on. You don't want to hear this. All my crazy memories.'

Alice smiled. 'No, go on. Mathematics and madness. My two favourite subjects.'

A few days later my father had told me to put on my suit and my mother had smoothed my hair with a spit wash. He took me to the City and we went into a building that was built like a shining castle, standing out amongst all the rest, its carpets deep red. We sat outside an office for some time before I was led in.

A man with deep wrinkles and thick black hairs growing upwards on the bulb of his nose looked at me over the desk. He asked me some questions about my family and what I liked doing. He gave me a few arithmetic puzzles which were so easy to solve they made me hesitate in case he was trying to trick me. When I spoke my voice disappeared into the fabric of the room, the carpet and the wood-panelled walls. I could feel myself disappearing with it.

'Good. Just one more thing: tell me, whom do you most admire? Which leader would you trust to show us the way out of the darkening chaos around us?'

I had looked at the portraits behind him, eminent people with stern expressions. There was a picture of the Queen and one of Winston Churchill.

'Karl Marx,' I said.

'I can't understand it,' my father said later. 'I was sure they'd offer you a job.'

'So, Alice, that was what came of my interview at Rothschild's. Imagine it. My life could have been so different. We could have been wealthy. Andrew at private school. Money to spend on art. We could have lived somewhere else. Dulwich. Hampstead maybe. All denied by my answer to that one question.'

Alice laughed. 'So you're a Marxist? You kept that quiet. You must be the only Marxist estate agent.'

'You'd be surprised. There's a network of us. We're entryists. We're taking over, putting all private property in common ownership.'

'You'd better make it fast, then.'

'Now you've got to work out who my successor is.'

I could see her thinking through all the staff, half playing me along, half enjoying the thought that what I'd said might be true.

'Beth,' she said. 'It's always the one you least suspect.'

'Maybe she's the cover. The one planted to bear the brunt of all suspicion.'

She was smiling, happy in a way I had not seen before. I felt a lurch of regret, for my age, for the impossibilities presenting themselves before me.

'You never see your family now?'

I nodded. 'The day I left that house was the last day I ever saw them.'

'And you never bump into them?'

'This is London. You don't bump into people. It can take three months before you 'bump into' your next door neighbours.'

She went up to the bar for more drinks. I watched her, taking pleasure in the shape she created, swaying her hips slightly as she stood there are the bar.

'So you were thrust together, you and Esme.'

'It didn't feel like it at the time. But yes, in a way. Even now it feels like a miracle. Why she would choose me? Strange looking. Ungainly. Without any distinction or wealth.'

I dropped my voice a little as I found I was revealing as much to myself as to Alice. 'I never thought she'd stay with me. Do you know that? I thought, this is it, a moment, then it will be gone. But somehow it went on and on. Until now there's an agony in having it continue. Wondering when the end must come.'

She reached across and gripped my hand in hers, enveloping it. 'That seems very sad. I always thought of you as an ideal couple. My ideal couple. My beacon of hope in the mess of my own family life.'

'You still see your father, don't you?'

'Not openly, but in secret. As if I'm doing something bad,

an act of betrayal. I never mention it. I've tried, but it makes them turn on me. My mother behaves as if I am trying to destroy her. I used to feel angry with him, but now I think he got out while he could. He had to get away from her. She was destroying him. He chose life over that shrinking decline my mother chose.'

'Is it women who make the choices? We go along with it, make the best of it. Somehow, they always force things to the point of choice. They don't decide, but they force a situation to a point where a choice must be made.'

She nodded. 'My father would have drifted on, carrying on with that succession of affairs that everyone knew about . . . except my mother. He had the excitement of being with those women, but always somewhere safe to come back to. She must have known, really, but one day it got too much for her. She took that safe place away from him. She left him stranded.'

I liked pubs. I wished I could spend more time in pubs. I had never really had a friend I could call on so we could wander down to the pub together. I had never been able to put in the effort and time to cultivate a local, where I could feel comfortable just turning up by myself, chatting to whoever was there.

'How's the cake looking?'

She nodded. 'Good. My sisters still don't believe I'm going to turn up. I've got the cake now. I have no choice.' She smiled, and I could imagine her running through the scene in her head. 'I am going to make another one. By myself. I feel confident now.'

'It will keep for a week in the fridge.'

'Yes, but I want to make one. Seventy years old. And she's been in mourning for twenty-five years.'

I had asked for a half, but she bought me a pint. I felt the alcohol taking grip, control slipping away. 'I'm not really much of a drinker. I'll have a gin and tonic in the evenings sometimes with Esme. But just the one. And I always have to make it. She has a strange sense of proportion when mixing a drink.'

The man on the opposite bench from us tipped his head back and began snoring, his mouth open wide. In front of him sat an empty glass.

Alice sipped her drink, smiling. Did she think I was suggesting that she, Alice, drank a lot? She drank some more of the wine and pulled a face.

'Do you remember the Stella house? Down Mayfield Road.'

I nodded. That house we sold where the guy had died. He had the sofa raised on bricks and had built a wall of Stella cans, a stockpile seven feet high.

'The smell of that place. Every time I went there that smell clung to my jacket for hours after. I couldn't help believing he died on that sofa. When I suggested to his son they should clear the room before trying to sell, he behaved as if I'd suggested a sacrilege. As if a wall of Stella Artois was a positive selling feature.'

'Maybe you've just got to find the right buyer.'

'It scared me. I thought of myself twenty years ahead, still living by myself, gradually drifting further and further into my own world . . . unable to see how remote everything had become.'

'You'll not be on your own.' I had a moment of fantasy, announcing to Esme that I was leaving, moving in with Alice. Esme would look up from her Spinoza, struggling to refocus in the real world, trying to puzzle out what I meant as I left to pack a bag and closed the door. She would be stuck in that chair, unable to move, unable to understand what had happened. 'You will find someone.'

She smiled sadly. 'Tell me about your son.'

'My son . . .' All the doubts I had had suddenly hit me: Esme's pregnancy and the dates that didn't seem to work out. I was just so grateful that she let me back I couldn't bring myself to work out the numbers.

It's always the numbers that get you, in the end.

The sleeping man had been woken by his own snoring and was shouting at the barman, accusing him of trying to poison him. 'It's the beer. You're trying to control my thoughts.' He slammed his glass on the counter.

'It's not the beer. It's the gas we pump in. It puts you to sleep and then I whisper words in your ear. That's what controls your thoughts.'

Alice shook her head. 'It's strange, isn't it, how these habits get passed down, generation to generation, and we are trapped in the cycle. My father's father was the same. He abandoned his family.'

I was a little offended by this. I looked down at her fingers, stretched out, as if her hand had replaced mine. 'It was different with my parents. It was a Jewish thing. You know, I feel sympathy now, more sympathy than I ever did when we were together. It is a fight for survival.'

'And you don't think you'll ever see him?'

I felt a shudder of something run through me.

Alcohol always affected me suddenly. One moment it was just a thirst that gripped me, and I was drinking to deal with the thirst, then, with no obvious moment of transition, I found myself sinking into the chair, powerless to rise, unable to move. I was looking ahead into a future spiralling off before my eyes, a cloud in which I could make sense of nothing. I looked straight ahead, barely able to raise an arm. I tried to get up and slipped; Alice grabbed my arm. 'Sorry, I'm not used to the drink.'

She leaned over and kissed me on the cheek. Then she was gone, and with her something else went. Something big, something enormous. My whole life.

I scraped a little more wood off over the top of the eyes. I had lost any sense of what I was aiming at, but now the horse's head was taking on its own form and coherence. It was solid, an uncompromising shape. The flow rising from the neck represented a surge of feeling, of joy. The flare of the nostrils, the angry blank eyes, the mouth that drew one as if fixed on the brink of saying a word. The word. I imagined it as an object of veneration, of it being discovered and adopted as the figurehead of a cult, a religion. A surly unforgiving godhead. Whatever entreaty its votaries made, still casting that same unseeing stare down upon them.

Esme appeared. 'So that's it? Are you finished?'

'Nearly.'

'I'm impressed.'

I smiled. Her compliments were rare, so difficult to take. I always felt an unsaid rider was on its way. I was impatient for her to utter it.

'Just one thing more.'

I gathered some dried-out hedge clippings, prunings from the apple tree and balls of newspaper, and lit a bonfire. The flames shot up rapidly, six, seven feet in the air, before dying back a little, creating a solid red heart that twisted and turned, pulsing with the small gusts of wind.

I went upstairs and brought down the boxes from Andrew's room, and tipped the first load of stuff into the flames. I knew I should have taken the things to the charity shop, but I couldn't bear to think of people picking through it, fingering their way through his books, holding up his jeans to their legs, checking the size, the shape, the degree of wear, then tossing them aside once more.

The sculpture wasn't great, but as a first effort it was OK. Not something to mount and ride out into the sunset on, but something on which to enter the arena, to announce your entry.

The balls of cloth hissed in protest before collapsing in the flames. The books were yielded more easily to give themselves up to the fire. Soon a power of heat had been generated. I took the horse's head and tipped it on its side, leaning its metal pole against a rock and resting another rock over the base of it.

I turned it, gradually, steadily, letting it char, splashing water over it until it became a black, angry mass.

So that was it, done.

Upright.

⚜

I woke up again in the night. My whole sleep pattern had changed. For years I would instantly fall asleep, stirring occasionally if I needed to pee, rising but not fully emerging from sleep, never reaching a proper state of wakefulness. Now I was wide awake, staring out of the window, down at the garden.

I heard something clicking, some insect maybe, and sensed

a whirring, like a moth chasing, just the hum of wings. A bright star glowed above the rooftop of the house behind, no, a planet, a solid yellow light, maybe Jupiter, maybe Saturn.

My head ached. It was a pulsing pain, advancing in a long, slow cycle.

Soon Esme and I would be in a place where the skies were bigger, the two of us still staring up at the same planets, following their courses that the ancients had plotted, but ourselves separated by the same unbridgeable distance. Esme would be in Sheerness, staring out across brown mudflats, delighted by a place unrelieved by any kind of comfort.

I turned her words over in my mind yet again. She thought it was all my fault. Even after everything that had happened, she could still get sucked back into the world as Andrew presented it. How could she not see that the whole dream would collapse? He was never going to be able to buy the house. He had no money. No desire to either raise the money or buy the house. All he had was the same destructive power he had nursed for all those years. Despite her dedication to study and her supposed clarity of vision, her observation of what lay at the heart of everything, her disencumbering of the truth . . . despite all of that, she could not rumble the crudest con artist, playing the oldest trick in the book.

I dozed sporadically, then sat on the back step as the sun rose. The transition from the first glimmer of light came fast, as if desperate for cosmic reparation.

I made a cup of tea. The air contained a dawn chill, helping me to focus my thoughts. I clutched the mug of tea for warmth and listened to the sounds coming from Esme in the kitchen. It was unusual for her to be up so early. She banged the kettle on the cooker, and I could hear her struggling to light the gas. I was about to go to her aid when I heard the pop and roar of the burner.

It would be a relief to get rid of that old cooker. I'd suggested many times that we should buy a new one, but Esme felt attached to it. The aesthetics outweighed the practicality. Always aesthetics overruling every other consideration. It was amazing that I was still around. To any degree. A miracle.

I had always been anxious about our relationship, insecure, fearful she would one day look at me and realise that she'd made a terrible mistake, condemned herself to living with a strange-looking Jewish boy with limited prospects and bad teeth. Now our house was our fortune, the fruit of the life we had made. All those things she'd professed she didn't care about could be bought now. I would feel secure; she would have no cause for resentment.

'Esme. Can I have another tea? If you're making one?'

There was a scraping sound as she pulled the chair back. She came out and sat down next to me. Except that it was not Esme.

Andrew handed me a mug of tea. He had remembered: just a small touch of milk.

'We didn't finish our discussion. So I thought I'd better come back.' His voice was croaky, maybe he'd been talking all night. He sat next to me, holding his own mug of tea. The tea was bitter from having been brewed too long.

The sun shone on the terrace that backed onto ours. 'Do you see there's an extra half brick in the course. It jumps, it was all done by eye in those days and if you look inside them, each house in the row is slightly different. They evolve as you walk on. The builders tried new little tricks as they built each house . . . more rounded stairs, more elaborately turned newels.'

He gave no sign that he was listening, instead taking a long sip of tea.

'You teach people how to live? How do you qualify to do that? Is there a college?'

He smiled and explained as if he was used to it. 'It's about stripping away layers, the stuff we hide behind, to get at what is inside, the creature within.'

'And what do you do with 'the creature' when you've found it?'

'You find out what it wants and you help get it what it needs.'

'Okay. And if it says it need a house?'

'You help it get what it needs.'

I could see him as a boy, standing next to me, holding my hand, watching as the car burnt in front of our house. Esme was rushing around talking to anyone who would listen. Andrew and I just watched, feeling that incredible heat. I was thinking, is that what the end of the world will feel like? When it comes? Will it be us all fixed together, as though we're melting together, merging. It sucks the will out of you if we all just watch.

How did it happen? That boy. Now become a man with a large, powerful physique.

'How would your inner creature buy a house? By working, saving up money? Or is there another way? Have you found a way to short-cut all of that?'

He smiled, as if being generous by not rising to my provocation.

I tried to get up, to go into the house, but my legs felt heavy, I was dizzy. I staggered inside and sat in the living room, on the sofa.

He came in and sat with me. 'You could never imagine anything good in my life, could you?'

'I just see what I see, not what I want to see. If I was going to sell you this place, how would you pay for it? Do they give mortgages to life coaches?'

He closed his eyes. 'It must be wearing, to be so sure of everything. Never for a single moment allowing doubt to intrude. An edifice of certainty, surrounded by waverers. It would do you good, to step back and allow some doubt in. To ask some questions.'

'But I forgot. Alice told me. You don't need a mortgage. You have compensation. What happened? It must have been pretty bad to pay you enough money to buy a house. You get five thousand if you lose a finger. Twenty thousand for a hand. You still have both hands and enough money for a house.'

'Not all injuries are visible.'

'So what was yours? Injury to your psyche? Disruption of your well-being? Do they give compensation for that?'

'It was a shattering . . . a destruction of self. These things are easy to sneer at, but the trauma is real.'

❧

He talked. He kept talking, long after I'd stopped listening. He kept talking.

He was like wayside preachers, those mad people standing

at the corner of the high street. If you listen long enough they begin to sound plausible.

I went into the living room and began to sort out paperwork.

Esme came in, looking ill, hung over. She settled on the sofa next to him.

She drank some coffee and flopped into semi-consciousness.

My tongue felt heavy in my mouth. In that moment I realised what was happening. He had drugged us. What was the name of that drug that took away the power of resistance?

Andrew was talking. It was a dream . . . a journey into horror, where the talking would never stop . . . like a visit I'd made to the theatre when I sat for hours, so much talking going on, but I had no clue what was happening until I drifted into a relaxed state in which the endless talking merged with my dream consciousness.

I was trying to get up, to escape, but my legs were too heavy. My feet were stuck to the ground. It felt as though my legs would lift, but my feet were still on the floor.

I could hear him talking, but his mouth was not moving. He was talking about compensation and how he was entitled to it because I had taken everything from him.

Esme was telling him he could have the house, that was his compensation.

'Where can we go?' I heard myself saying. I don't know if I asked that, or just thought the words, but no-one answered.

I reached across to Esme, wanting to hold her hand,

thinking that if we could hold hands we might find enough strength to get up and escape. Could Spinoza help us?

Andrew seemed drugged, too. He tried to get up and fell sideways next to her on the sofa.

In my head he had always been there, shaking out the can of petrol, shaking it so thoroughly, then stopping briefly to look at his handiwork, looking at me, then back at the pooled petrol. Holding the matches, striking them, the first, the second. It was the third one that worked.

I'd mentioned the story about the caravan to Alice. She was going away with some friends, to stay in a caravan in France, somewhere in the Dordogne, for a few days. I just wanted her to beware. She'd come back at me, saying it could not be true, that a sufficient concentration of gas could not be pumped in to paralyse the campers so they could only watch as they were robbed. 'If that's what you want to believe,' I said. 'If that's what makes you happy.' I could see us, stuck in mudflats, sinking into collapsing ground, all around brown rivulets running through, half-light from the sun.

What most amazed me was that Esme had stayed. Throughout my life. I had never expected her stay. I always thought I would come back one day and find that she had left, that she had found someone else, moved in with someone who had more money, more class, more prospects. But she stayed. She was still here.

I drifted into a haze. Andrew kept asking things, starting discussions then abandoning them, and all I could feel was anger. The two of them were goading me, Esme too, as he told me how I'd wrecked his life. Now I must pay. He talked and talked.

So much talking.

Suddenly there were flames everywhere and the place filled with smoke. His talking stopped at last.

The fireman once told me that even if you know there's an escape route only yards away you can't step through that smoke. You stay in a place where you've been secure, rather than saving yourself.

3

CAROL: I AM HERE.
WHERE ARE YOU?

I CAN'T SAY what it is . . . some instinct . . . some primal sense . . . I hear the phone ringing, but I can't bear to answer it. I know it won't be him. He never rings that number. It could be my mother: she will ask about everything until she comes to that last question, the one she can't avoid any longer, 'So how is . . . Andrew?' Always that little trick of hesitating, as if she can't bring herself to say his name.

Or it could be a sales call. Who ever responds to them positively? How can cold calling be worth the effort? Someone called the other day about a dating site . . . 'No,' they said quickly, 'this is not for you, but do you have a friend you could recommend as a potential girlfriend or boyfriend . . . for a no-strings-attached trial?'

'I don't know. I'm not sure I have any I could recommend as friends,' I said, and there was a pause.

'You're joking, right?' said the woman at the other end of the phone.

'I don't make jokes,' I said.

The phone stops ringing. I chop vegetables for a stew. I can picture the grimace on Andrew's face, as if he can see from wherever he is that it is 'another bloody vegetable stew'.

'Yes, but there's ways . . .' he says, 'ways to give it some flavour.'

He is right, of course. He finds ways. That Ethiopian meal we had the first time we went out. I will not forget that, those flavours, the hot buttery spices, the cinnamon, cumin and ginger. It's a memory tinged with sadness.

It's always bad news on a landline. Or no news.

⌘

I met him at the food co-operative – I went to the meeting – we had so many meetings that went on forever and the goal always seemed further away at the end than at the start. It was always a shambles: no-one stuck to the agenda, they all jumped in with whatever was on their mind, and at times there seemed to be more opinions than people in the room. The chairperson spoke calmly, but with a choked frustration that made some of the group even more on edge. Phyllis, who dressed in a ragbag of clothes selected to clash . . . bright red dots on her t-shirt then smaller white dots on her shirt, topped off by a large scarf wrapped tight around her neck embellished with pink polka dots.. She always had something to say and she said it again and again. A long rip in her T-shirt exposed a stretch of her stomach streaked by a vivid red scar.

'You just doing it for the rich people innit. Just the rich. Forget the poor. We don't want this stuff. Basic food. Olives. We don't need olives. Capers? I don't caper. Not no more. Not no more.' She cackled and clapped at her own joke.

The chairperson stopped to reassure Phyllis that the poor

were very much in her mind, but now they needed to get on with the items on the agenda.

'Agenda . . . I never get the chance to speak. You're always cutting me off with your agenda. Always silencing me with your agenda . . . '

Finally, we muddled through it all. A collective sigh of relief spread throughout the room. People began to gather bags, find cigarettes, turn their phones on again. Then the chairperson said, 'There's just one more item . . .'

Andrew. I had noticed him earlier. He had seemed to be brooding as he stood there watching everyone. His head was shaved in a razor cut which contrasted sharply with the dreadlocks or floppy fringes of the other men there. There was a coiled energy about him. He was slightly bent over, his hands clasped in front of him, as if prayer, but also as if he could rise to his feet in an instant.

He raised a hand and the room went quiet. The silence was immediate. I had never known the hubbub to be stilled in this room: there was always some distraction, some conversation bubbling in the corner. He let the silence linger as if it was something to treasure, only breaking it reluctantly.

'Today I want to talk to you about well-being . . . .'

He talked only briefly. He made well-being sound scary, something you wouldn't want to embrace unless you really had to; but we could not escape the hypnotic effect of his talk. He was going to help us do it and because he said he would, we all wanted to. The intensity of the way he spoke left me in thrall. He only spoke for five minutes, but when he'd finished I went straight across to enrol with him.

I had, in fact, absorbed little of what he said. If someone had asked me afterwards what it was all about, I would have been unable to offer anything coherent. There was a music in what he said, a steady rhythm that carried me with it. If I had been taking notes they would merely have said, 'he spoke about life-stuff,' but I knew it was an emotional journey he had taken me on. I wanted to be a part of it; a part of *him*.

My family had never been people who embraced life. They lived solitary lives, regarding each other in silence, rarely deviating. Each day like the last, no change foreseeable in the future. Each night they mutely congratulated each other that things had not changed. No better, but also no worse. All the potential disasters in the world had passed them by for another day. They expected me to live the same way; any suggestion I might adopt a different pattern of behaviour was perceived as a threat.

I had been a disappointment to them. My father had dreamt I could be a musician. I think he saw me as a member of a church orchestra, playing the same pieces each week, rehearsing in the evenings, attaining a simple perfection. I went along with the idea, thinking something would happen to prevent it. My school offered free loan instruments and free lessons, though getting an instrument involved engaging in a free-for all, and my diffidence meant I ended up with a violin with black gouges in the wood. No-one else wanted to play an instrument that took so much effort to produce an acceptable sound.

That violin was the perfect instrument for my feelings about communication. You keep quiet until you have something to say. You express it in the most perfect way you can. Then you stop. My father listened to my playing as he tried to read, persuading himself that I was improving.

The violin gave me an excuse to lock myself away in my bedroom; and it taught me something profound. The difference between something wonderful and moving and something painful is subtle, very subtle, not even a pressure, a tension, just a feeling of tension.

I embraced the idea of becoming a musician. I practised three or four hours each evening. I set my alarm early so I could run up and down the fingerboard with the strings muted, the bow bouncing gently as it produced the quietest sound.

I thought that painful period of learning would wear through my father's patience, but he didn't tire of the sound the way I had expected. There was a sudden shift in my proficiency: I found myself able to play in tune, to shift each note from one of painful discord to one of moving emotion.

All this happened with no sense of direction or personal ambition on my part. It had not occurred to me that this could be a way of life.

One day, in passing, my music teacher mentioned the possibility of music college; then she rapidly assumed it was the only path my life could take. I went home fired up, wanting to talk about it to my mother but afraid to say anything. Then one day I spoke out and my parents agreed to support me.

Being at music college was a terrifying experience. From having been the stand-out pupil, the one who was serious about music, I was a minnow in the pool. The competition was intense. Every day we each battled for recognition while also affecting an air of nonchalance. The dedication to practice was beyond belief. Playing was like breathing to most of my fellow students. They made no conscious choice: it was what they expected to do, most of their waking hours.

Then I had a revelation. I would ignore the strident male composers and instead would concentrate on gentler, subtler talents. Amy Beach, Clara Schumann, Fanny Mendelsohn. I would play women composers exclusively and eschew the males.

My tutors were encouraging. I had found a niche: I knew my chosen repertoire so well. I had created arrangements from the works of my chosen composers, so broadening my repertoire. I had memorised that music so it journeyed with me wherever I went. I could sit and replay it in my head, my fingers twitching in time with the journey. But in the latter part of my third year I hit a crisis. I was walking along a corridor when I heard a pianist working through a piece I had played a few times before my conversion: Felix Mendelsohn's *Variations Serieuses*.

It shocked me because I was drawn into its world with an intensity I had not felt for a long time.

For a year, I continued to put forward my argument about women composers having been unjustly neglected. We had an end of year recital. I played my pieces and there was polite applause. I bowed, holding the book at my waist, seeing the lithograph of Clara Schumann on the cover. I struggled to walk off stage in my high heels. Then the next performer played the Mendelsohn variations and as I listened I realised that I was done with music.

The phone again. Eventually I answer it, but the ringing stops just as I pick up. I stir the stew again. I really should have gone out to get some herbs, to make it taste of something more than tomato and sweet potato. Yam. Some okra. Callaloo. Ackee.

I left both college and my parents' home. The focus of my life had gone and I needed something to fill the void. Music had let me down. Instead I chose God. I read Thomas Aquinas and Meister Eckhart and found a profundity in their exploration of presence and absence that inspired me. At first it was Evangelical Christians who seared with fervour and intensity. I created an idealised image in my head of a group fired up by wrath. I wanted a finger to point at me. I wanted to feel the fear. In reality the group stood for something quite different. At meetings I was trapped in corners by boys with bad breath who backed up what they said by flicking through a bible, always searching for that reference from scriptures that they couldn't find. It was as much of a let-down as music had been. 'No, really, it is here, Corinthians, the description of love . . . it is profound . . . it is moving.'

I was always faking my belief in God, and I felt no love for my fellow believers. I could not maintain the pretence. I had to move on again.

I travelled into a different world: one of action, of socialist enterprise. International socialism. Trotsky was our role model.

I threw myself into this angry leftist group. We relished any disturbance and claimed it as our own. We all pretended that we were in control of the masses, that under the power of Marx we could discern the forces driving them, and see within the great unfolding of history, the march of the inevitable. We were confident in our beliefs but decided sometimes that history needed a bit of a nudge.

I wore monkey boots and a donkey jacket with orange

high-visibility shoulder patches. This gave me kudos, suggesting connections with actual workers. But the Socialists became increasingly like the Evangelists, just with different reference books. I was passing John Buckle Books one day, and on impulse I picked up a set of the works of Enver Hoxha. Something about the picture of Comrade Enver and his paranoid world view attracted me: his protection of Albania from attack by littering the countryside with concrete pillboxes and gun emplacements and instructions that the road signs should be pointed in the wrong direction to mislead invaders. He was a tragi-comic figure, this grand orator with his artificially constructed version of history and imperialism; but through the cloud of propaganda and inflamed rhetoric, I thought I discerned some clarity of vision. The arc of history will reveal the rightness of our course and the folly of imperialism. If only we could share that view...

'Left Wing Socialism – an Infantile Disorder', 'Dialectical and Historical Materialism,' 'The Fist of the Marxist-Leninist Communists Must Also Smash Left Adventurism.'

In my head Albania became an idyllic land, a place of both purity and menace. From the rubble of Zog's destruction Comrade Enver had built a country of promise and paranoia.

But not even my small radical Marxist-Trotskyist-International-Socialist cell could share his vision. Especially not them. They would not have been more horrified, more puzzled if I had declaimed from a copy of 'Mein Kampf'.

Then I became part of an ecological group, but it lacked the intensity I needed. I sensed the existence of a secret group within the group, planning action, planning a fight, but its members did not trust me enough to invite me in.

I became convinced that the fight was not about ideology

but about community. It was about working with others to discover a worthy course of action. The collective will. So I became part of a collective, working with them to build up a community, discovering the cause as we built it.

The co-op had become my outlet. I worked there as a volunteer. I sat in the work-room on the lumpy donated sofa and used the Wi-Fi as we worked on stock control and waited for the inevitable collapse of capitalism.

The trouble with community was that other people were so annoying.

I would look around the room, hearing the same arguments every week, and realising that the people who joined groups were just as dysfunctional as my family, but being dysfunctional collectively gave them validation, a semblance of normality.

⁂

The day I met Andrew was different. When he talked, Andrew was not reciting thoughts received from elsewhere, a doctrine from on high. He offered words as if they had just occurred to him. I looked round the room and saw everyone else was as gripped as I was. I felt jealous. This was my moment. He talked about explosions of will and the fire of intensity that drives us and I felt he was directing his words at me alone.

When he had finished I felt devastated. I wanted him to go on; I could have listened forever. Discreetly, he placed his business cards on the table. He had leaflets but he did not distribute them. He pointed at the one on top. 'There's a mistake,' he said. 'I must have missed it in the proof-reading.'

I smiled at him. 'I want to get involved. I want to help you.'

He reached out, his warm hand enveloping mine, our two hands folding round each other; somehow, he never let go.

After all that apparent confidence and self-assurance, at first he was embarrassed; but an hour later we were in an Ethiopian restaurant and he was telling me about teff and its importance for the world economy.

He had taken me to the restaurant without consulting my tastes. It hardly looked like a restaurant: there were no menus and the door was locked. When he tapped on it a woman with cinnamon-hued skin and wide-open eyes drew us in as if we were old friends. She indicated a bench and brought us honey wine. There was no need to order: she brought what she thought we needed, and explained the dishes in a soft murmur, as if to remind herself.

The room was warm and lit by low lamps with pierced copper shades. The air was rich with the mix of spice and burnt butter. She came to check on us every so often, smiling, deciding what else we might need. Then more food would appear. There was a central tray on which had been arranged a large teff pancake, spongy and sour, dotted with vegetable stews, piles of beans and leaves, shredded roots and sprinkled seeds. As we ate some of the food, she brought more to cover the gap we'd made: smoky aubergine, mashed sweet potato and honey, green banana and herbs.

She kept topping up my cup with the honey wine. I kept telling myself I would drink no more, but then felt compelled to sip it again.

Our interaction with her was practically wordless, just nods and smiles of satisfaction, but we never felt awkward.

'I have a theory,' Andrew said. 'It's probably not original, but if so I don't remember who told it to me. It is that language evolved with the need to lie. When we lived as hunter-gatherers, there was no need for language, no need for abstraction. The world around was all the expression that was needed. But then a cunning member of the group, probably an aggrieved outsider, realised that he could separate language from the world and create stories that made him powerful. Language favours the person with the best stories. Language was developed to create lies and to deliver the power they brought.'

I looked across at the cloth paintings adorning the walls, telling mystifying stories in cartoon form. Groups baked bread, fed their daughter to crocodiles and greeted visiting kings with more bread. I pointed to them. 'Stories like that?'

'Ethiopia is where it all started.'

The woman appeared, presented some grey coffee beans to us for approval and crouched over a pan she'd placed on a little charcoal burner, turning the beans with a long brass spatula until they turned brown. She crushed them in a mortar and poured water on them and while it steeped she dropped a piece of myrrh onto the charcoal and spun the two cups in the white feather of smoke that rose.

'There's something about this place. It makes you feel in touch with what is deep inside yourself. This is where humanity started, isn't it? Ethiopia? Just being here, eating the food, seeing that woman, so beautiful, so at ease with herself, it feels like you could learn lessons about how to live . . . how to just be.'

He nodded. He was silent for a long time, but it was not an awkward silence. Although we had only just met, it felt as if we had always known each other.

'I read about a psychologist who was researching where

people perceived their consciousness to be located. For some cultures, it was the head, for others it was the heart or the belly. There were some for whom it was in the groin. But there was one group in Java who maintained it was located outside them, in the forest. The psychologist assumed they had misunderstood and got the interpreter to ask again in a different way. Whatever way he put it, he got the same answer. 'It's out there.'

The woman crouched again to pour the coffee and gave us a fragment of a sweet made with baked honey and nuts. She looked up at us, handing us the sweetmeat in a ritual movement as though by asking us to accept it from the same plate, she was binding us together. I imagined her smile was to celebrate our union.

He told me he could not work at the shop any more, because they would not commit to a policy of no meat products.

'You don't eat any meat?'

He looked astonished that I wasn't committed to vegetarianism.

'It would be tough for them, because they serve the whole community.'

'You need to have the courage of your convictions . . . to stick by what is right. Other things follow from that.'

I was terrified that I would not see him again, but once we left that restaurant we were never parted.

I would help with Andrew's talks by preparing the hall, putting out the projector, the flipchart, the microphone. I was happy to do that. I enjoyed my supporting role.

He would sit in silence in a back room to let his mind clear.

When people started coming in I would slip a sheet of paper under his door. One star, two stars, three stars, depending on how good the crowd was. I didn't just focus on numbers, but on how good I thought they'd be as an audience.

If you hear the same speech again and again, you begin to notice the subtleties. How long a moment is held. The rhythm of a phrase. There were times when I caught myself speaking along with the words, under my breath, becoming a part of Andrew's message.

I noticed it was changing. It had been about the development of self . . . the inner core of being. But now it was more about understanding what you wanted and ways of getting it. About finding the things that blocked your fulfilment of your wishes, the excuses you made to yourself.

I thought it sounded more selfish than before, but I could see it was popular. I tackled Andrew about it.

'It's just the presentation of the message. What I am saying is still the same.'

I wondered about that.

After we'd left the Ethiopian restaurant we walked back down the Edgware Road and through Hyde Park. I told him that there had been two women who were struck by lightning there, that they were vaporised. All that was left was the wire from their bras. 'I can't imagine how that can be possible. To disappear in a moment like that.'

'You can disappear, but the trace remains.'

'The trace?'

'Every action, every interaction. Every movement produces waves that ripple through the universe; they travel: a billion years into the future, those waves, those dots of light, will still be travelling. An observer could reassemble your life from those actions. Nothing gets forgotten.'

We caught a bus. He took me somewhere deep into south London, a place I had only heard of because I'd seen the name on the fronts of buses. His flat was there, in a thirties block whose corridors smelt of floor polish. Every surface in the communal area was decorated with warning notices or prohibitions.

His coffee was from Yemen. It dripped slowly through the filter paper. We watched it together. It had barely begun to cool when he came to take me in his arms. I moved closer, sinking into him.

'In a moment. Gone forever.'

When I kissed him, I moved my tongue into his mouth fast, as if we might both disappear and the act had to be completed before that happened, as part of the unfolding of the course of the world he had described. It was a puzzling thing, that dance of the tongues: it had shocked me the first time a boy slipped his tongue into my mouth, but now it was my tongue that was leading.

My hands journeyed down his chest to his groin. I opened his fly and reached in to hold his cock. It lay soft in my hand.

I found it reassuring that he needed me to stimulate him, that mentally he was elsewhere and needed drawing back to the present. I had spent so much of my time with people who pretended to be elsewhere but were actually horribly focused on one place and one thing. I found his state of otherness alluring.

By the time he was erect I was impatient. I took my jeans and pants off and sat on top of him, felt him pushing deep, rocking gently forward and back.

I cried when it was over. I turned away, so he would not see my tears. He touched my face and felt them but knew better than to ask why. I lay down on the sofa with him behind me. It was uncomfortable, but I didn't want it to end.

As the dawn rose I was still awake, numb but still wanting to stay like this forever.

Eventually I had to get up to pee. I sat in that sad, damp bathroom and there was music playing in my head.

Fanny Mendelsohn. A sonata that I had battled with. Now I know that the secret I had thought was locked in that piece was somewhere else. It was out in the forest.

※

How did it happen? There could be long periods of drudgery in life when nothing happened as you wanted it to, and then suddenly you would experience something wonderful, a frenzy of illusions and imagining, a trick of the bored brain. Fantasies you wouldn't have believed possible. Then you had to breathe through the dream and hold on to it.

One evening we were sitting reading. I was locked in an Anne Tyler novel that was still building an idyll of married life for the heroine that you knew was soon going to be shattered. Andrew never read a book from cover to cover, but always had a stack of books beside him and would dip into them, jumping between Wittgenstein and Tagore, Kierkegaard and

Hölderlin. Reading was not a restful activity for him, but a flurry of book-swapping. It was a journey, a search, a hunt.

'Where did you get that habit from? Did no-one ever teach you to just read one book at a time?'

He looked up at one point, his gaze following the coving where the lumpy ceiling met the cracked wall.

'We should buy a place.'

'Together? How can we?'

He looked at me, smiling, as if there was a lot I did not know. And there was. A lot I did not want to know. I did not want to examine my life at that point in case this dream collapsed. He had hypnotised me; of my own volition I had surrendered my powers of control, of healthy scepticism.

When I realised everything was falling apart, I was frightened of asking the wrong question in case it drove a wedge between us. 'How could you not tell me? How could you think it would stay hidden? Even your name was a lie.'

Even his name. Well, strictly it wasn't a lie. He had changed it legally. But it was a monumental thing to do, throwing off family history that went back generations.

He'd told me his story. His battles with his father. How they nearly destroyed him.

I told him it did not matter. We could stay in the rented flat. We had other, more precious, intangible things. In some ways staying in the flat would be better than moving to a place so loaded with his past memories.

That evening had been a difficult one. Andrew was giving a presentation at the community hall. He knew it was going to be tough. In that part of South London money was tight and people were inclined to scepticism. I had invited Alice to come. She had shown an interest, but I thought just out of politeness. 'Do you think she'll come?' I said, as Andrew packed up his materials.

'The estate agent? Her sort promise something and have forgotten it as soon as the words have left their lips. She won't come.'

I watched out for her, just in case.

I was still shocked at how quickly this moment in our lives had collapsed. I did not want to make small talk.

There was a group near the back of the hall who'd clearly come to make trouble. They were talking loudly to each other, laughing, holding cans of lager. Andrew had dealt with lots of individual troublemakers before, but a group was more difficult. Why they should want to spend their evening in a community hall mocking a life coach was something of a mystery to me.

I could sense from the start that it would not go well. There was a sinister energy surrounding the troublemakers that I didn't like. I often felt that Andrew was holding something in. I'd get a glimpse of it when he was angry, when I did something that enraged him. Then the rage would pass and he would smile once more.

I had prepared the form we used to gauge audiences with one star for the crowd and a question mark to show I thought that things might get awkward. Then I screwed it up and put three stars instead.

He came out and looked at me, I thought accusingly.

Then he began his talk.

'What is it that holds us back? Why do we not achieve the things in life that we want? If you imagined your life was a picture, a work of art, an epic picture unfolding, how would it end? Can you imagine the moments in it?'

'Excuse me,' someone said.

'Could I take questions at the end? In a study on attitudes, those who rated themselves as optimistic were found to have attitudes that were delusional with respect to outcome. Even those who considered themselves pessimistic were considerably more optimistic than events proved they should have been. The world is a grimmer place than we imagine, and it is only by confronting that we can begin to achieve . . .'

He was interrupted by a sneer and a ripple of giggling. The voice was insistent. 'So, if you're able to achieve all your goals, how come you're here?'

'Excuse me?'

'Why are you here talking to us? Why aren't you living your dream on your yacht in the south of France?'

There was tittering. I looked up at the brown patches where water had leaked through the roof and stained the plaster and saw Alice sitting at the back. She looked worried; she was near the doorway, keeping the way clear for escape.

He turned to me as if I would be able to help. There was a long pause. 'This is my dream . . .' He looked at me and smiled. 'This is my dream.'

❧

I forgot everything and listened again to Andrew's words, as if for the first time, and what I heard is a doctrine of capitalist self-reliance, a rejection of social cohesion, a spurning of communicative action. It was about focusing the self and personal desire. Constructing an edifice around them. It sounded like everything I hated.

I could not listen. I went outside into the cool air and I heard the rumble coming from inside. It had an unpleasant energy to it. I felt anger building inside me, anger that for all his talk of focusing on your desires and building a plan to fulfil them, he had very successfully shattered ours. How had I ended up here?

⚜

I caught sight of Alice as I stood outside. She had left before the end and was embarrassed to see me.

'You came . . .'

'I was interested.'

'He didn't really get going. Normally it's much better.'

'I'm sure. When there's troublemakers . . .'

'One or two is okay. When there's a group of them . . .'

Alice was always earnest when she spoke; she had an intense way of looking at you that made you feel that speaking to you was the most important thing in the world to her. She gripped my hands; I could hear Andrew's words ringing. 'She's selling. She's always selling something.'

'I'm sorry about today,' she said. 'I don't know what to say.'

'If she comes, don't speak to her about it,' Andrew had said earlier. 'But she won't come.' I had vowed to myself I would say nothing. He was still talking. There was a faint rattle of applause.

'Alice, you've got to help us. That house . . . it's really

important to Andrew. It's the place where his story happened . . . he needs to finish it there. It means resolution for him. He explained it all to me.'

She gripped my hands again and I could see what she was thinking: if he could lie about who he was, what else could he lie about?

It was not really a lie. It was an omission, but made for good reason. He had explained it to me, and I thought it made sense, but Alice raised a sceptical eyebrow. She made me consider again whether I believed in Andrew and his path to wish-fulfilment. Did I believe it more than I had believed in the argument of the radical left? Was I just attaching myself to another framework for action in the face of despair? I didn't believe in belief anymore. I was no longer capable of it.

'Sometimes it's the things that seem most secure that are most vulnerable to collapse,' Alice said softly.

I wondered what had brought Alice there that evening. Did she want to learn how life coaching could help her fulfil her potential? Her air of confidence suggested that she was doing that already.

'I will talk to the Guralnicks. I'll see what I can do.'

'Thank you.' She released my hands, letting them fall.

'Do you want to see Andrew? He's almost finished.'

'No, I'm going to head off.' She smiled, hesitating a moment, and then she was gone.

I waited, watching the passers-by make their slow way along the road, in what seemed to me a parade of despair.

As the last few members of Andrew's audience loitered in the lobby, Andrew appeared. He took the presentation equipment out to the car – legs of chrome and black plastic tied by rolled banners and twine. I began to speak but he raised a hand to silence me as we drove away.

I had bought teff flour that morning and I left it in a bowl fermenting so that I could make injera. That ripe acid smell suffused the atmosphere in the flat. When I looked into the bowl the mixture was frothing up high. Nothing said love like Ethiopian food.

❧

He sat at the kitchen table. The only light was from the small bulb over the cooker, which cast angular shadows across his face.

'It doesn't matter. I'm still happy here. We don't have to move. I know I was keen, but it doesn't matter. I spoke to Alice this evening. She's going to talk to your parents, though. See if she can persuade them. She seemed hopeful. She thought . . . she said not to rule it out, that's all. She thought it might be better if you tried talking to them. She said he . . . your father . . . he flies off the handle but then five minutes later it's all forgotten, like it never happened.'

'That's what she said?' He smiled. 'Like it never happened.'

'What have we got to lose? Will you try?'

'OK. It might be more of a problem than she imagines.'

He took the presentation equipment to stack in the bedroom. I wanted to ask him what he meant. But I never got the chance.

❧

It takes two days for the mixture to prove. When I try to cook the injera, they stick to the pan and fall apart when I try to lift them. They become small fragments: just a mess on the plate. Then I remember what the woman in the shop had told me. 'Low, low, low. Very cold pan.' I try again. Very low. The darkness arrives and I lie on the bed and I write in pencil on the wall. We will have to repaint when we move.

Words dictate themselves to me. The old certainties.

We see the beginnings of the collapse of capitalism into socialism

The inevitable emergence of the dictatorship of the proletariat.

The inevitable course of history.

The emergence of the dictatorship of the proletariat...

The merit of Stalin . . .

The end of history . . .

Make the rich pay . . .

The heroic and consistent fight of true Marxist-Leninists

. . .

The transition to a socialist economy

The collapse of capitalism into socialism

The open degeneration of pseudo-Marxists...

Make the rich pay for the financial crisis.

Make the rich pay . . .

Make the rich pay.

It is all right. I can wash it off in the morning.

He will come back.

I will wait. I am waiting.

ESME: THE VIOLENCE OF METAPHYSICS

W E HAD JUST turned down Jockey's Fields, into
Emerald Street. The traffic was beginning to ease.
It was 7.20 when David told me he was going to hand in his
notice. I was looking at my watch and noticing how long it
took my eyes to readjust to a change of distance. It was a
shock to hear his words: I had always imagined he would carry
on forever, struggling on in that determined way, complaining
endlessly but never able to extricate himself. I thought he
would continue in the way that street names survived: bearing
a trace of a geography lost in the generations, they preserved
a mysterious under-city beneath the changing top layer. I had
imagined that, despite his mutterings of dissent after Alice's
take-over of the business about the changes she had made, he
would stay on forever. To change this was to break the rules
. . . our pact.

'Really? You want to stop work? You're going to leave?'

He nodded, watching me, as if he needed my approval.
He halted and looked me in the face. A man in a 'Death
Rage' T-shirt pushed past us, muttering to himself about our
blocking the pavement. It struck me that we never looked each

other in the face any more. Maybe we were scared of what we might see.

'Are you sure? Won't you want to keep dropping in every time you go past?'

His face. Had it changed? Of course, the skin was saggier, and hung differently. There were pores and wrinkles and a generational gravitational pull south, but also the quality of a boy seeking approval, something I must once have found appealing. Still found appealing.

'No. There's something else. I want to move away. To the coast. I've had enough of London. We've got stuck in a rut here. Being somewhere with . . . air . . . and sky . . . it would be different. And we'd have some money if we sold the house. What do you think?'

What did I think? One thing my reading of philosophy had taught me was to be suspicious of thinking. And feeling. These are activities we don't own but observe from a distance, because they seem to belong to us, they seem to be us. But they actually belong to someone else, to a stranger we have barely encountered.

We arrived at the gallery. It was just off Lamb's Conduit Street, a section of the terrace reassigned to the business of art. The studio no longer had a visible door. There was no obvious means of entry, although through the vast window we could see people carrying glasses of wine and catalogues, which showed there must be some way of getting in. We stood for a minute before I noticed a camouflaged panel in the wall, discernible only by a slight change of texture and its six black holes for communication. I passed my hand over it and spoke into the holes. There was a buzzing and a lump of the concrete wall began to slide open, making a faint scream of protest at its first lurch, then letting out a blast of warm air along with the roar of conversations.

I didn't know why we had come. There was nothing in the invitation that suggested it was going to be any more interesting than the other half-dozen exhibitions I had seen in the last month. Had the exhibitions got duller, or had I become less receptive to what they offered? Had the parade of work become more derivative, leaden in its references, joyless, or was it just that I had become cynical, yet somehow still committed to my endless quest for disappointment?

And still I dragged David along with me. Actually I think he had started dragging me; although he liked to adopt an air of reluctance, he would remind me about exhibitions I'd received the details for if I showed no sign of attending them.

He would look at me for a reaction, but he knew better than to press me for a reply: he would always bide his time, often for so long that I would begin to think he had forgotten. He never had. Eventually, he would hit me with a barrage of references and reminders until I had to make a decision.

We admired the door, the drama of its opening, more impressive in its monumental scale . . . its mass . . . its material presence than anything inside the gallery was likely to offer. We went in.

There were crowds massed around us, no-one giving more than a glance at the artwork. I glanced through the catalogue. The girl on the desk, wearing outsize red glasses and a line of inflamed cheek piercings, had smiled as she handed it to me, but I understood the calculation going through her mind. Why was I here? Was I someone important from the art world? Was I an investor? Was I the mother of one of the artists? Everyone here was united by a similarity of purpose, even if it was only the language of aesthetics and a basic appreciation of the works on display. Why, then, did I feel so isolated?

David had gone off on his own. He used to hate these events: I would find him sitting in a corner with the paper folded over at the crossword. I found his new enthusiasm disturbing. It made him garrulous; he engaged in conversation with the artists without any kind of inhibition. I was always wary of catching an artist's eye, worried about getting trapped in a thinly disguised sales pitch, cautious of building up expectations that would be shattered when they realised I had no money to buy art. Or not their art, anyway.

He read the artists' statements and asked the unforgiveable question: yes, but what does it mean?

I grabbed a glass of wine and began my tour of the room, my mood of despair growing. We had spent ninety minutes travelling here and now we had arrived it was just like so many other exhibitions I had been to. A decade of dreary art work.

I was looking at a glass dome containing a black pile of charred matter of no discernible form. I looked it up in the catalogue. The artist had bought the goods from her daughter's favourite pages in the Argos catalogue and burnt them. The art was a display of the debris, charred fragments bedded on grey ash in a glass box: a searing indictment of the consumer culture. But it was her daughter's choice. It struck me she should have paraded her daughter before us and made her account for herself.

A white-haired woman with a tight face approached me, as if recognising a kindred spirit, then changed her mind and hurried away, suddenly finding a burning item of interest in the far corner of the room.

'I believe that nothing that exists can be temporal, and that therefore time is unreal.' I had had a jolt that afternoon, reading a student's essay on Spinoza and Leibniz that focused mainly on the illusory nature of time. I had drawn a big red cross through the statement. 'This is not relevant,' I had written. 'Not relevant.' Double underlining. But here we were, back in a strange time, a merged world.

I stopped in front of a landscape painting, green grass punctuated with pill-boxes, precisely modelled. 'The inhabitants of this "Land of the Eagles" have been considered a savage, barbarous people,' was its title. It contained no people.

'It's a landscape of a place in Albania. I am from Albania.' The woman stood in front of me, her hair sternly cropped.

'Albania. That's nice.'

Something in her facial expression told me it wasn't, or if it was, we should pretend it wasn't. So I pulled away, and headed for an outsize deflated leather telephone with paper streamers hanging from it. They were printed with traumatic messages from torture victims, and emoticons representing their words of trauma.

David was there next to me; we were standing between two groups, the young friends of one of the artists, all shrieking and laughing, and the gallery owner's entourage: the moneyed clients and the critics, gently mocking each other in fey tones.

'Have you seen the work in the conservatory? I think there's something special in it.' His cheeks were flushed, telling me he was beyond his third glass of wine. He always professed to drink just a single glass of wine, but his behaviour belied this claim. When he drank too much he suffered an inner collapse, a loss of energy: similar to the deflated phone, his communication system became frozen. Maybe it was genetic pre-disposition, maybe a lack of sustained exposure to social events with alcohol. He would suffer for it in the morning, which meant I would suffer more.

'Really? I didn't notice. What was it you found interesting?'

'Can't you just come and look at it?'

'I'll come in a moment. Tell me first. I'm interested in what you saw in it.'

I had seen it already: a sculpture of rough animalistic forms, crude and unappealing to me. But the artist had mountainous black curls and a hungry look in her eye.

'She has an innate sense of structure and form. She uses distorted animal forms to bring to the fore the trauma of our relationship with them.' He said it with conviction.

'Are you sure that's not just what she put on her artist's statement?'

'Well, maybe, but she's just saying what I thought. She puts it better, though.'

'Right. I will go and have a look in a moment.'

'Actually 'the innate sense of structure and form' was what she said about me. She said I had that.'

I could detect his pride. We had both been to too many of these exhibitions. 'She obviously has great insight. That ability to appreciate the finer qualities of potential customers is an underrated talent in an artist.'

He put his glass down and began to head towards the door. If he could have worked out how to get the door open, he might have stormed out.

'You can laugh. You just like to think you're the only one that has any appreciation of art. Just because I'm not taken in by all that conceptual stuff. 'Untitled 17' - the contents of someone's sock drawer tipped on the gallery floor. 'Threnody for Malcolm X' – a black matchbox with ebony matches and white heads. I'm sorry . . .'

'I'll go over and see it in a moment. I need another glass of wine if I'm going to get through this.'

I went over to the wine table. A long line of glasses was poured ready. The gallery owner approached me with the sort of welcoming smile born of desperation, his eyes all the while darting behind me in case someone more important materialised.

'Esther. Good to see you. You wouldn't want to miss this.' I had reached an age now where people thought I must be hugely wealthy and were consequently over-friendly. 'There's some really key works here. I think in a few years we'll be looking back at this exhibition, proud to tell people we were here.'

'I'll look forward to it. I love living in the supplement.'

'Yes. The supplements. There's someone from the Observer here. I'll introduce you.'

I rested in the future, alone with Derrida, leaning against the table, watching a video piece exploring isolation, despair and emptiness, feeling very happy to be alone.

'We can go if you want.' David was suddenly at my side.

'Do you mind?'

I turned round as we left, looking back, and it felt like a significant moment, probably the last time we would come to one of these openings. It was the end of hope for us, the end of the prospect that we would find something enriching, rewarding. The room was full of hope; plenty of hope, but for other people.

In the street I realised I hadn't been to see his favoured artist. I apologised. He nodded. 'She was just trying to sell me stuff.'

I also hadn't answered his question. What did I think? Moving to the coast with him. Think? It wasn't a 'think' question. It was mood question. My mood was one of terror.

We battled our way through meandering tourists to get to the bus stop.

'It is interesting, though, how you think it's impossible that I could have an aesthetic sense.'

'What's bugging you?'

'You sneered when I was talking about my innate sense of form. I saw you.'

'It wasn't that. It was just . . . let's get the bus.'

We joined a queue of over-excited tourists who were dancing around each other, photographing each other in different combinations.

'I'm going to enrol in a sculpture class. I went to see the tutor. She's booked me in.'

'That's good.'

'And I've already worked out what my first piece will be. It's going to be a horse's head on a spike, its nostrils flared and its mane twisting into flames.'

'It sounds very . . . impressive.'

'You think it sounds terrible. It will be carbonised. Charred black.'

'What are you going to call it?'

'Untitled four.'

'Four? What happened to the other three?'

'They all got carbonised a bit too much. You can never have 'untitled one' in the art world. There has to be a beginning, a root that is unreachable. Who wants a point of origin that is accessible?'

'I think I may have had enough of art exhibitions for a while.'

'Do you mean . . . ?'

'I mean I may have had enough of art exhibitions. For a while.'

The bus came and we pushed past the crowd and fought our way upstairs. Kids sat at the back, playing rap on a phone with a speaker that buzzed like a bluebottle raging in a jar.

The window was steamed up. I wiped it with my glove, to look out on the street and watch the activity below. So much activity to so little purpose.

I was still churning over his question. Moving away from London: I had not suspected this would happen. We had often gone on day trips to the Isle of Thanet or Whitstable and walked a few miles across along the shingle. We'd stared out across the seafront at seagulls and fish and chip papers trapped against lamp posts. We'd sat on benches where bored youths hung out, watching them smoking roll-ups, drinking ESB, waiting for something to happen. Anything. Then when it did, wishing it hadn't. But we had never stayed overnight. I always felt a sense of relief when we caught the train home. Now we weren't planning a day trip, but the rest of our lives.

'That piece that I saw, the wood was hacked and mutilated, as if she kept changing her mind about what she was trying to convey. I said to her I could see the anger in it.'

'There's always anger . . .'

'Well, she nodded; she didn't want to argue, but she didn't think there was any anger in it.'

'Where did the anger come from?'

He shrugged. 'I guess the anger came from me.'

Sometimes I like to play these little games.

'You want to move away?'

He was looking at me, plaintively. He would never do it, when it came to it. He was too much tied to London. South London. That bit of South London.

Maybe if it had been a better exhibition I would have said no straight away, that I couldn't bear to leave, that I needed to live where we had always lived. Because that was where it all started, and it was to there we must return. Where we would all return. Where Andrew would return. But the more I thought about the exhibition, the angrier I became. It made me feel as if my life was all over. Burnt out.

'I'm still thinking about it. I've not said no.'

He nodded, and I detected a note of triumph. He had his answer: the lack of a refusal was enough for him.

As we rolled into Kennington the kids from the back seat rushed through the bus, banging into David. A small boy, aged eight or nine, hurried behind them. 'Wait, wait,' he shouted, getting trapped by the people in front of him. The doors closed and he was forced to travel to the next stop.

'What do you think Alice will say when you tell her you're leaving?'

He grinned. 'She's probably got a bottle of champagne on ice, waiting for the day.'

'I thought you and she got on.'

'She takes the time to listen to me, get the benefit of my experience. Then she ignores it. It's a culture thing. It's like relationships now. Everything happens in a night when it took us six months, a year, just to hold hands.'

'That was just you. Everyone else was getting on with it.'

'Just me?'

'Us.'

'She doesn't want to take time to understand what the client wants. She slams a load of stuff in front of them, whisks them round the properties, if they don't put in an offer she forgets about them.'

'She's doing all right, though.'

'I've never cared for pushiness. I always thought of selling houses as a subtle art. I was probably fooling myself.'

'We all fool ourselves. The whole time. It's the only way life is tolerable.'

He looked directly at me. 'In what way do you fool yourself?'

I wished I hadn't said it.

In what way do I fool myself? In the illusion that Andrew will return and the entire family relationship will be magically healed. In the illusion that I have stopped being angry and resentful toward David. In the illusion that we could head off into the sunset, holding hands as we walked along the seafront, the waves crashing, a lone gull crying, salt spray burning our eyes. These were some of the illusions I tried out for size.

The image of those charred horse heads stuck with me. It was a long bus journey home. At times it felt as if we had ground to a permanent halt while an argument raged. Someone refusing to pay. Someone without change. A drunk passenger falling over into a heap. I still preferred it to battling on the Tube. It gave me space to think, in the rhythm of that journey, lurching forward, the distractions, the drawing back to thought.

We passed a small bin fire, eager flames rising up a lamp-post, a lady pulling a Jack Russell past it as he barked, his eyes catching the orange light.

Questions of art obsessed me on this journey. I was teaching aesthetics, struggling to find any texts that would work for me. The standard essays that we made students read and discuss each year seemed to skirt around the edges, never really homing in on any kind of answer. The power of art . . . like phlogiston, something invented to account for a mystical transformative force for things we do not understand. The breath of angels transforming an object torn from the place from whence it derived its status to suspend it in isolation. Art had once seemed like a controlled outlet for rage, revealing dark desires, releasing them in orgies of slaughter. Meat joy.

Sometimes I wondered if that was what drew me to David first of all. Ours was an unlikely match. I recognised in him a person on the edge, just holding on. It was exciting, but became disturbing when we had a young child. He appraised Andrew like a critic, an artist horrified by his own creation.

I felt guilty. What kind of thinker prefers mystery to clarity? If the transformative power of art could be reduced to essences, to chemical reactions, transfers of electrons across energy levels, vibrations of atoms, surely this was better? I feared the truth was that it was all in our heads. There was nothing actually there, just the sadness of our imaginings, our wanting to love and be loved.

The bus jolted and there was shouting downstairs. I felt the familiar dread of getting mixed up in a late-night confrontation, and all the passengers being dumped into the street, to battle with the crowds for another bus. I would walk the rest of the way if that happened. Two miles in the darkness. Space for thinking.

'Okay.' The words emerged, surprising me as much as him.

He was fired up with momentary hope. 'What . . . ? Are you saying . . . ?'

'Let's do it. We'll move to the coast.' I had spoken the words but I didn't know where they came from. My real decision was quite contrary to this: it was that I could never leave that house, that I could not bear the prospect of Andrew finally returning after so many years to find that we had gone. I knew the prospect of his return was so remote that I should not even allow myself to think about it, but this was how I felt all the same.

David's face was gleaming, as much at the triumph of persuading me to move as at the prospect of a new life.

'Let's go tomorrow.'

He looked alarmed at my keenness, not recognising it as a cover for my dread.

'If we're going to do it, let's do it.'

A drunk man loomed over me and stared into my eyes. I could see I was shifting in and out of his focus. He raised a hand, about to say something, but forgot what it was. The bus lurched and he toppled forward, first on his knees, then flat on his front.

Behind us the kids were laughing and mocking him. He began a slow, caterpillar-like crawl towards the stairs. I watched, fascinated by what might happen when finally he reached them.

The bus passed the Portuguese bakery, now shutting up for the night. The owner was outside, crumbing the last of the ring loaves to toss to squabbling pigeons on the skate park.

The drunk man reached the stairs and suddenly sprang

back to life. He got up and appeared fully restored, except for the bus grime trailing down his cheek and the front of his coat.

'So you're going to start in a sculpture class? That's interesting.'

'You can pay week by week. They'll have classes there, as well.'

'Where?'

'Broadstairs. Or wherever.'

'How could they not?'

'I've arranged to attend twice a week. Tuesdays and Thursdays. I've said I'll join the beginner's and the advanced class at the same time. She said that was fine. As I was keen,' he confided, as if wanting praise.

'That's great. Well done. When does it start?'

A horse's head on a metal spike. That's just what the world needs.

Suddenly he wanted to move away to the coast. We'd talked about it from time to time, but I thought it was an idea that would always recede into the distance as other things took over. I had a picture in my head of walking along vast empty beaches with a big sky and clouds that reached from here to forever, a lone figure on the beach with a dog, walking, but never progressing.

In the same way that he thought they would always need him at work and that, faced with the reality of his departure, they would beg him to stay, I had never imagined having to embrace the idea of life away from London. I was confident that something would always prevent it.

'Are you sure Broadstairs is the best place? It's a bit . . . there's people . . . it's busy. It just seems a bit too . . .' Happy was the word that came to mind. I hated the prospect of all those happy, seaside faces.

'I thought you liked it there. Where did you have in mind? Sheerness?'

'We'll see.'

He was still fired up with enthusiasm for the exhibition. 'That was a good show. Normally the only thing that impresses me is their power of salesmanship, but this one . . .'

He was distracted, leaving his sentence hanging as the gang of kids moved up the bus to sit two rows behind us and noisily played with their mobiles. They turned on one boy, mocking him, spitting out successions of rhythmic insults, sucking their teeth after each burst. I thought for a minute David was going to remonstrate with them and laid a calming hand on his arm.

'But it's . . .'

'Yes, and so is everything. Somehow we go on.'

What was this new-found compulsion to craft dimension out of concept . . . to breathe spirit into structure? A cold flame ran through me, sucking me dry at the thought of David carving his rage out of a lump of wood.

Finally, the bus rolled up the high street and stopped just past David's office. We got off, moving out of the steam and the shouting into crisp evening air. The bus roared away and there was silence. David peered in through his office window.

'Will you miss it?'

No cars were moving. An empty street. Just a bird in the cemetery singing a mournful repetitive cry. A moth wove in crazy spirals around a street lamp. A background scent of smoke and fish emanated from the black shed in the fishmonger's yard; they had shown me round once, treating it like a place of secret worship, a scene of regular rituals of burning and preserving. On the walls the blackness of forever. A sailfish's head with a four-foot beak the owner had picked up from the market lay half out of the bin, bloodied and rotting, black with flies.

David shook his head and we marched up the hill. The wine seemed to go straight to my knees these days, as if it sloshed around in the joints, making my calves heavy. I reached for his arm, but he ignored me and strode ahead.

As we turned into our road I could see David still felt anxious, his eyes glancing from side to side, checking for signs of some kind of attack. The tension would last until we were safely inside.

David opened the front door and waved me in.

He turned on the gas under the kettle, searching first for the igniter, taking a moment too long so that a blue ball of flame shot out with a pop.

'Please. Don't do that. My nerves are bad enough.'

'I'll tell you one thing. We'll buy a new cooker.'

That would be my last evening viewing. The exhibitions took forever to get to and there was so little reward in it. The hope, the promise that they used to hold for me had evaporated, vanishing even before I began the journey. There was nothing new and exciting any more.

'That gallery owner's losing her touch. She used to find more interesting stuff.'

He grunted again. I could tell he disagreed but didn't want to provoke an argument so late in the evening.

※

I was never serious about him until my parents put the pressure on me. My father would shake his head mournfully while my mother cornered me and spoke in hissed whispers about the problems of marrying a Jew. 'Oh, there could be trouble. There's a lot of differences . . .'

'What? Like circumcision . . . . I think I know about that . . .'

'Oh, it's much more than that. There are expectations you're not aware of. A Jewish wife has to put up with a lot of humiliations . . .'

'Like what?'

'I'm not telling you every detail. But it's your own bed you're making. Don't say I didn't warn you . . .'

I would never say she didn't warn me. She warned me on an hourly basis, and when she finished warning me she jutted her jaw at me indignantly to let it sink in. Then the whole episode would be repeated again.

When we decided to marry I saw that same look he'd had when I took him to art exhibitions, as if he'd got on a ride and wanted to get off. Fast.

I was also taken aback by the speed at which things happened. When his family found out about me they threw him out. He was in a desperate state, living in a tiny bedsit where the wall was alive with black mould. We communicated via a call-box in the hallway where there was a little blackboard for messages. The messages were thinly disguised gay innuendo. 'Terry called - needs his pipe inspected. Simon - at home but all tied-up. Philip - wants to discuss a matter of HUGE importance.'

It felt as if he had given up everything for me. We spent evenings sitting on the cold lumpy bed, or cooking on a Baby Belling, stuffing shillings into the coin meter.

'This is an awful place.'

He nodded. 'I don't know what to do.'

He was working in a turf accountant's, where his quickness with figures was appreciated, but he didn't earn much. He wasn't a great prospect for me, but we were living in a new era, by new rules.

I was already anxious about our relationship, worried that we were too different, that all we shared was a cynical view of the world and a liking for opera. Now I believed I was facing the inevitable. I was carried away by the romance and drama of the situation, but I knew he would never ask me to marry him, so I proposed to him.

He dared not refuse: his philosophy was that anything life offered should be accepted. He didn't believe in God, but in a simple unfolding of fate that we should not struggle against.

Soon after we got married we moved into the house. I remember I was surprised; I could not understand how we could afford it. He had gained a small promotion at the turf accountant's, but I couldn't imagine they paid him enough to buy a house. I was still at teacher training college and had no money myself. Despite my determination to live my life in contrast to my mother's meek acceptance of whatever my father said, finances were not my forte. I had an innate fear of numbers and did not question him further.

※

We were drinking tea. He began fiddling around in the cupboard. Sometimes I wished he could just sit quietly, he was always moving things around, reorganising. He dug out his metal boxful of paperwork and began to flick through it.

'Think of it,' he said. 'We could be looking out at the sea. A sky that reaches from one side to the other without buildings blocking it out. We could see the stars . . .'

I was focusing on a closer alternative reality, documented in precise detail: letters from solicitors and building societies. This had been his domain and I had never wanted to venture into it. Until now.

He looked at me warily, stretching and yawning, trying to make me feel tired. His behaviour only spurred me on to try harder to unpick the story this succession of documents told.

'Well, I'm going to bed,' he said, without moving.

I flicked through the papers.

'So the mortgage is all paid off.'

'It's all paid off.' He pointed to a piece of paper from the building society. 'We have the deeds.'

I saw the letter confirming it, but there was more: a statement of account from the solicitors. 'But the mortgage was only half of it.'

He looked worried.

'What do you mean?'

'The mortgage was only half the money. Where did the rest come from?'

'Do we really have to go through the accounts at this time of night?'

'Where did the rest of it come from?' I felt a cold horror rising in my back. 'Did you steal it?'

He looked embarrassed and I could see him casting around for a plausible lie. He was unable to lie convincingly.

'My parents gave me the money.'

'Your parents?'

That story he'd told me with a quiver of emotion in his voice!

'You said that as far as they were concerned you were dead. Better if you had never been born, they said. Their history started again without you. They stacked up all your possessions for the bin men to take away. Your bicycle, your clothes, your books, all out in the street. No-one was ever to mention your name again.'

He nodded.

'Then they forgot all that and gave you money so that you could move in with me?'

He couldn't look at me. His voice was that of a young boy's, one who's been caught lying and thinks he can get away with it by telling an even bigger lie.

'They were angry. But then . . . they helped out as an end to their obligation.'

I felt the years fall away, collapsing. All those years. Forced together.

'So we've been living in a house financed by them?'

'It was nothing to them. Not a gift of love. Their extraction from an unpleasant contract.'

'We've been living a lie. They didn't throw you out.'

'You know they threw me out.'

'I know you told me that. It was a lie. It's all lies.'

I felt the years slipping away. I thought we had been thrust together by the romantic tragedy of his exile for my sake.

I remembered the moment when he told me he was joining the merchant navy, to build up some money . . . to start a business. At first I was horrified by the prospect of his disappearing for months. I told him I was going to do some more studying to fill the time while he was away. He nodded, smiling at some private joke, and said to me, 'My mother always warned me about marrying a clever girl.'

I thought of my own mother's warning. 'Did she? When did she say that?'

I saw his fleeting look of regret; he had let something slip and needed to backtrack. 'It was a family saying.'

I let the statement slide back into the pool of general puzzlement about his past. He barely talked about his childhood, but anything that slipped out was always full of contradictions . . . his teetotal father getting roaring drunk on Christmas Eve; their suspicion of outside influence but his father's reverence for books, his mother's sentimentality about animals but her insistence on gutting and dismembering chickens, their soft half-formed eggs popping out and rolling over the kitchen floor.

I had thought of our relationship as a distress sale, born out of a crisis; and that it had been my responsibility to save him.

Over the years I had suspected that he made occasional visits to his family. Sometimes he disappeared without explanation. He didn't have friends to visit; he didn't have hobbies. But he would go off for several hours without a word and when he returned he was silent and thoughtful for a long time, as if he was contemplating an alternative life, trying it out for size mentally. I had worried that he might have a lover; that he might go off one day and that would be it, but then when I tried to picture his attempts at seduction the fear faded. And I grew to look forward to my time alone.

The house we had bought gave substance to our relationship: it was a place of dimension, with locks. Substantial locks.

Looking at the walls now, at the skirting boards, architraves, the woodwork we had stripped down, I could recall the weeks we had spent together, scrubbing the place, then sanding down and then painting, while the radio banged out classical music. Even now I could barely hear a Shostakovich symphony without feeling the need to start sanding.

Then, when it was all done, we had one night together in the newly decorated house before he announced he was off to the merchant navy.

I had been dreading his departure, but when the time came I found I liked living without him. There was a liberation in being alone but married. I was studying and developing focus: my concentration built and intensified; for days I was locked into an area of thought. I was free of his musings, of his habit of citing interesting stories from the paper that always finished with an implied 'so there', as if the story proved some point of his about the ways of the world. I would have to fight my instincts to avoid getting drawn into discussion. I loved that world of silence and focus.

His letters came, telling me how he was struggling to adjust; that his seasickness had not gone away; that everyone hated him and he hated them. I wrote supportively to say he should try for a bit longer, that it would get better.

I started work, teaching at a local school. I got used to the freedom, there were social evenings, trips to the theatre and dances.

When he wrote to say he couldn't stand it any more, my reaction was one of rage.

I went to a dance where I stayed too long with the same man, a chemistry teacher who could dance well. He gazed down into my eyes with such a clear confident look that I had to ask myself what I had done with my life. What had I done?

I came home late. I'd had one glass of wine too many and dropped my keys opening the door.

I sensed straight away that something was wrong. There was someone in the house. I stood still, waiting for some movement, then tiptoed into the front room.

He did not say anything. He was sitting in the dark in the living room with one case on either side of his chair. The moonlight was reflected in his glasses, so I all I could see was a black form with two flat white disks for eyes.

If I had had a weapon to hand I would have probably killed him at that moment.

'Hello Esme.'

Relief that he wasn't about to attack me was quickly replaced by something else.

'Why are you sitting here in the dark?'

'Waiting.'

He stood up, kissing me awkwardly on the head, then the lips, recoiling because he smelt the wine I had been drinking.

'I've come back,' he said. 'I've come back . . . for something.'

When you have had a place to yourself for so long, sharing it can be difficult. I was hypersensitive about small things. Books were dropped on the table, the kettle landed on the stove with a metallic thud and the water sloshed around in turbulent waves.

I was sick before I left for work next morning. I could sense him standing outside the bathroom, listening. The same thing happened twice more. Then he came in as I was washing my face. 'You've got to stop drinking.'

I didn't tell him it was morning sickness until three months later, after it had passed and my belly was beginning to look round.

He must have made the mental calculations. He must have worked out the dates, asked the question, was it his? Worked out when his last fleeting visit had been. And probably I had the same answer as he did: there are some questions it is best not to ask.

I began going to museums and art galleries because I loved the peace they offered, the space to think. I became more and more interested in art, not just the old stuff, but the new art, work that challenged you not to like it, that seemed to threaten you and at the same time promised that it was saying something really important.

I also threw myself into study. I had noticed how often the pupils at my school would ask me questions for which I could only supply a stock answer. When my child asked me questions I wanted to give the best answer I could.

I started to buy philosophy books again, looking for answers but instead finding more questions.

༄

That was all I had now. All those years of study. A geometric method to give dimension to my life. Questions and still no answers.

I looked at the figures again, the solicitor's statement of account, and then at David. 'When we sell the house should we give the money back to them? Give them back what they gave us? Or should it be half the value of the house?'

He ignored the question and began put the papers back

into the box. 'Half the value. How much is that? Are they still around?'

He slid the box into the cupboard. He took out a full bottle of gin and put it on the tray, even though the one already opened was still a quarter full. He slammed the cupboard door.

'You lied to me. Your family never threw you out. Was that the way you thought we should start our relationship? I barely knew you.'

His face was drawn tight in panic. 'People lie in relationships. At the start. They pretend to be funny, clever, cultured, appreciative. Nice. Then you learn about them. You learn the truth. You learn what they are.'

'Liars.'

I went upstairs and pulled my suitcase from the top of the wardrobe, tipped out the winter coats on to the bed and filled it with clothes. Then I grabbed the books from my bedside table and stuffed those in too. I closed the case and lifted it down.

I would be able to carry it ten yards. No more. I would have to ask him to help me. I took half the books out, but it was still too heavy.

One Saturday, we'd had an argument and he'd come back with a bag of bagels, as if that solved everything. The row had made me hate him so much I couldn't bear to see him. He went to work and as soon as he'd gone I had packed a case for myself and one for Andrew and we had gone to my mother's. I pretended it was a new game, although Andrew sensed something was wrong. 'Are we going forever?' he asked.

A few hours with my mother and her smug relief at the

collapse of our relationship convinced me to go back. I rang him. Just visiting. Back in the morning. You didn't you see the note?

That night I hardly slept. I was torn. Divided. There are at least two answers to every question. We went back the next morning and pretended nothing had happened. He knew, though. I heard Andrew go into the kitchen where David was, I heard him say to Andrew 'Did you have a nice trip?', and in reply Andrew said to him, 'Why can't you just go?'

At the time I thought I'd probably misheard or misunderstood the context.

Why can't you just go?

⁂

I emptied the case and put it back on the wardrobe. The thing I had now was philosophy, and I embarked upon my struggle to grasp something always just out of reach. It was like an uphill journey where the peak is always just ahead and when you reach that point there is a further, higher peak hidden behind it.

Here in the bedroom, where I had lain awake beside his sleeping form for so many nights listening to his spluttering and snoring, I wondered what I was doing there. I thought of the world of Spinoza and his idea of mankind unified in a great single substance, heaving with individual desires and urges. I was sinking into a hole, a state of emptiness.

When he couldn't sleep, he moved through the house, the noisy ghost of a past he couldn't let go. His perambulations confined me to the bedroom. I could not bring myself to get up, to go to him and ask him, 'Can't you sleep? What is it that's keeping you awake? What are you thinking about as you move in the darkness?'

I looked out at the bay window that had once lit up in terrifying orange: a foreshadowing of the end of the world. David's appalled face, Andrew's calm, fascinated, as fire entered his being.

The neighbours were jabbering about it, a year's supply of gossip unleashed in a single night.

'Three kids . . . it's no wonder . . . right under his nose like that.'

'If the tank had been full . . . that's what he said . . . a big hole . . .'

'That's his no-claims bonus up in smoke . . .'

All through this, the neighbours bringing us tea as the fire brigade dowsed the car . . . 'Bad luck he parked it outside your house . . .' Bad luck . . . and Andrew sitting silently, in a daze. I thought he was half-asleep, sipping sweet tea in his red winceyette pyjamas decorated with pictures of buckets and spades and sand castles.

When Andrew was born I could see the resentment on David's face straight away. He was no longer the focus of attention and he didn't like it. I couldn't leave the baby with David, because immediately he started to wail. In those days you expected a man to be hopeless with a child. I liked the fact that I was the one who was always needed, but even so . . . sometimes I wished I had some time to myself.

When David was with Andrew, I could not stop watching them. If I was working in the kitchen I needed to rush back every ten minutes. What was it that scared me? I sensed David's instability, that he was on the brink of exploding.

I still find it hard to understand what made me feel this way. David was never violent to me; he never behaved irrationally. But there something: he was too controlled.

For the first three years I seldom left Andrew. David was a mere observer of his upbringing. He did try to contribute, but each time he attempted to do something I would find myself stepping in. Andrew began to pick up on my fear. He became fearful and cried. If David tried to feed him he would cry and shut his mouth tight in refusal. If David tried to change his nappy he would struggle and writhe, preferring wet nappies to his father's attentions.

Was it my fault? Was I unconsciously transmitting my fears?

As Andrew got older, things seemed to improve. They would go off to the park to kick a ball around, that kind of thing, and they seemed like two versions of the same person, united by their mannerisms, by their same slightly awkward physical presence. When I saw them together there was no sign of conflict.

One afternoon I was walking down by the side of the park when I spotted them and knew that something odd was happening.

I waved but they didn't see me. Then I moved to the cover of the bushes. I approached gradually for the pleasure of seeing them playing together, father and son, until I realised that while David was frantically rushing about kicking the ball around, Andrew was standing motionless, his mouth curled with contempt.

Eventually I couldn't stand lying there any longer. I put the light on and began to read, a controversial new book that was drawing connections between Spinoza and post-structuralist thought. It was a mistake to read philosophy when I couldn't sleep. My brain got fired up, eliminating hope of any further rest.

I went downstairs. David was in the kitchen, warming some milk. It hissed on the flame. He was swirling it round as if by doing so he could hurry it along.

'We'll move.'

He nodded. 'Shall we go tomorrow and look at some places?' He looked at his watch. 'Today?'

I nodded, too tired to think of a reason not to. Other than that our whole relationship had been founded on a lie.

※

He was working on his magnum opus: the sales details for the house.

We caught a train to Broadstairs. I couldn't read during the journey. I could only look out of the window and feel the world slipping away.

David led the way from the station, striding ahead of me along lines of terraces with front walls containing gardens in which crumpled boats, bikes with missing wheels and bits of hi-fi had been abandoned.

David tapped on the door of the house and a woman in her thirties opened the door. A child clung to her. She smiled apologetically. 'I'm sorry,' she said. 'He's a bit under the weather.' A bubble of snot appeared from the boy's nostril by way of confirmation. She apologised repeatedly, for the state of the house, the fact it was the size it was (not larger), the decorations, the weather.

In the main bedroom the bed was still unmade. The house was full of laundry.

We went into the garden. 'It's perfect', said David. Looking out from the corner, you could see the sea. There were lines of courgette plants with canary-yellow fruit and bulging shiny green skins. There were rows of ripening tomatoes, also rhubarb and gooseberry bushes.

'Esme likes gooseberries,' David said to the woman, and pulled a face. 'And rhubarb. I could never see the point of a fruit you had to cover in sugar to make it edible.'

I did like them. All my favourite foods involved sourness and bitterness. Only with drinks would I introduce some sweetness.

಄

Th woman was quiet with a desperation that David failed to notice. 'I'm surprised you can bear to move. Why are you selling?'

'We're splitting up. Me and my . . . I've got to find a flat . . .' She left it hanging, as if we might offer her one if she waited long enough, then grimaced. The boy gripped her arm harder, as if he sensed impending disaster, and left pink hand prints on her flesh.

಄

'Well?' David said. He pointed to an old Wills cigarette machine fixed to the side of a corner shop that looked as if it might still contain cigarettes. At the front of the shop wooden crates were stacked high with cauliflowers, the yellow curd peeping through gaps in their leaves. Rows of clay pots were filled with cherry tomatoes, yellow and purple. It was as if he were citing evidence for why we should move there.

'It's the first place we've seen. I've hardly been into the town.'

He stared ahead.

'It feels a bit . . . comfortable. I just need to think about it.'

He was crushed. 'What more do you want?'

'I just want time . . . to grow used to the idea.'

'You want something difficult, don't you? You want urban rage.'

'Give me a little time.'

He moved away. 'I'm going to walk on the beach for a while. You take all the time you need.'

I stood on the front looking down at the sand below. The tide was low and the children were playing in the distance, too far away to be heard. A woman wheeled her buggy past me, smiling as her daughter waved.

'Won't you miss the art exhibitions?' David asked on the train back.

'She seemed very nice, didn't she? I liked the way she presented the house,' David said, as though the woman selling the house was part of the deal.

She had dabbed her eyes with a tissue or her sleeve when she thought we weren't looking. She had barely been holding things together.

'Shall we go for it?'

I had not answered, but maybe I had nodded, a nod

induced by the rocking of the train as much as conscious choice. I felt separated from the gesture and its consequences.

That was it.

❧

The next day I travelled down to Sheerness, stepping out of the run-down station on to an empty street as it began to drizzle. However I arranged my collar, the rain managed to wet my face. I walked along past the shops, the varieties of pound stores and discounted dog food stores. I passed bleak guest houses, whose signs advertising 'vacancies' seemed redundant: there would always be vacancies here, and a banqueting hall with a special offer, Thursday Banquet, £9.95. I followed the path out to the shingle and the mud flats which merged into the mist before they met the sea.

A man sat on a bench flying a drone. It hummed mournfully and was turning in circles over the beach, first in one direction, then the other, while a boy dug for ragworms further out, the water rising to splash over the sandbank on every seventh wave.

Each of the benches was dedicated to the memory of someone; most were adorned also with elaborate flowers, plaques, children's toys. A rainbow-coloured windmill was spinning above a picture of a boy with pudgy cheeks and a winning smile . . . Timothy, snatched away in a moment of madness, aged twelve. But surely too old for a windmill?

The Bax sisters, Pamela and Jane, who both fell asleep on June 16th.

Joyce, much loved triplet. How cruel the loss . . .

Far out to sea you could make out the looming shapes of

the Maunsell forts, there to protect the estuary from invasion.

I liked the bleakness of the Isle of Sheppey. The wind was blowing and it was hard to imagine that it ever stopped sweeping across the shingle, carrying away the loose sand, sucking the moisture out of people, leaving them as crisp as the shells.

I saw a couple of German teenagers sitting there, cans of beer in their hands, staring at a terraced house that was flying a Union Jack in an upstairs window. The white paint was flaking from the front door. The house looked out on to the long grey wall of the sea defence.

When David had suggested moving to the coast this was the type of scene I had imagined. A place where you could pass way your life without having to love it, or praise, or show gratitude for being there. Where you could stare into the grim, soupy greyness of estuary waters, the sea a stern unforgiving father who refused to engage with his children for fear of making them weak, choosing their destruction over softness. It was the perfect place to abandon your family and drink yourself to death.

I could not imagine starting this new life. I needed space to think, not in order to bring us together more, but to stop us slipping further apart. No distractions. No classes helping people to churn out sculptures of heads, torn between the agony of relocation and their own failing talents.

Someone had created a little cairn from the rocks, just large enough for a seagull to shelter in.

A man was training his mastiff to be a fighting dog, pulling the stick in its mouth with both his hands as the dog's eyes widened with rage. Then he raised the stick so high that the dog was hanging from it, fastened on only by the grip of its own jaws.

Two young boys were surreptitiously drinking Red Bull fortified with vodka from a quarter bottle one of them had under his coat. They were throwing stones at an empty can, but their shots were wayward and half-hearted. 'Can you feel it yet? Can you feel it?' they said to each other.

Behind them a muttered conversation was taking place. 'I got this shitty Nokia thing cause I had this iPhone 5 I dropped and I took it to the phone shop and he gave me the Nokia and now that's been nicked and he won't give it me back. Cause I've been away, eighteen months, gave me three years, three years for motoring, driving while disqual. Driving under, and due care and attention. Woman judge. She had it in for me. What a joke. For motoring. Yes, I did hit the copper but that was just the drink.'

And now here I was, in my true spiritual home. Grey skies, smiling at me. A ketch bobbing on the waves in the distance.

I was not going to move with David. It was the one thing of which I was certain: I would never move to the coast with him.

∂℃

There came the time when I woke in the night to find the space in the bed next to me empty. I listened, hearing just the rhythm of speech, no words. David was talking with Andrew.

I checked the time. It was two o'clock. Andrew had been waking a lot at night. One consequence of toilet training was that he would wake in a panic and sit upright, terrified he might lose control of his bodily functions. Sometimes the fear passed, but on other occasions he would collapse into tears of frustration and fury. I would go and settle him: a few minutes of my holding him were enough to get him back to sleep.

David couldn't do it. He couldn't bring himself to hold him, as though there was a battle between them and he would lose it if he held him. Instead he sat next to him and talked in a long low monotone.

I had always wondered what he talked to him about. That night I stood there by the door and saw that Andrew was awake, his eyes staring towards me, wide in wonder, but not seeing me.

David was pointing through the window, up at the stars. 'Those tiny dots everywhere . . . explosions of light . . . the brightest light you can ever imagine . . . an explosion so loud we can still hear the echoes . . . the frozen solid wastelands . . . the huge expanses with deep courses of rivers . . . dried for a billion years . . . the solidified echo of that sound.'

He stopped. Was he looking at Andrew to see if he was getting sleepy? Did he notice that his son's eyes were wider than ever?

'The fragments . . . tiny shards of light . . . spinning . . . buzzing round each other . . . each searching for its partner . . . each with only one it can meet and extinguish . . . snuff out forever . . . united. All united. Then it explodes . . . and the whole thing starts again.'

Andrew stood up in his bed.

'It explodes? Does everyone die?'

'No. They've already died. They have already gone.'

'They all have to find each other. What if they can't?'

'The world waits for them.'

'How long does it wait?'

'As long as it takes.'

'What if it takes forever?'

254

'Then it waits forever. And a bit longer.'

Andrew looked at me, his face drawn and scared.

'I don't like that.'

David nodded. 'We've got a long time to wait. Do you see that group of four stars? They are the truth-seeker stars. The four men who went into the woods to find the truth.' He pointed upwards and Andrew looked at his finger rather than following its path. 'One crumbled under the burden of his own body, one was lost in the wilderness of the wood, another in the wilderness of his own mind. But the fourth came back with a fragment of light . . . a glimmer of truth. The miracle was that when he spoke the words came out before the thoughts they invoked.'

Andrew was crying now.

'There's no reason to be scared.'

Andrew collapsed on to the bed, over-dramatically, and David put a hand on his chest to steady his breathing. I went back into our bedroom. I heard David go downstairs.

I waited for ten minutes until I heard the distant clock ringing out the half-hour, and returned to Andrew's room. He was lying on his back, his eyes wide open, a shuddering coursing through his entire body. I lifted him up, wrapped him in sheets and blankets and carried him into our bed. I curled myself around him, trying to stop those violent tremors running through him as if I could squeeze them out of him.

Eventually he became still. The only remaining sign he had been disturbed was his breathing, which would race intermittently in little gasps. Then his eyes would open again, startled, as if he was seeing the terror of the end of the world.

Eventually David returned, and seeing Andrew in the

bed grunted his disapproval. He went into Andrew's room and lay on Andrew's bed, no bedclothes now there to cover him.

🐝

Sheerness wasn't quite bleak enough. It was a bit desperate, people there fighting just to hang on, but the place felt petty, not the grand empty expanse I needed. I walked down the road out of the town and round the island, peering into the haze of the estuary, sensing the distant ghost cranes within it, endlessly loading and unloading boxes carrying stuff from one side of the world to the other. Brown water trickled down in rivulets, the surface flicking up in long fingers . . . the wind was running across it.

A line of holes led towards the sea, as if someone had headed out to drown or sunk deep into the mud, submerged, the holes closing over them.

Behind me was a pumping windmill, a section of its circle of sails collapsed on to the ground below. It was trying to turn in the wind, the remaining part of the rotor rocking from side to side.

This was the place I wanted to be.

🐝

When I answered the door, I was surprised to see Alice standing there. 'Have you come to pick up David's notes . . . the details? I'm sorry. He's still working on them. You know what he's like.'

She shook her head. 'Between you and me, there's no hurry.

I've got enough to work on. Didn't he tell you? He's going to teach me how to bake a cake today.'

I smiled. It struck me as funny that he was passing it on to a Greek girl who had eased him out of his work the one thing he was able to offer from his heritage.

'He's just upstairs. I'll need to clear up the kitchen first.'

She came into the kitchen with me and I began to stack the soiled plates beside the sink. I moved the stack into a bowl and put it on the kitchen table. She picked up a tea towel. 'You wash. I'll dry.'

I took the tea towel from her. 'Just talk to me. Why are you learning to bake?'

'Two things are essential in my family: cooking and finding a husband. I thought if I made an effort with the first . . .'

'Did your mother never show you?'

'There were four girls in the house. I was back of the line when it came to domestic skills. When it was my turn . . . she drove me mad . . . everything was so slow . . . chaotic . . . she kept forgetting what she was doing . . . losing something she'd had in her hand two minutes before. I wanted to explode.'

'You'll be okay with David. His technique is cooking as a military operation. You might regret it and wish you'd gone looking for a husband instead.'

'My sisters are all beginning to find out about their husbands' affairs. For them, it's not about the hurt and betrayal any more. It's all about a place to live and how to care for their children now.'

'So you made the right choice of career.'

'Tell me, Esme, have you started looking for places to live?'

I nodded, trying to smile enthusiastically. 'We saw somewhere. Yesterday. David's keen.'

'But you're less so?'

'I could live anywhere. It just seems a big step and I'm not sure why we're taking it.'

There was something miraculous about her hair. She could shake her head and her mane would look chaotic and a moment later be perfectly aligned in a black bob. She leaned back in the chair and began to scrape at the table with her nails, making a paler line in the patina.

'On the way here I saw a guy with facial tattoos. He was sitting on the wall with his hand outstretched, asking for my charity. I reached into my purse to hand him some coins and he just keeled over in front of me, lying on his side, his hand still out in front of him. I had to step over him.'

'That's what happens sometimes.'

'I worry about this neighbourhood. Where it's going.' She did look genuinely concerned.

I could not help laughing. 'No, you don't.'

'You're right. People will still buy the houses. They like 'edgy'. They think they're getting a bargain. Something up and coming.'

'I will miss it, though.'

'But what about the broken windows: the stuff on the door? You're not going to miss that?'

'He told you? He said he wouldn't tell anyone about that.'

'He never told the police?'

I couldn't explain that a mood of resignation had descended on him, as though the violation was something we deserved, something which we had brought upon ourselves and now had to live with.

'You've no idea who it was?'

'He thought it was neighbours . . . there was a house with

258

some drug dealers. He had words with them at one stage. He blamed them.'

'But you didn't?'

'The drug dealers couldn't focus enough to close their front door at night, despite all the metal cladding they'd fitted to it. Getting their children dressed for school was beyond them. Retaining a grudge for five years after they'd moved on seems unlikely?'

Alice was troubled.

'It's not that serious. A broken window now and again. Dog shit on the doorstep . . . a bit of scribble in marker pen.'

'If it was anti-Semitic you should definitely involve the police . . .'

'Why is one form of hatred worse than another? I find it almost comforting that it's not personal . . . but that's another thing . . . how would the drug dealers have known he was Jewish? It's ascribing to them a higher level of ethnic awareness than they could have had.'

'So who was it?'

'Do you think he's going to include it in the details? He does like to be thorough.'

She gripped my hand, laughing. 'What?'

'A neighbour we've crossed in the past? A disgruntled house buyer who thinks he was lied to? Maybe an artist we've annoyed, retaliating by turning us into their own little art project.' I suddenly took that idea quite seriously. 'Maybe I gave someone too much encouragement . . . they believed that I was wealthy . . . built it into a multi-layered grudge. A mailing list revenge. It's a minor thing. It hardly happens any more. It's a bigger deal for David, but it's mostly big in his head. It's not that that's driving us away.'

I gave up on the dishes and sat opposite her. She gripped both my hands. 'You don't have to go.'

'I can be anywhere. If I can read. Walk occasionally. Alone.'

'Are you going to be happy with local church hall exhibitions of watercolour seascapes?' Her face was earnest, terrified at the prospect of life outside the M25.

'You know what? The other day I went to an exhibition up in Southwark and I saw that stuff . . . glass boxes of debris from lives, and I read about the word and object and the separation and space between them and I thought, thank goodness it's over. Thank goodness I don't have to do this anymore.'

I put out a bowl and the scales.

'You understand art. It makes no sense to me, most of it.'

'My sense of wonder has gone. I think the more I see, the less I understand of it. It's a bit like the property market. But with no property . . . a mental landscape. Maybe this is how we'll be in the future. All lined up like people in an old folks' home, exploring a mental landscape.'

'That could wreck the property market.'

Strangely, we were still grasping hands. Desperately holding on to something, trying to grip it, something that was slipping away. It was so long since David and I had held hands, that innocent uncomplicated form of contact.

David came downstairs. He was surprised to see us talking together. Without a word he took the almonds and began to grind them. I left them to it.

When Andrew turned up here, I was not surprised. When I heard that a young couple was coming to view, a couple starting out, buying their first house, I cast my mind back to how it was when David and I were in the same situation. Then I thought of Andrew, how he was at that age, imagining what he would be like now. I was always thinking about Andrew: where he was, what he might be doing with his life, what belief system he had constructed, how he spent his days . . . what he thought about . . . what he thought about us. Everyone I saw, I saw in relation to him: how much older or younger they were than he was now . . . how they might interact with him. If I saw a young family I asked myself whether he had a family now. What age were his children? Did they have scarves and gloves on strings like that, or would he have spurned that kind of childhood accessory, as if he believed childhood was something to rush through as fast as possible? Did he have a buggy like that or would he have rejected it as the trappings of an over-equipped society? Everything was about technology. Every social happening.

Everything I saw was filtered through reference to him and measured by the likely differences. When he turned up, therefore, it seemed the most natural thing in the world. The picture of his homecoming I had built up in my head turned out to be exactly how it really was. His return had been my constant expectation, but endlessly thwarted, making me resent every other visitor for not being him.

When he came in, when they came in, it was a miracle, but not an unexpected one.

I was frozen, unable to speak, unable to react other than to look at them and be suspended in this unreal moment, a moment so much anticipated that it was impossible to believe it had arrived.

In my head I was rushing towards him, hugging away the

years, holding him, feeling the weight and muscle of his body, inhaling the smell from his skin and hair, hearing the sound of his voice. In reality I stood there as if I had no idea who he was. I smiled to Alice and nodded and shook hands, first with Carol, whose hand was soft and warm, then with Andrew, his hand firm, hard, engulfing.

I sat down. We all sat down, observing the peculiar formality required of such occasions.

'Really, yes, I was a primary school teacher at first. Yes, for a while.'

I was gripped by a terror that David would walk in at any moment.

'So, it's a pleasure to meet you.'

'Yes . . .' Carol's face was fixed in a big smile, as if it really was a pleasure. 'We love the house. Andy's really excited too. Although he doesn't show it.' She gripped his hand. 'You should practise what you preach.'

'I don't preach. That is one thing I definitely don't do.' He smiled at me and I felt a warmth in his smile. I wanted to say something, to rush over and hug him, but his look kept me away. Like fishing. I had never fished, but I always liked the idea of it. Sometimes ideas were like that; you began to grasp a new concept and you wanted to rush in and embrace it, but you had to hold back, keep your distance, let it come to you. Gradually, gradually.

'All right, then. What you say. You should do what you say.' Carol smiled proudly at her redundant clarification.

'What do I say?'

'I don't know. I can't remember.' She shook her head, looking at me. 'He thinks we should be more spontaneous.

262

He talks about accepting your desires and feelings. Focus on them. He has a whole system built around it. Understanding what you really desire. He likes precision in language.'

I felt a surge of joy. I thought of what I might have said on those tapes that I'd sent after he'd gone. I had often cried myself to sleep thinking of him lying somewhere far away and listening to them. This was it. He had come back.

He had not changed. Well, a little. He'd lost the lean, hungry look of his youth. He was muscular now, powerful. His eyes didn't twitch about, looking all over the place for potential attackers. He had a calmness, a generosity. When he smiled at me I felt as if nothing had happened in all those years since he'd left. It had all been a terrible dream: this was the reality.

I was about to end the pretence. I was about to rush over to him, hug him. Kiss him, let the tears come and the years flood away. They all looked at me, knowing something was about to happen: Alice's smile fixed but questioning, Carol suddenly faltering mid-sentence as she prattled on about how much she liked the simple colour scheme. Andrew was looking at me, still focusing on that desire.

The door banged as it bounced against the restraint of its hinges.

David came in.

He glared at Andrew, then at Carol and Alice, and then at me. Conspirators. The air was sucked out of the room. The back door could also be heard banging.

Only Carol seemed unaware of the change in atmosphere, but maybe she was just putting on a brave face. Maybe Andrew had primed her. She stood up. 'I love these artworks,' she said, walking through the living room, taking a moment to stare at each one. Suddenly I felt embarrassed by them, wondering why I had bought them, what I had been thinking of. Now I was stuck with them: they were a part of my life. I didn't know how to get rid of them.

David had behaved in an entirely opposite way from me. He had purged Andrew from his mind; he never mentioned him, as if his son had never been born.

At the moment of David's entry into that room, the life he had blocked out had reasserted itself.

David sat down quietly, looking at Andrew, a hunter regarding his prey, his face screwed up as if David was a puzzle he had to solve while we made small talk.

'Do you like art?' Alice asked Carol. 'Esme knows all about it. I know nothing.'

'Yes, but when I do an art project with the kids I sometimes think . . . if only . . . if only I'd had the . . .' she lost the word. Carol told us about her teaching job and how she loved the kids, but a lot of them came from troubled families . . . they were out of control . . . in fact, it was usually the parents' fault . . . how she worried what the kids would be like in five years' time.

'That goes for all of us.' That was the only thing David said.

'We can always rely on David to bring some sunshine into the room.' Alice was fighting a giggle.

'And what do you do, Andrew?' I asked.

Life coach. Carol said it quickly, as if he might have wanted to come up with some other term instead. He probably could guess that it would be one of those job titles that would drive me into a rage, like the various new-age made-up therapies that require the suspension of all reason. But I did not react. David furrowed his brow, probably trying to conjecture what I might think about it.

Alice was smiling, talking nonsense, with Carol chattering back about the house and what a perfect place it was for a young couple and how it could be a wonderful family home, how they'd never want to move again because it was ideal. If you're happy with a place why would you move away?

'And the area . . . well, let's say it's colourful. There's variety without you feeling you're living on a powder keg.'

'A powder keg?'

'Some parts of London, they seem all very nice and then it's as if there's a chill wind comes over the place. Forces are unleashed. I was down at the corner of Brockwell Park the other day, as it was getting dark . . .' she shuddered at the memory.

'Zephaniah Mothopeng park,' David said.

'Pardon?' Alice did not like to be interrupted in full flow.

'They renamed it. After a South African revolutionary. That was the council. We have to call it that. Everything has been renamed.'

'That was years ago. They renamed it back again.' Alice had obviously encountered his insistence on this before, David making some point about it she didn't quite understand.

'I still like the old name. The South African name.' He smiled at Andrew, as if issuing a challenge.

'Is it like that here? A ferment of revolution? It always seems very quiet around the school.' Carol looked concerned.

'No. It's calm here. There's the odd thing . . . but no, it's quiet.' Alice smiled.

Andrew and David shared a look, as if both were about to disagree.

'It was a proposal. They never renamed it. They talked about it,' Andrew said. 'I think they wanted to start the debate?'

'What debate?' David was picking fights.

I got up. 'I'll make some coffee. David?'

He ignored me. Instead it was Alice who accompanied me to the kitchen.

'I mustn't forget my cake. David wouldn't let me move it until it was completely cold. They seem nice, don't they?'

I was trying to listen, to hear what David was saying, wanting to rush back into the room again. He was dangerous unsupervised.

She tried again. 'Don't you think they seem nice?'

I found the wrapped cake in the fridge and handed it to her. 'Lovely. For your family gathering. Lovely. Like us. Happy families.'

Alice pulled a face. 'Do you think every family only looks harmonious and well-adjusted from the outside? That it's when you're part of it that it feels like you're living in a horror film? In every hidden space something lurks.'

'Probe below any surface, there is something you would not dream of. Secrets, desires, lies, damage.'

'The answer is to stay on the surface . . .'

'That's it. Never go deep. Never probe.'

She smiled and gripped my hand. 'I look at you and David and I think it's not all bad. There is hope.'

I smiled, finding tragedy in her words. 'David and me. He told me once that I was all he had in the world, that I was the one thing that gave him hope. Like most hope, it was misplaced desperation. But what the heck?'

She smiled sadly. 'That's touching. The two of you against the world.'

'Believe me, it can be a lot easier on your own. You've got a business. What comes, comes.'

'I've got three sisters breathing down my neck. As if there's going to be a shortage of children of Greek descent if I don't start breeding fast.'

The coffee began to hiss on the cooker. She stacked cups on the tray.

'I went to a speed dating event the other day. I couldn't imagine anything worse, but my sister Helena made me go. Those guys . . . I could look at each one and see why they were still single. I started a little game in my head to spot the defect as early as possible. Lack of ambition, stutter, smarmy, egocentric. That about covered it. Three minutes can be forever.'

The coffee bubbled through on the Moka and I swirled the milk around in the pan to warm it. Alice stacked the cups on the tray. I turned off the gas ring.

'What did you say Andrew's surname was?'

Alice picked up her clipboard and flicked over a couple of sheets. 'Williams.'

'Right. Like the singer.'

She looked blank. 'What? You think he's someone famous?'

'No. Tell me more about speed dating. The world is in a hurry.'

'The women were all lovely, but the men . . . it seems so unfair. I thought what has gone wrong, that this is the state of things? If only I was attracted to women, my problems would be solved.'

'There would be different problems when your family found out.'

'That would solve two problems, because they would disown me. Still, there is hope. Look at those two. Carol told me they only met three months ago.'

'Nothing is ever quite what it seems.'

Alice picked up the tray. 'We'd better get back before David starts showing them the circuit diagrams for the boiler.'

When we returned Carol was talking to David about the local schools and he was expounding his views on how the world was collapsing around us and he was the only person who understood this. Carol nodded politely and told him about her school, which wasn't collapsing. It didn't put him off his stride.

I was puzzled, watching David for signs of imminent explosion as I poured the coffee.

As I handed Andrew his cup, he took it from me and gripped my hand, enclosing mine completely. He had warmth in his eyes. There was something in his look I recognised from many years ago when I was a young teacher, something that happened when you had made a connection with a pupil and helped them through a barrier, and you were embarking on a journey together. Times and feelings had faded; everything was now a mere echo of them.

Alice drained her coffee in one gulp. She gripped David's arm. 'Why don't you take Andrew round and explain the plumbing and electrics to him? We'll help Carol measure up the windows.'

'I haven't brought a tape measure,' Carol said.

David watched Andrew, watched his feet as though he was leaving a trail on the carpet. I didn't want David to leave, fearful of what might happen. 'Do you need to? Because David put all the window sizes in the details.'

'You should always double-check the dimensions,' David said.

'I'll find one.' I reached into the cupboard by the fireplace, but David strode to the door, scowling at Andrew, who flashed a look of helplessness at me. Engulfed in the world.

David was looking from me to Andrew and back again while Andrew stood up. I had not noticed how substantial, how physically powerful he was now, even though at that point his expression was one of alarm.

I thought to myself, 'It's going to happen, then.' I thought he and David would leave the room together and we would hear the furore and envisage with dread what was happening; but David left the room alone, closing the door behind him.

Andrew walked around the room's perimeter, feeling it for size, no longer listening to us.

Carol was apologetic. 'I had thought that we'd get a flat. But one of Andrew's dictums is that you should focus on what you want and not compromise. If you accept something less than your ideal, your life becomes a series of compromises.'

All around me I was surrounded by compromises.

'So you saw this place . . . and that was it?'

'I didn't imagine we could afford a house, but Andrew saw this and he told me we would be able to.'

It all seemed very familiar. Who wanted to think about money when someone else could take that responsibility away from you?

I tried to draw him back, to make him pay attention. 'Andrew, tell me about being a life coach? What does it involve?'

He ignored the question, still surveying the walls, carrying out his architectural inspection of the plasterwork. Then without a word he left the room.

Carol smiled, and dropped her voice, sharing a secret. 'I was part of a grocery co-operative. We were trying to undercut the big supermarkets and when we had a meeting it all got very fraught. People can get very involved, emotionally, at such gatherings. We went from heritage carrots to . . . I don't know what . . . the disappointments in peoples' lives, how everything just keeps going wrong. Then the chairwoman stood up and she said there was just one more item on the agenda.'

'There's always one more item on the agenda.'

'Andrew appeared and I saw straight away that he had a way of taking control of the room. Everyone stopped talking. "I'm here to talk to you about well-being," he said. I remember that. It sounded mysterious and a bit scary. When he had finished I was convinced that I was destined to work with him.'

Alice had put down her phone. She was sitting forward in her chair, making her hair swing over her face. 'I can imagine that,' she said.

I created a mental picture of his work. I thought he must be like a counsellor, but instead of listening to hours of verbalised despair, inadequacy and delusions, he would take stock, intervene and tell people how to sort out their lives. Not giving advice . . . he gave instructions, orders . . . 'this is what you need to do . . .'.

'Afterwards I stayed to talk to him, and somehow we were never really apart again.' Andrew, having returned, sat between Carol and me on the sofa. She gripped his hand. David reappeared and I felt a stiffening of tension run through Andrew.

David handed Carol the surveyor's tape. 'You turn the

handle,' he said. 'It doesn't have a spring.'

She held it, perplexed by this disc of hard brown leather, having forgotten what problem she was trying to solve. She sat tight-lipped, staring at the windows.

'We had to replace that pane in the centre. If you look in the right light, you can see it's modern glass.' I could not understand why he was telling her that.

David sat on the chair opposite, glaring at Andrew.

'So,' said Alice, 'do you want to talk furniture?'

David smiled as if he found the whole thing funny, his lip curling unpleasantly. 'Furniture?'

'Not just furniture,' said Carol.

Andrew nodded. 'Not just furniture.'

I suddenly felt anxious about the price David would ask for it. He always overvalued everything. 'We can't sell you the cooker. We can leave it but it's old . . . We couldn't take anything for it.'

Carol jumped in. 'We haven't really got any stuff so . . . anything you can sell us . . . or leave us . . .'

'You really want our furniture? What, all of it?' I would have expected my reaction to be one of delight, to be able to leave everything behind and start again, but instead I felt pangs of regret, an emotional connection with some of these things, as if moving without them would be like living in a hotel for the rest of my life.

Andrew narrowed his eyes. 'We want it all. Just as it is. Leave it all as it is. Everything on the walls. Everything on the floors. I want it all just as it is.'

Up until that point I had been optimistic, believing that perhaps Andrew had arrived at a point of stability, that it was just a twist of fate that had resulted in his searching for a house just as we were selling . . . and that pure nostalgia had made him want to buy his childhood home. But now there was menace in his words.

He settled back in his chair.

'Just as it is?' David smiled. 'Just as it is. And at what price?'

'Tell me the price.'

'I will tell you the price.'

Andrew narrowed his eyes as he waited.

I knew David was going to name a ridiculous price. It couldn't be that easy for him.

'Ten pounds. You can have it all for ten pounds.'

Alice was checking her phone. She stopped mid-tap, her focus moving rapidly from the screen. 'David . . . ?'

'Ten pounds. For everything. Ten pounds for your childhood. Is it worth that?' His face broke into a smile, as if it was all a joke and the rest of us would laugh at it in a moment. But it was no joke.

Andrew reached in his pocket, pulled out a ten-pound note and threw it on the table. Alice's gazed shifted from son to father, then back to her phone, as if it might contain the answer. She panicked when things got out of control.

Carol was unpicking the puzzle in her head, examining David's face as if this would provide the answer.

'Ten pounds or ten thousand pounds. It makes no difference.' David grinned, and tried to draw me in. 'Esme, he's wasting our time.'

He got up and I noticed how rounded his shoulders were. He was starting to develop a bit of a stoop. 'Alice, you should check out your clients more carefully. He's not going to buy this place. He can't. He's got no money.'

He went over to the window and gripped the steel bars he had fitted. He put some weight on them, testing them to see if they had any give. 'I'm sorry, Alice. It's all been a bit of a waste of your time. If he brought the money here today in a suitcase full of cash, I wouldn't sell this house to him.'

Alice had put her phone away. Now she picked up her cake, as if she could use it as a weapon if necessary.

'He was useless when he was a boy and he's useless now.'

Andrew rose; I could see how he towered over David. David's spitting fury . . . his jabbing finger, snarling words . . . were no match for Andrew's strength. Andrew was tall, powerful, in control.

'Go on. Offer me more. Offer me any price. I won't sell you this house.'

Carol's face collapsed in a stream of tears; she was shaking her head from side to side. 'What's happening? I don't understand,' she wailed, looking at me for help.

Alice's face was white with rage, and not knowing where to direct her anger she came over to me. I held her arm and hissed the words in her ear. 'He's our son. Andrew is our son.'

Andrew met my eyes as if he was looking deep into me. It was as if the words had triggered a long-forgotten memory. If the circumstances had been different, I would have suspected a trick, a party-trick demonstration of mesmerism . . . his eyes were sending out light, firing it deep into mine . . . so I was transfixed. Then he kissed my forehead and left, banging the front door behind him.

David followed him into the street. We watched Andrew pass the window with its modern, replacement glass and disappear down the road.

David came back into the hall, slammed the door behind

him and stomped his way upstairs. I heard him pacing around above us in the room that had been Andrew's room, then stop and let out a roar of rage.

Carol looked from me to Alice and back to me, pleading with us, begging us to fix this problem for her. With a further wail of despair, she ran out after Andrew.

'What just happened?' said Alice. 'Tell me what happened.'

'Family life. Family life just happened.'

The more I heard David knocking things about upstairs, the more I thought about his dream, his coastal idyll. I would let him go on with his dream, help him build it; then the more we built that dream, the harder I would eventually stamp on it.

❧

It sounds more terrifying than it actually was, that fire in our bedroom. When such things happen you can be surprisingly cool-headed. I was waiting, as if instructions would surely arrive from somewhere. The smell was the first thing I noticed, an overwhelming smell of petrol that took over my dream. Then my eyes opened and the dream became Andrew standing over us, shaking as he tried to light matches, flicking them. The first ones fell dead to the ground, harmless. The next ones didn't.

David leapt out of bed, reacting instantly, as though he'd been expecting it, as though he had the whole rescue plan mapped out. He turned the burning bedspread in on itself and threw it into the bay window. For the second time in our lives that bay window exploded into light and heat, a new sun emblazoning fire at our bedroom window. He whisked me out of the room, grabbed Andrew and slammed the door behind us. He pulled us downstairs and into the garden. I reached up to feel my forehead. The front of my hair was singed. My fringe had gone, reduced to a stubble; a fragile frizz came away in my hand. My eyebrows and eyelashes disintegrated as I touched them. David's arms were burnt – he rubbed them as if the only problem was that the hairs had been singed. Andrew was leaning against the wall, twitching and weeping. I went over to him and put my arm round him. He began to shake; I took him further into the safety of the night air. I could hear David calling from the hall phone. Ambulance, fire and police. As if he had worked out the order of priority. I felt I should gesture to him to join us, but I let him finish the phone call first.

I remembered seeing David's face in the moonlight as he looked towards us when I wrapped my arms around Andrew. I've never seen such utter disgust. As I flinched under his gaze I could feel that my son, although at that moment held in my arms, was slipping away.

※

At first the firemen were unimpressed by our fire. It had burnt itself out quickly, turning the covers to ash but spreading no further. Then they saw the petrol can and began to speculate on what could have happened if the can had been fuller. 'You're lucky. You're very lucky.'

I didn't feel lucky. I was surprised they never asked why we had a petrol can in our bedroom, even if it only contained an unimpressively meagre quantity of fluid. They removed it and promised someone would drop off a 'Safety in the Home' leaflet.

The police were perplexed: one of them actually used that word. I imagined he was not often perplexed in his work. I thought most of what they saw must be depressingly straightforward. David appeared unable to explain what had happened, so they assumed we must have had an intruder. They said they would ask the neighbours if they had seen or heard anything. I was left with Andrew and a police-woman. She came over to me and nodded at him. 'He did it, didn't he?'

At the time the police were busy in the area, dealing with drugs raids and street robbery. They didn't want to get in-volved in family trouble unless they couldn't avoid it. We would be offered family counselling. The policewoman gave us the address of a counsellor. I got in touch with her.

I had a feeling of dread about this from the start. From the moment I heard her voice on the phone, I felt fingers of despair pulling me down. David told me what to say. What not to say. I walked out of the room. He probably tried the same tack with Andrew, but his son had not spoken to him since that night, so whatever he said was unlikely to make any difference to him.

I heard David later, speaking to him, choking out the words. 'What you did . . . I think you must have been sleep-walking . . . I fail to see how anyone could do such a thing otherwise.'

He continued. 'The thing is, I don't feel safe anymore. You need watching. You need constant watching. This condition of yours. It makes you unsafe.'

We had our therapy session. The woman asked us ques-tions and I answered as honestly as I could. 'It's all perfect-ly normal,' she kept saying. 'That is normal, to have those feelings'. But at times I zoned out. She would ask Andrew a question and then wait for the answer that would never come.

David's replies were brief and non-committal, pre-screened to ensure they gave no possibility of an interpretation that could reflect badly on him. I found myself thinking through work problems, areas in Spinoza that I needed to revisit. My world was a world that could be structured. Axioms, propositions, proofs. We did not choose the actions that made up our lives. They were events we witnessed. She was trying to pinpoint a cause, a concept: that to me was unacceptable.

I kept looking at the carriage clock on her mantlepiece. I imagined her being presented with it when she left one of her previous jobs.. Twenty-five years of making families normal again. Now, at this new moment in her life, this further opportunity to give something back, to save us, to lead us out of our darkness. But I knew as I sat there she was not going to lead me anywhere. I imagined her keeping a large blue book containing testimonies from previous satisfied clients. 'We were very happy with the way she was able to get to the root of our problem. We will definitely be back next year.'

Definitely back next year. We managed two weeks of counselling, then David took Andrew to an army recruiting office. Andrew must have seen it as a means of escape. More sullen silence. We never returned to leave our comments in her book.

I had sat down with Andrew, his bags already packed. 'You know you don't have to go.'

He looked back at me, his face heavy with tragedy, shaking his head. 'You know . . . you know . . . you know.'

There was no acknowledgement of his father. In those remaining days he behaved as if his father did not exist. David, allegedly made into a non-person by his own parents, faced this as if it was a natural thing, a relief.

I bought Andrew a going away present: a CD and tape player. I wrapped it up and put some tapes in the box. I had recorded some tapes for him.

What did I say on those tapes? That was the terrifying thing: I could not remember. For all my years practising structured thought and argument, and founded reasoning, I knew I had spoken off the top of my head. Did I give him advice? Did I give him directed messages? I do not know. I recorded some music for him. Beethoven's late piano sonata. String quartets. Mahler songs. Stuff he would hate, but I had a hope that he might come to love it. One day. That he might come to it, eventually, and appreciate it much more than my recorded words. Then a couple of years later I was caring for a friend who was dying and I realised that the music I'd recorded was the music you'd choose for someone who was facing death. It was something of a comfort to me to think that in his darker moments he could listen to music on that tape-recorder, at first maybe just his own music, then perhaps moving on, and that the day would come when he would put on that tape I had made and would listen to my words.

I probably talked about being trapped, stuck in a place where we have no will with which we can control our actions. We can only witness them: we have to step back and watch them unfolding. There is a spirit that binds us, that unites us. That can be terrifying, but we can't escape it. That is the thing that terrifies us most. We are the thing we most rebel against. I talked about his father, trying to get him to understand, to forgive. I tried to find things that would help him rebuild his life, get the things he wanted out of it.

Whatever it was I said, I remember feeling very calm afterwards, while I was putting the tapes in their boxes and labelling them. What did I write? I held my pen poised for a long time and when I wrote I was embarrassed by my words. It was a horribly new-age message. Like those booklets you see by bookshop tills and in card shops. 'A little book of calm'. 'A little book of terror'. 'A place of safety,' I had written, and immediately regretted it.

I worried for a long time afterwards about what I might have said in the tapes. I was trying to be honest; about myself, about him, about David; to give Andrew the benefit of my honest, uncensored thoughts. It wasn't easy. So much of our thought consists of accumulated fragments absorbed from the world around us.

Sadness. The world can seem sad, unbearably sad when you're young. Does the sadness fade? Does it ever fade? I don't know. The sadness may shrink into the background, waiting for its moment, but I think it's still there, looking for a way in.

What I might have said on the tape troubled me more than it should have done: Andrew's philosopher mother rambling on, providing him with incomprehensible nonsense. I needed to keep close that image of him sitting in the darkness, listening to me, finding something in those words, taking some comfort from them.

What advice can you give someone if you don't accept the concept of a will directing action? Behold the mystery: there is no moment of decision, just a projection and a retelling. I would not have been a good witness in court; in my world no-one is ever responsible for a crime. We are only ever observers, and pretty unreliable ones at that.

A person can be defined by their absence. Every day that

he was away I felt a seething rage. A directed rage. A hatred of the void and everything that was associated with it.

❧

'I still don't understand. What just happened?'

I raised my hands, and she knew not to ask any more questions. She gathered up her papers. 'Don't worry, Esme. You'll be out walking along that beach before you know it.'

David pointed to the orange and almond cake shrouded in its silver foil cover.

'Tell me if they like, it won't you? Everyone likes it. But tell me anyway.'

'I'll give you a running commentary on every bite they take. And . . . we will find you another buyer. A proper buyer. I'll check them out . . . make sure they're completely . . . completely . . .' Alice tailed off, not sure what she would be checking them out for.

'It's life. What it throws at us. It's not the end of the world. It's just another moment. That's all that happened.' I smiled at her reassuringly.

'You see?' Alice said to David. 'That's why we should all study philosophy. Then you can just face a situation with equanimity and . . . it doesn't affect you. That's why I'm going to take classes. In fact, Esme is going to teach me.'

'Cake-baking classes are more useful,' I said.

She laughed. 'For fattening up Greek women, maybe. Not for the rest of life.'

Alice left.

❧

We went back to Broadstairs. We walked on the beach for a while. The tide was out; the sea, a long way distant, was exposing the mud and the rocks, still gleaming with pockets of water and damp with green seaweed. It was quiet, but the sort of brooding calm that suggested it might be whipped up into a crisis. There was the pungent smell of decay, fostering excitement in a gull who was digging around for the bugs in the tangled mass of rotting weed.

You could not tell where the sea met the sky at the horizon. Both combined in the mist in a silver-grey glow. We walked along the beach, stepping uncomfortably on shingle caked with patches of thick brown mud. Here were grey leather bundles of sea kale and brown scraps of sea beet, dried out by the constant wind.

We walked in silence. We'd hardly spoken during the past few days. Then David began to talk, suddenly burbling inconsequential chatter. 'I liked that woman who was selling the house. Maybe we should go and see her? She was pretty. She reminded me of you . . . that smile.'

Seaweed caught round my foot and trailed behind me. 'She was in despair. Didn't you notice? She was crying into her sleeve every time she thought we weren't looking.'

He stomped on. 'Maybe not, then. I just thought it would be friendly. Update her on the situation.'

'I'm sure she'd love that.'

He pointed at the scrubland. 'Is that the remains of a pill-box over there? It's not hard to imagine this area under attack, is it?' He rushed over to the stained lumps of concrete, ugly ropes of rusting steel twisting out of the gashes running between them. 'It must have been huge. I wonder if it got hit or whether its ruin is just the effect of time?'

The effect of time. Taking us and smashing us up. Quickly or slowly.

Whathappenedwhathappenedwhathappened . . . the wind shouted. I stepped through the barbed wire tangle of seaweed, dried into black brittle coils.

'I knew he would amount to nothing. The only thing he ever developed for himself was a sense of entitlement.'

'He has established a life. He has a girlfriend. He wants to settle down.'

David was striding ahead. He always did that. 'A girlfriend. That's some kind of achievement, is it?'

'He's got nothing he has to prove to us.'

'So why did he come back?'

I stopped and let him march off into the distance. The truth was I didn't know. I could not understand what Andrew had hoped to get from his confrontation. I didn't believe he meant to taunt us. Perhaps he really did want to buy the house: some part of him wanted to live in his childhood home. Maybe his memories weren't tipped towards the grim times, as I had imagined. We never found out whether he could afford to buy it, because David chased him out.

David. The figure accompanying me, marching off into the mist. Fluff from the waves had gathered into big lumps of foam and flew along the beach. A dog snapped at them, a new game, his head shooting from side to side as he tried to guess where they would come from.

'You never gave him a chance.' I shouted this at his back, now heading into the distance, knowing that he would not hear. Could not hear, even if the sounds reached him.

I would never move away with him.

It was a shock when those words entered my head. I hardly

knew where they came from, or who they belonged to. How they would work out, what they meant in practice.

I would never move away with him. From London. From that house.

I could no longer see David. I took a path off the beach that led into a copse. All the trees were dried out and dead. Brown leaves hung from them still, as if some catastrophe had sucked the life out of the place. There was a wooden hut selling tea and snacks. I went inside and the woman behind the counter looked up, surprised, but continued her conversation with an older woman who was sitting at a table midway down the room, still using the same monotone. The older woman was anchored in her seat, clutching a large mug of tea. She had a bulky scarf wrapped high around her neck.

I ordered tea and a Buck Rarebit. The presiding woman sloshed tea from a big aluminium teapot. The tea was darkest amber in colour. She added a splash of boiling water. Then she turned on the grill, the Calor gas burners roaring. I poured a drop of milk into the tea and stirred it with the teaspoon attached by Sellotape to a frayed bit of string tied round the table leg.

The cafe walls were lined with paintings, large dramatic fantasy scenes, dragons being attacked by superheroes with bulging muscles. Swirls of purple mist merged into maidens' dresses and hair. The earth had disappeared; the battle was the only thing there was.

'He paints them.' The woman behind the counter nodded towards the back of the café, as though I should know who was out there. 'My husband. Day and night. I tell you last night he woke up at three in the morning and got up, went downstairs. After an hour I went down to see what he was up to and there he was, painting. I'd rather he was looking at pornography. It would be more . . . normal.'

'They are for sale,' she said, as she delivered my mug of tea and buck rarebit. 'If you've got the right place, maybe a corner which is out the way . . . I don't mean that you want to hide them, just you'd want to keep the sense of mystery. Or that's what he'd say, anyway.'

The food tasted good, maybe because I was hungry from being blown about on the beach: the cheese sauce had the right soft consistency, bearing the tang of mustard; the toast was singed to just the right degree, with a hint of smokiness. And the tea was strong and astringent, cutting through the fattiness of the milk and cheese.

As I paid, thinking I should make an effort to find David, the woman gripped my arm. 'Follow me,' she said.

Behind the café there was a workshop and inside were huge figures assembled mainly from wood but armed with what appeared to real metal swords. Horses' heads, wild beasts raging with clawed fingers grasping at their foes. Within their forms you could see the shape of kitchen utensils: the holes of colanders, blades of spatulas and bowls of ladles. There were human forms constructed like superheroes with taut muscles and misshapen faces, all too big ever to inhabit the real world. The single door (I calculated it must be about six-foot-six high) at one end was the only exit but it would take a powerful magic to allow them to pass through it.

'See what I mean? Pornography would be a relief. Less banging around. Quieter banging, anyway.'

I was impressed by the scale of what was before me. But what was the myth her husband was connecting with? What was it that was drawing him? What values? What were the stories?

I went back to the beach and saw David in the distance. He began running, an uncoordinated whirl of flailing arms and legs. I was about to offer a playground insult, but he arrived gasping, doubled over.

'I thought you'd gone . . . I thought you'd left . . .' he said.

'You went ahead without me.'

'I didn't know where you'd gone . . .'

'I was waiting.'

'You could have called me.'

'I wasn't looking for you.'

He looked at his phone, pushing his glasses up and peering at it. 'There's no signal. What would have happened if I hadn't seen you?'

'You don't get rid of me that easily.'

He nodded, smiling, reassured.

On the train we sat opposite each other. He was following the route on the map, looking at the printed details and then scouring the landscape for the corresponding features. 'Over there . . . do you see it?' he kept saying, pointing a gnarled finger. As I followed that finger I wondered how I hadn't notice it changing, that same finger that pointed, directed, admonished, explored my body, my genitals. (Even now he still seemed to find them fascinating, probing the flaps of skin, as if there was still some mystery yet to be discovered.)

'When do you start your class?'

'Wednesday. I'm looking for inspiration.'

'Horses?'

'Anything but horses. I'm looking for something terrifying. Something that makes you feel like you're all alone in the world.'

'Lost and engulfed by it. That's going to be tricky to convery with a horse's head.'

'It's all about the world slipping away. Providing an anchor to hold on to a single moment.'

'Is that from an artist's programme?' I immediately regretted the jibe.

'You think you're the only one who can have any appreciation of art. But you know what I think? I think art's become a habit to you. I don't think you even like it any more. You just think you should. You're out of touch with it.'

'You're probably right.'

He was looking at me sadly, in confusion. I gripped his hand. 'We will buy the house. It will work out.'

He nodded. And that was it.

※

That night I woke from a deep sleep. I sat up, an ache running up and down my spine. I was wide awake. Whereas it normally takes me many minutes to emerge from sleep, I was instantly conscious. Aware of everything, and with clarity.

I thought of something that had never occurred to me before: that Andy might have been to blame for all those mysterious attacks and other hostile episodes. That he had been lurking in the neighbourhood, bearing his grudge . . . his rage . . . awaiting his opportunity to attack . . . prepared to disregard any impact it might have on me. His rage against David. Or maybe his rage was directed at me, too. Those dehumanising years in the army may have brought their toll.

❧

I was finishing breakfast. The coffee was bubbling through on the Moka when I heard someone knocking at the front door. It was Alice. She always managed a crisp, fresh look in the morning, as if she had just stepped out of a shower, a look I could never achieve, no matter how much I washed and scrubbed. As if that mass of hair respected who was boss, whereas my hair, although cropped short, still always seemed to be sticking up in odd directions when I looked in the mirror. 'I just wanted to drop by, to check everything is okay. Listen, don't be depressed. There's been a lot of interest. Believe me.'

'But not quite enough for anyone to come and see it?'

She smiled. 'Things are a little quiet. But a lot of people are thinking about coming to view.'

'Alice . . .'

'So aren't you going to make me a coffee?'

I poured her some. We sat on the back step, nursing a cup each. She had brought some sweet pastries. 'They're very sweet. When I eat them they always make me want to go and kick a dog. All that sugar.'

'Kick your staff instead.'

'It would wake them up. They might sell something . . . I'm not sure I could cope with the excitement.'

'You're missing David? He tells me he kept the place going.'

'You'd be surprised.'

She crunched on the final bit of her pastry. 'All Greek food is about fattening up the women. Providing a sweet contrast to their bitterness.'

'How did you become an estate agent, Alice? I'm sure there must have been other professions that could have attracted you. Motivational speaking, for example.'

'I think your son has cornered that market.' She looked embarrassed, worried by my reference to Andrew. 'How did you become a philosopher?'

'I'm not a philosopher. No-one ever claims to be a philosopher. I teach philosophy. I mark essays that bear some passing reference to the subject, that have at least some twisted view suggesting the students read the first page of the reference text. But I was going to be a singer.'

'Really?'

'A classical singer. I had a good voice when I was young. I had a wealthy boyfriend who paid for singing lessons. My family had no money. My teacher was given to a florid turn of phrase, but he behaved as though a great singing career was a foregone conclusion. But then I noticed something disturbing: a crack in my voice. Just around certain notes. I mentioned it to him, and I could see he had noticed already. There was a coldness in his manner from that day. No more descriptions of my future glittering successes.

'I continued with the lessons. The crack was getting worse.

'It was about that time I met David. I used to go to the opera, climbing up to the cheap seats, so high that it used to terrify me. I had to hold the seat backs and work my way along the aisle, never looking down. I noticed him after a while. He always seemed to be there. It wasn't that he was in any way striking, but he had an individual look. I would hear him arguing with people in the interval and after the performance had finished. It was always about the things he hated about the production. Have you ever been to the opera?'

Alice shook her head.

'I will take you some time. Anyway, one day, it was Don Carlos, I remember that, the Inquisition, cleansing by fire. At the second interval I was walking along the aisle and I looked down and I was terrified. The drop to the ground was so deep. I could not move. He was behind me. As the final applause died away people wanted to get past me, but I was too terrified to move. He gripped my arm and told me to close my eyes and he led me out. He made them give me a brandy and let me sit down. He crouched in front of me with such concern.

'Afterwards we went for coffee in Soho. We went to the opera together, several times. He could talk for hours about what he'd seen, and what was wrong with it. I would contradict him, just for sake of talking, and I began to like to argue.'

Alice had a tear in her eye.

'What's the matter?'

She shook her head. 'My sisters are right. I'm missing out. What happened to the rich boyfriend?'

'I don't know if it was that I was no longer going to be the singing star he had imagined, or if his interest would have waned anyway. I think his parents probably thought he could do better. I deliberately became less interested, less available. Then, when David's parents threw him out, we were suddenly thrust together, so to speak.'

'So that was it?'

'A story without an end. Yet. Although every story has a notional end. We all have an end we're heading towards, even if we don't know what it is.'

Alice stood up. 'This is killing me,' she said, stretching her back. 'Now I'm stuck with my sister who has turned into a mad man-hater. I just wish . . . you mean it about the opera?'

'Of course. I'll check what's on. I won't make you sit in the top seats, either. We've got all that equity to spend.'

I was working my way through a set of essays by students who thought it easier to make up Spinoza than to read it for themselves. It was beginning to disturb me.

I rewarded myself with five minutes' reading for every thirty minutes' marking, but it was becoming harder to drag myself back to the scripts.

There was a sound. I looked up; Andrew was standing behind me. 'Did you come through the back door? I keep telling David to keep the gate locked. This is South London he's in, not the village idyll he wants to move to. He keeps pretending we've moved already. He used to be the one who was obsessed by security.'

Andrew sat down in the chair opposite. 'It's been a long time. And then twice in a week. In the words of that family therapist . . . is there anything you want to talk about?'

He looked at me, challenging me to break the moment, to speak first. Eventually he leaned back.

'Tell me about philosophy. You never told me anything about Spinoza.'

I held up the essay on the top of the pile. 'In his argument about substances he said that everything was one substance. Our thoughts, our bodies, rocks, lumps of wood. It was all a big cosmic soup.' I smiled. 'That's philosophy. Wading in the cosmic soup.'

'That must limit your options.'

'There are no options. It's very thick soup.'

He nodded. 'He's making you to move to the coast?'

'Who? Spinoza or David?'

'Do you want to go?'

'It's probably for the best. After so many years here, it will be good for me to go somewhere else.'

'He always knows what's good for people. He knew what was good for me.'

'Andrew, it's all a battle. Sometimes what he says makes sense. Sometimes it doesn't.'

He stood up and began to examine the pictures on the wall, working his way from one to the next, his face creased with puzzlement. 'This house hasn't changed. I thought you might have repainted the walls. Gone for some colour. I'm surprised.'

'He's not one for change. And I . . . don't really care that much. White walls are fine. Occasionally another coat. I like to move the pictures around. The pictures have changed.'

He peered at the painting by the door. I had started to hate it, a tricksy collage with heavy-handed symbolism intended to represent the slipping away of time and the approach of death.

'I like this one.'

'Well, you can have it. When you move . . .'

'When we move.'

'When everyone moves. I like Carol. She seems nice.'

He moved through the hallway, glancing at each picture briefly. 'Mmm. I worry about her.'

'What do you worry about?'

'I wonder why she is with me. What she sees. Is what she sees something very different from what I am?'

'That probably goes for all of us. How many relationships would even start if you could see what would unfold?'

'Speaking of which . . . where is he?'

'He's upstairs. In the loft. He's sorting some stuff out. You know what he's like. Always sorting things out. Putting our rubbish in alphabetical order.'

'He likes his stuff ordered.'

'When we first got together he told me his parents threw all his stuff out.'

'The Jewish thing.'

'The lack of the Jewish thing. My lack. He told me in detail. Everything he owned. His clothes. His books. His pictures. His bicycle. Out with the rubbish. He could have gone across the road and rescued them. But he left them. To embrace his new life.'

He nodded, indulging me. He must have heard the story before.

'Are you're going to try to persuade him? To change his mind? That won't be easy. Even for a life coach.'

'You could try saying it without the sneer. What future did you have planned for me? An estate agent? An artist? Keep up the family tradition?'

'Do you believe in it?'

'Belief is overrated. Self-belief is even more over-rated.'

'Why would you want to come back here? There's so much pain trapped here.'

'Why do you want to stay?'

'I'm not staying. We're moving. Remember that bit?'

He looked sceptical. 'I thought he'd stopped that.'

'Shall I tell you how to persuade him?

'You have the key?'

'He's not that complicated. Tell him you're sorry. Tell him it was all a mistake. Show a bit of humility. Listen to his plans.

Don't lay down what you want. Let him tell you about how to bleed the radiators, how to change the sash cords. Let him show you his instruction manuals and explain everything. He'll tell you about how a blackbird got stuck in the chimney breast and he had to knock out the air brick. Nod as if it's the first time you heard it.'

'It is the first time.'

'Don't ask for anything. Give him time and he'll come round.'

I reached forward and gripped his hand. I felt a shiver run through him, and my instinct was to pull away. But I left my hand there, looking down at it, embarrassed.

'He will come round.'

Andrew went upstairs. I heard the growl of him talking to David, each of them repeating the same rhythm in what they said, again and again.

I needed silence. I needed rest.

☙

It was dawn. After the longest night. It was a long time since I'd seen dawn. I used to have trouble sleeping when I stayed at David's bedsit, confined to that single bed. Often I had to escape the physical closeness. I would get up in the night and try to read a philosophy book. I had just started to get interested in philosophy, and I would spend hours staring at the words in the hope that at some point they would begin to make sense. I would go outside and walk in the darkness, walk across Tower Bridge, see the river community start to wake up, the mist still hanging over them, and up past Aldgate, where straggle-haired men gathered round coffee stands, their coats held together with string. Still I'd walk, up to the bakery, to that steamy warmth, the smell of dough and chopped herring and the staff barking the orders back at their customers. 'Salt beef bagel, gherkin mustard no butter. Onion platzel. Six, plain.'

I would buy bagels, looking up at the sign that showed you the price per dozen, all the way to twenty dozen with no discount for quantity. It felt like they could never put the price up, because then they would have to remake the sign. No matter what the time, even at four in the morning, you could join the queue of policemen, taxi-drivers, tube-workers and nightclubbers in eccentric outfits. Everyone would make jokes about everyone else's garb. 'Nice uniform. Who lent it to you? What time does he want it back? Don't stretch it with your bulges.'

I would buy one smoked salmon bagel and a dozen plain ones, all still steaming, and walk back biting through the crisp crust, chewing the soft strips of salmon. As dawn rose and I walked alone I felt the inadequacy of philosophy. What place was there in the geometric method for this moment? What place for the moment of getting back to the flat, dropping the bag on the kitchen table and getting back into bed, feeling the warmth of another person's body?

༄

Andrew had left his room at last.

'Is he still talking?' David whispered to me. His voice was low and soft, as if he was drunk. 'If only he'd stop talking. I could take anything else.'

My tongue felt fat and heavy. I began to shape it into a reply but gave up before any words emerged.

Andrew was now in the kitchen, but his commentary continued. Was this how he spoke when he did his life coaching talks? Did people sign up just to get away from him and stop having to listen to the words? It reminded me of the great communist leaders, Castro, Hoxha, Khrushchev: they would make interminable speeches lasting four hours and more, their listeners obliged to pay attention and stand up and cheer in the right places. I would readtranscripts of these speeches – accounts of Western intrigue, imperialism and plotting – and realise they sounded convincing. But they went on for too long.

'What do you think he wants?'

I shook my head. I think I did, anyway. I wasn't sure David could see. It had been a long dark journey through the night. I was just relieved to have a bit of quiet. A bit of light.

'I wonder if he would make some coffee.' Maybe not all those words came out.

'You and your coffee.'

'I'll make some. When there's a pause.'

'A pause.'

I wondered if it was a hallucination. Does it still count as hallucination if it is a smell rather than visual? Anyway, there was the smell of coffee. Andrew came in with a tray of coffee and biscuits. He put it on the table in front of me and smiled. I thought he had made it just to torture me, not intending me to drink it, but he poured out a cup and held it, smiling, to my lips. 'Let me know if it's too hot,' he said. He tipped some into my mouth anyway.

'I can see why you want to get rid of that cooker.'

The coffee was too hot, but I drank it. The tingle of pain in my mouth stirred me, brought me back to the room.

'You see. I just need to understand some things. There's questions in your life . . . Things that you want resolved. Things I need to know.'

He'd made the coffee the way I like it. How could he come and make it just how I like it when David could never get it right, after all those years, all those times of my showing him, explaining to him? He was someone who loved the detail of a process but could not make a decent cup of coffee.

Now Andrew was holding a biscuit to my lips. Shortbread. It suddenly made me aware how hungry I was.

'What about Carol? Does she know where you are?'

He looked puzzled. 'Carol?' he said. 'Carol.'

I wasn't used to feeling hunger. Not that deep, absorbing, pit of the stomach hunger. It was one of those sensations that features in your life when you are young but disappears as you take control of your world.

※

There was a time when I could have escaped. We were young; David had just returned from the Merchant Navy and he didn't want to go to a party. He didn't want me to go, either. I had bumped into a friend of mine down the Walworth Road. Kevin was part of a crowd I knew who'd left art college five years before and had, to his surprise, discovered that not many people wanted to buy art works constructed of rotting food, even if it had been dried out and varnished. He looked desperate, almost destitute, but I felt curious about seeing my old fellow students again, so I accepted the invitation to his party.

I was apprehensive when I reached the address he had

given me. It was a house in a run-down terrace. The music was thudding out: psychedelic-era Pink Floyd. Incredible String Band. Blues. The door swung open when I knocked.

'Esme.' My friend Christine came and hugged me and seemed not to want to let me go. She led me into a room where everyone was sitting on cushions arranged on bare floorboards. There were some flashing lights. The whole place reeked with the powerful smell of boiled meat.

The walls were covered with paintings of meat, all in shades of grey. Every gap was filled, the smaller spaces containing pencil sketches. All the works were of meat: haunches, piles of offal, half-dissected animals.

'There's food. I've made food.' Kevin appeared with a stew pot. There were long grey bones emerging from it, as if it was a cannibal's cauldron. He began to ladle the khaki liquid it contained into bowls.

Someone muttered that he must have killed one of his tenants and boiled him up. It was only half a joke.

'Why's nobody eating?' Kevin wailed.

We went out to the garden. Some of his guests had dragged old sofas out there. Christine and I perched on the corner of one of them.

'Married. I can't believe it. You.'

'Sometimes these things just happen. I wanted to stop deciding things. Just let them happen. See what unfolded. And that's what emerged.'

'But married!'

There was a bang. Someone had stuffed fireworks into one of the sofas and someone else had lit a fire underneath it. We went back inside as it began to erupt into flames. Rockets shot out, most sliding along the grass and hitting the fence in fury;

bangers erupted in a shower of dust and sparks. Christine and I dug around in the back of the fridge in the kitchen for cans of beer.

'Aagh. What is that?'

'Blood bags. He's been draining off his blood for a project.'

The deep red plastic sacks in the base of fridge put me off the beer. The window shattered as it was hit by a firework.

Later, we stood outside again, still sheltering from the random explosions of fireworks. Someone had found the blood bags and began to throw them at the others. Kevin had tears in his eyes as he rushed about trying to grab back the bags. Some merely bounced off the people they were aimed at and slid across the pavement. Others burst, leaving elongated red stars where they had landed.I thought, this is where I want to be, this where I want to be forever. Yet I felt the pull, the force of something growing inside me.

'How was your party?' David asked when I got home. I settled into bed beside him, not knowing what to say. How was my party?

⚜

I was cold. My arms were stiff. I wanted to reach for a blanket.

'Do you want to hear something funny?' David loomed over me, triumphant.

'Not really.'

'He wants us to give him the house. As compensation. He'll very generously take a mortgage for half of it. He wants us to give him the rest. I told you, didn't I? I told you there was no way he could afford it.'

'You did. You were right. You're always right.'

He nodded, managing to restrain himself from saying more.

'Always right. And that's why I want to do it.'

'What? What do you want to do?'

'I want to give it to him. Compensation.'

He stared at me, and staggered away, collapsing into the armchair.

'We'd have nothing . . . we'd get a tiny flat if we were lucky.'

'Compensation,' I said again, 'I want to give him compensation.'

He closed his eyes, unable to contemplate the horror that was unfolding.

I felt unbearably heavy: I could not lift my arm. My lips were so thick and swollen that words deadened under their weight before they could emerge. My head was still firing thoughts, but none quite made it into words.

❧

What do you want?

What do I want? What do I want? What do you want? That's what's interesting.

What do you want?

David was weary, close to sleep. 'Is it? Is it interesting?'

❧

Andrew was outside, in the shed, standing there as though he could absorb something valuable from the fumes of petrol, Jenolite and weed killer, as if some essence from many years past was embedded there. Occasionally he turned a circle, performing slowed-down Sufi worship, receiving inspiration from all directions of the universe.

❧

'I just wish he'd stop talking. I can stand anything but the talking.'

❧

'Andrew, on those tapes I left you messages . . . I told you everything I could think of that might be useful, that might be helpful. I wish I knew what I had said now. Or maybe I don't. I would probably be deeply embarrassed by whatever words I had offered. I sat for a long time in the darkness of our bedroom, still damaged by smoke, still tinged with the scent of terror. I talked, but I don't know what I said. I don't remember a word of it. I must have said 'I don't blame you'. I understand what it is like to be overwhelmed by anger . . . to be choked by rage. I understand. What use is understanding, though? It's counsellor talk. I hear your anger. I hear that you feel rage overwhelm you. I share your anger.

I share.

❧

He's more like you than you can imagine. There's more and more of you I recognise in him.

David looked at me, incredulous.

❧

A fox shuffling under the wild rose issued a murderous yowl, tearing at baby flesh then panting and growling, panting, panting.

❧

I just need you to listen to me. I need you to listen.
    He shook his head. Listen . . .

❧

A chilly wind rushed past us and blew through the house, carrying with it the scent of gin and smoked fish. There was a roar as it banged the back door closed.

❧

What does he want?
    I'm so tired.
    I just wish he'd stop talking.

❧

He's more like you than you can imagine you know. There's more and more of you I recognise in him.
    Andrew looked at me, incredulous.

❧

Once David told me a story about a couple in a caravan. Thieves came and pumped in poison gas, paralysing them so that they could only sit in chairs and watch as their possessions were taken.

'I don't think that's possible,' I had said.

'How can it not be possible? It happened.' David had pointed at the newspaper article.

'Things that aren't possible happen every day,' I said, flinging the newspaper back at him. It was happening now.

Andrew sat on the floor cross-legged, rocking backwards and forwards with that frighteningly intense concentration.

I wanted to go and hug him. I would wrap my arms round him, envelop him, and it would be just him and me. I could block out the cold universe forever. I wanted to pull myself out of this poison gas haze and hold him.

David lay dozing on the sofa. He mumbled something but the words came out in a fuzz.

I reached into the drinks cabinet. It was also where David kept his papers.

'Wow,' said Andrew. 'He still has all those papers stashed away.'

'The documentation. Of our relationship. From the start. It's there in every detail. You could reproduce our whole lives from this. From our dimensions on the plans. Our energy consumption quarter by quarter.'

He smiled. 'Would you want to reproduce it?'

I felt a moment of anger as I looked across at David. 'You resulted in a bit of a blip, I'm afraid. Bill by bill. Every receipt. If anything was broken, damaged, stolen, the evidence was all there, so we could replace it.'

I felt a surge of cruel mischief. I took the top document and screwed it up into a ball and tossed it into the fireplace.

David reached out a hand in protest. He was weak, his hand flailed ineffectively.

Andrew took out the service manual for the boiler. He tore out the service history page and rolled it into a ball. Then he stacked both bits in the grate.

'Tell me about your life-coaching. What is it? Philosophy? Spiritual growth?'

'Something you'd like or something you'd hate? It's somewhere between the two. Which probably means you'd hate it all the more.'

'Do you believe in it?'

He looked puzzled, as if this was the first time he had considered this question. 'It's not a question of belief. It's what is there when you strip away belief.'

'That's philosophy.'

'But not in the sense you would understand it. It's the philosophy of a frightened child stuck in the dark and discovering a chink of light to follow. It's founded in fear, not the comfort of a university.'

'What I don't understand is how you have the confidence? I've been studying for forty years and now I cannot tell a person how to apply for a bus pass. You are telling them how to live their lives.'

'The philosopher finds ways to say nothing, knowing it's all wrong. The artist finds ways to say everything, knowing it's all wrong.'

'You're an artist?'

'An artist. A con artist taken in by my own trick.'

'I was going to come to your meeting last night, but somehow time slipped away. Alice came, though.'

'Carol saw her.'

'Carol . . .'

'Carol.'

'I worry about Carol. She seems too fragile.'

'Too fragile for me? What do you think will happen?'

'She will build up hope. That you are something different from what you are. And she will be destroyed by it.' I leaned towards him. 'What's going on? What do you want? Why are you here? You don't want this house. Of all the houses in London, this is the one you least want.'

'Perhaps it's the trick of nostalgia. You see things in a new light.'

'There's nostalgia and there's delusion. You want to endlessly relive moments from your childhood?'

'That's what we all do.'

'Isn't that what you save people from?'

He nodded slowly. 'Something like that. How did you know?'

'No-one's going to teach you to stay trapped by childhood.'

He stood up, stretching up to his full height, executing some kind of twisting manoeuvre, releasing his spine. He looked so tall when he went to stand beside David. 'So . . . moving to the coast. I would never have imagined it. Won't you miss all that London stuff? All the art exhibitions.'

'Art . . . is a something we share . . . a communal activity . . . but when I go to those exhibitions I don't feel a part of it anymore. I feel like a spectator at an orgy, like a priest who still practises the rituals but who's lost his faith.'

'So how would it be? Endless walks by the sea with him? What else would you do?'

'It would be . . . endless. I realised the thing that stopped me moving away wasn't leaving art behind or even the fear of being alone with him. It was the fear that if I moved away I would lose any chance of seeing you again.'

'And now it's happened, now you've seen me again, has it liberated you?'

'Yes, but the thing about liberation is, it's frightening. It's not freedom at all: too much responsibility. I'm free to leave. To go anywhere. You know he lied to me?'

'Dad?'

'He created a fiction of his family being so shocked by his relationship with me that they threw him out. It forced us together. I couldn't really turn my back on him when he'd been thrown out to live in that horrible bedsit with damp dripping down the walls.'

'How do you know he lied?'

'He let something slip that got me thinking, that made me realise he still had some contact with his parents. I went through the papers. He never thought I would look through all those reams of paperwork. Bank statements, letters. They gave him money to help us buy the house. They gave us half of it and he didn't tell me. There was a trust fund. Not much, but something . . . a monthly payment enough to make this possible . . . this house . . . our life. Of course, things were easier in those days. But it means our whole relationship has been founded on a lie.'

'What will you do?'

'All those years. His time in that awful bedsit. Those strange early years of marriage. Not peaceful. We were always arguing. First of all, about nothing, then when you came along, about you. Even later, as the anger dissipated, the attacks came from outside. Bits of graffiti on the door. Burning paper through the letterbox. Smashed windows. That's why we put the bars up. David said they were random attacks. He said everyone suffers them in London. It's a part of the madness of the place. For some the madness goes into art, for others it explodes into violence. But I found something hopeful in it. I thought it was you. I thought it was you and that eventually it would burn itself out.'

I pulled out all the papers from the metal box and began to roll them up into balls. I created a pile of them in the grate and held a match to them.

'Won't you need some of those? For the move?' He touched my hand, moving it away.

'For the move? But you can't buy the house, can you?'

He shook his head.

'What did you think was going to happen? Did you just mean it to be a joke? Did you think we would just give it to you? Compensation for a damaged childhood? Or did you fall for your own rhetoric?'

He helped me screw up more papers. 'All of those.'

'What will you tell Carol?'

There was a smell of burning. 'The coffee.' I rushed into the kitchen. The Moka pot was glowing a dull red. The kitchen smelt of bitter black coffee, the stench of plastic and rubber burnt dry into a charred mass.

'I can't believe it.' I wanted to grab it, but the handle had burnt away. I began to cry.

Andrew was behind me and put a hand on my shoulder. 'It's just a coffee pot.'

'It's a relationship with a physical thing. It's everything in the world.'

We were looking out on to the shed where he had spent those appalling nights.

David was quiet now.

'I'm so tired. Did you put something in our drinks?'

Andrew smiled reassuringly and held my hand.

The fire was blazing now. I seized huge stacks of the papers. In a frenzy, Andrew and I tore up reams of documents and threw them into the fireplace. The burning pile grew higher. Shards of paper began to spill out over the hearth, while the flames grew higher, yellow tongues licking the front of the fireplace wall.

David's eyes opened briefly. He put out an ineffectual hand.

Colour beyond colour.

I was trying to grope for words, Parmenides, his proof that change was impossible, not being was impossible . . . all of us unified in a single moment of being. Names. Being and passing away, being and not being, change of place and alteration of bright colour.

Andrew shuffled over to the cupboard and pulled out another pile of papers and instruction manuals. We scrunched them up in the fireplace, on the hearth.

David let out a gasp, trying to protest.

The flames rose, a fearsome orange leaving a curling black trail in its wake. I thought I might get closer to the warmth, then realised I was warm enough already.

The flames were high, so high. I stopped shivering.

Andrew sat close to the fire, cross-legged, calm, his eyes closed. The flames were reaching higher.

He pulled away and continued rocking as before, impervious to the fire, which was now beyond control.

David rose and groped his way through the smoke to the windows, rattling those steel bars. Then Andrew was with him; they struggled together with the bars.

We should have gone years before. Left the house. All those years of attack. That feeling that I was trapped there.

'Andrew,' I whispered. 'Was it you? Was it always you?'

I was so heavy. I could hardly raise a hand to lift myself up.

I looked out and saw a kind of oblivion. There was always a dark side; at least it was more than just a void of being.

Andrew was lost in concentration. Then he collapsed on to his side and it was over.

THE END

ACKNOWLEDGEMENTS

THANKS TO MY family and friends for their help in the development of this book. Thanks also to Jacq Molloy, Beth Miller, New Writing South and Linda Bennett. Finally, thanks to Brixton and West Norwood for providing locations and inspiration.

This book has been typeset by
SALT PUBLISHING LIMITED
using Neacademia, a font designed by Sergei Egorov
for the Rosetta Type Foundry in the Czech Republic.
It is manufactured using Creamy 70gsm, a Forest
Stewardship Council™ certified paper from Stora Enso's
Anjala Mill in Finland. It was printed and bound by
Clays Limited in Bungay, Suffolk, Great Britain.

LONDON
GREAT BRITAIN
MMXVIII